DIRTY
LITTLE
MURDER

A Plain Jane Mystery

This is a work of fiction. All characters, places, and incidents are used fictitiously. Any resemblance to actual persons either living or dead is completely coincidental.

Proverbs 31
House

Dirty Little Murder: A Plain Jane Mystery
Proverbs 31 House LLC
Paperback Edition
Copyright 2013 by Traci Tyne Hilton
All rights reserved
Cover Design by Andrew Rothery
Cover Photo by ariwasabi

DEDICATED TO DANIEL FOR HIS LONG SUFFERING, HIS KINDNESS AND ALL OF THE DISHES HE WASHES.

CHAPTER 1

JANE ADLER SCRAPED THE GUNK out of the u-shaped pipe and flicked it onto the newspaper on the floor. She spread it thin with her gloved fingertip, but the missing wedding ring wasn't hidden in the blob of gunk. Either it hadn't fallen down the drain or it had washed away. She wasn't a plumber, so she couldn't vouch for the ring's ability to wash away, but it seemed unlikely. Especially with the huge diamond attached.

A tight knot had formed at the base of her neck, so she rolled her head from side to side. The sink parts had to go back together before her client came home, no matter how her neck felt.

Jane rocked back on her heels. According to the Youtube video on her phone, the plastic pipes should go back together without any kind of putty or tape. Jane started with the pipe from the drain to the pea trap. Despite the slippery sliminess of her gloved hands, it fit. So far, so good. If the pea trap would connect to the drain from the other side of the double sink, she was good.

It almost did.

She pushed it gently toward the back wall, and snapped it into the receiving end of the other pipe. She let go of it, and slid the screw connector into place, but the threads were crossed and it wouldn't twist on. She slid it up again. The pipe that led from the pea trap to the drain popped out.

Jane's phone beeped.

It was Isaac.

She tried to take the call, but the phone wouldn't read her latex and slime covered finger. She pulled her glove half way off, then changed her mind. Time was short, her boss was picky, and her boyfriend could wait.

She forced the PVC pipe back into place, but that made the pea trap pop out of the first connection she had made. She tried to slip it back up into the cap, but it wouldn't go.

She took a deep breath. She relaxed her shoulders. She thanked God that she wasn't the one who had dropped her client's wedding ring down the sink.

With slow, measured movements, she unconnected the twisty connection ring that supposedly held the pea trap in place, and slid it back onto the pipe in the right order, noting how much easier things came apart than they went back together.

She tested all of the connections. They were solid.

Then she pulled her gloves off and called Isaac back. "Sorry about the delay. I was plumbing."

"You know how to live."

"My client dropped her ring down the sink and wanted me to get it out." Jane crumpled up the newspapers she had used to protect the marble floor.

"And you tried, because you are awesome like that." Isaac had a chuckle in his voice, but the phone call was breaking up.

"Let me guess, you taught a class of eager, enthusiastic young seminarians under the shade of a grass roof, and then went to the beach to swim in the clear waters."

"Close. After class we went out back and kicked the ball around."

"Are you in heaven?"

"Are you kidding? You're not with me. It's paradise, at best, but it's not heaven."

Jane flushed. "I wish I was there." She mopped up the drips of grimy water that had missed the newspaper. "Only forty more days until you come home."

"Yup."

"Man, I do wish it was the other way around." Isaac's voice sounded far away, which was fitting since he was more than four thousand miles from home.

"You wish you were forty more days away from going away?" Jane rubbed her forehead. She wanted to engage in romantic banter, but she had limited time to get the plumbing mess put away.

"I wish you were coming here in forty days."

"I see! Sorry." Jane pushed the box of organic home cleaners back under the sink. "I'm thinking the Seminario Christiano de Costa Rica doesn't approve of girlfriend visits, though."

"They'd keep a close eye on us, that's for sure. But…"

Jane smiled. "But I could come, say, just for a week, right before you head home?"

"You could."

"Do you know how many houses I would have to clean to afford a trip to Costa Rica?" Jane swept the kitchen, though at first glance, it looked clean.

"Your parents?"

"Are about as excited for me to run off to Costa Rica with my boyfriend as your employers would be."

"Point taken. But I miss you." The phone crackled again.

"I miss you, too." The worst part of their summer apart was the patchy international phone calls.

"And I love you."

"I know."

"Jane, I'm serious." Isaac's phone crackled.

"I know. I'm just up to my armpits in Ajax and about to face a client who isn't going to be happy with me." Jane hedged. Love. Sure, she "loved" him, or she couldn't have spent the last year dating him. But after a point, love means the rest of your life, and that's where she hesitated. The phone fritzed again. "I do, too, Isaac. You know I do."

"I've got to run. Call me later?" His voice was distant. Jane wanted to blame the phone, but she was pretty sure it was her own fault.

"Definitely." Jane racked her broom in the pantry. It was a balancing act, and no one knew it better than Isaac. Island life was getting to his brain, and she couldn't blame him. She hoped his summer away would light a fire for missions in his heart that matched her own, but only time would tell.

In the meantime, Caramel Swanson wasn't going to like it, but there was no ring in the kitchen sink pea trap.

Jane checked the house room by room to make sure all of the lights were out before she let herself leave for the day.

A bright red convertible pulled into the driveway just as Jane was locking the door. She had hoped to get out before Caramel returned, but she was a moment too late.

"Jane! I'm so glad you are still here." Caramel swept out of her little car, her heels clacking on the brick driveway. "Did you find the ring?"

Jane grimaced and shook her head.

"Did you take the sink apart to look?"

"Yes." Jane never knew what to say to Caramel. Isaac's mom had recommended Plain Jane's Good Clean Houses to the Swanson family, to replace their regular housekeeper while she was on vacation for the summer, but the thirty-something Caramel was as different from sixty-year-old Mrs. Daniels as a yappy little Chihuahua was from an Airedale.

"Did you check the mudroom sink?"

"You said you dropped it down the kitchen sink." Jane checked herself before she said, "Ma'am." Caramel's husband may well have been sixty years old and a former mayor, but Caramel was clinging to her youth at all costs.

"This is a very expensive ring, Jane. I assumed you would stop at nothing to find it."

Jane snuck a peek at the time on her phone. She wished with all her heart that she had to rush back to class, but nope. Her first year of business school was over and done. She had no reason to rush away.

Jane weighed the missing ring on a quickly manufactured scale of emotional importance. Her personal goal was to treat each family like the mission field, serving them with the heart of Christ... but finding a trophy wife's missing diamond didn't resonate with her.

"You were hoping that I would keep checking even if I didn't find it where you thought that you lost it." Jane went with "reflect so they will feel listened to" to buy herself some more thinking time.

"Indeed I did. And since you claim you didn't find it, I hope you have good insurance."

"Excuse me?" Jane took a step backwards.

"You claim you didn't find the ring. It went down the drain of my sink last time I saw it, so if it's not there now, there is only one reason."

"I'm sorry, what?" Jane couldn't reflect that sentence. "Are you accusing me of stealing your ring?"

"You tell me. Did you 'find' the ring in the sink or not? I would think if you honestly didn't find the ring you would have kept looking. That ring is worth half a million dollars."

"But, ma'am." It slipped out. Jane didn't intend to make Caramel angrier than she already was. "You told me to check the kitchen sink because you thought you dropped your ring down it. I took it apart, cleaned it out, and didn't see anything. You didn't ask me to look anywhere else." Jane's hand went to her pocket, where her instruction notes were folded carefully in a wallet, just for that purpose. Isaac Daniels' father was a small claims court judge, and getting to know the family over the last year had made Jane wiser and more paranoid. Apparently, just in time.

"You can get back in that house and find my ring, Jane, or you can leave, and hear from my lawyers." Caramel's cheeks were flushed pink, her red lips were parted and puffy, as though they had recently been shot full of fillers. Her eyes had done the buggy, crazy-eye thing they did when she talked about her husband's ex-wife or her neighbors.

Jane prayed again, begging God for the right words. "If you would like to have me come back tomorrow to help look, I can schedule you in." She exhaled slowly. "But I think you could get all of the sinks checked faster with a plumber."

Caramel stood between Jane and Jane's car. Jane measured the distance with her eyes. At least twenty steps, if she tried to barrel past her, but double that, or more, if she attempted to swing wide, walking around Caramel.

"My husband won't put up with this." Caramel put her hands on her hips. "When I tell him what happened here, you'll never work in this town again."

Considering Portland had half a million people, or more if you counted all the surrounding towns, Jane didn't take the threat seriously.

"Don't underestimate me, *Jane.* My husband may think you are the cutest thing ever, but that won't stop him from putting you in your place."

The husband.

Jane doubted that Douglas Swanson thought she was the cutest thing ever, as she had never met him, and didn't have a picture of herself on her website or flyers.

"So, would you like me to come back tomorrow or will you be calling a plumber?"

Caramel narrowed her eyes. "My husband won't be back for another two weeks, you know."

Jane nodded. "What time would you like me to arrive?" She attempted to smile. If she truly was coming back to dig through every sink in the Swanson house tomorrow, she'd be bringing Holly, her new employee, with her. When half million dollar rings were at stake, a witness seemed super important.

"Be here at 7:00 a.m. sharp." Caramel swept past Jane, pushing her into a concrete angel. "I'll be home the whole time, so don't think you can get away with putting the ring back. I'll be watching you."

Jane ran to her car. She drove away from the Swanson house as fast as she could. "Quirky," "spirited," and "particular" were the words Mrs. Daniels had used to describe the new Mrs. Swanson. They must have been synonymous for utterly bonkers, otherwise Mrs. Daniels was at risk for false representation.

The Swanson paycheck was a welcome addition to the bottom line, but Jane was willing to forego name brand coffee and other luxuries if it meant she could quit this job tomorrow morning, as soon as all of the sinks in the six-thousand square foot mini-mansion had been put back together.

Jane parked at the apartment she shared with her cousin. She had to take off her house-cleaner's hat now, even if the current situation seemed to call for some serious planning.

In a few short hours, she had coffee and dessert with her church's Mission Coordinator. Jane decided to spend as much time as she could this afternoon praying, listening to God, and reading the Bible.

Jane didn't know what Paula Ehlers had in mind, but a coffee and dessert get together with a couple of other mission-minded people and the woman in charge of the church missions program was something she needed to prepare for.

CHAPTER 2

AT SEVEN O'CLOCK SHARP, after two hours of prayer and petition, a nap, and a hastily eaten sandwich, Jane found herself in the cozy living room of Paula Ehlers, head of the missions department at Columbia River Christian Church.

While her time in the Bible had been solid, the scene with Caramel that morning had shaken her. She sat on an overstuffed leather chair across from Pastor Ehlers, feeling out of place and lonely.

The other two would-be missionaries sat on the matching sofa. Jane shifted in her seat. Long fingers of the bright summer evening sun filtered through the half-shut curtains, blinding Jane. Plus, she was hot. A fan kept the air moving around the room, but she was glistening and damp.

Paula was a thin, tan woman with wise eyes that crinkled when she smiled, and soft, straight hair that fell to her chin. Paula had a slow, steady way about her that spoke of the many years she had spent overseas, and reflected a life of patient obedience to God. She was exactly who Jane hoped to be someday.

Jane held a stack of papers on her lap that had crumpled a bit in her hot hands. She tried to smooth them out. A combination personality-test/resume, Paula had given a set to all three women a couple of weeks ago when they first met each other.

Paula gathered each set of papers. "I'm glad to see you all had a chance to finish the packets. We've found that a little time spent learning about our missions' candidates goes a long way toward helping them succeed on the field." Paula squared off the stack of papers and then slid them into a messenger bag that sat on the floor. "After I've had a chance to read all of them, I want to get together with each of you alone and chat." She folded her hands on her knees and leaned forward slightly, giving them the impression of rapt attention.

"I really enjoyed the opportunity to think and pray over the questions." Kaitlyn, a petite blonde woman sat across the room from Jane. Kaitlyn had a fifty-watt smile, glossy blonde hair, and a prosthetic hand, something Jane hadn't noticed last time they had met. "My fiancé is already overseas." She dropped her gaze to the diamond engagement ring on her fake hand. "I've been taking my future ministry for granted. It was good to step back and consider what God has prepared me for, instead of what I expect I'll be doing."

"Were you surprised by any of the answers you got?" Paula relaxed back into her chair. She picked up her tea cup and sipped it.

"Nah." Kaitlyn laughed softly. "It was really good to see how well my hopes and my talents align."

"Remind me what Spencer does. I know he's in the Philippines, but what's he doing?" Valerie, sitting on the corner of the couch so she could face Kaitlyn while she spoke, was a plump, cheerful woman in her mid forties. Her eyes almost disappeared in crinkles when she smiled, and her curly hair bounced as she nodded her head.

"He runs a youth shelter in the Philippines. We're going to get married when he comes back on furlough next year, then I'm going back with him." Kaitlyn's prosthetic hand rested on her knee. Jane did her best not to stare at it.

"Congratulations on the upcoming wedding." Paula, herself a newlywed, glanced down at the simple gold band on her own left hand. "So what did the packet say you should do when you get to the Philippines?" Paula chuckled, and Kaitlyn and Valerie joined her.

Jane didn't feel like chuckling. She wanted to, but the missing ring kept worrying at the back of her mind. If Caramel decided to say Jane had stolen the ring, she could lose everything she had worked for this far. Trying to fight such a claim was one thing... but an arrest record would look terrible on an application for overseas mission work. Jane swallowed. A criminal record would likely keep her out of the closed-off countries called the "10/40 window" as well.

"I'll work with the women already there, leading Bible studies and Sunday school stuff," Kaitlyn said. "He will keep his focus on the young men, and I'll try and reach their mothers and younger siblings."

"What would you do if there wasn't a Spencer in the mix?" Valerie lifted an eyebrow. "I mean, it's awesome that you have a built-in ministry waiting, but what if you didn't?"

Kaitlyn lifted her hands, palms up. "Who can ever answer what might have been? I know that before I met Spencer I knew I had to go overseas. He was on furlough." Kaitlyn blushed. "It was pretty whirlwind, but our hearts and minds on ministry were pretty identical, so it wasn't hard to see how our lives could easily be joined."

Jane looked down at her hands. She rubbed her thumbnail. It was cracked from spending so much time in hot water. She knew she could wear gloves to protect them, but she always felt gloves kept her from feeling if surfaces were truly clean. Kaitlyn and Spencer. Two perfect missionaries joining forces. She sighed.

"That's fair," Valerie said. "I was just wondering. It seems harder for us single gals, if you don't mind my saying. I've wanted to go overseas for a long time, but found it hard to get the wheels in motion."

"I think that can happen to anyone." Paula gave her attention to Valerie. "And I don't think it's a bad thing. Sometimes God plants a seed in us because he knows it needs to germinate for a long time before it comes to fruition."

"Like you and Mark!" Kaitlyn's already happy face broke into a smile so wide Jane thought she might need sunglasses to look in her direction.

Paula glanced up to a huge photo hanging over her fireplace. "Yup," she said with a slight blush coming over her. "Just like me and Mark." After an embarrassed pause she started again. "Turning in your packets was a good sign that your intentions for missions are serious. Let's face it, dozens of students think they want to go overseas, but not all of them are willing to fill out fifty pages on the off chance their church will help support them."

"I bet not," Valerie said.

"We at Columbia River Christian Church get very excited about sending out missionaries. Kaitlyn, you probably already know this, since we support Spencer, but we feel it is our duty, as a sending church, to provide the bulk of your support."

A thrill raced up Jane's spine. The bulk of her support? That was unheard of, almost. She had taken a class called Perspectives during her days at Bible School and had heard that a few churches around the country had adopted the philosophy, but she hadn't known Columbia River was one of them.

"We don't make that public knowledge. For one thing, we get dozens of requests for support every month as it is. We prefer to get to know the missionary hopefuls in our congregation, invest in training them up and then support them in such a way that they don't have to spend their whole furlough drumming up more money."

"Furlough is much better spent resting and getting married," Kaitlyn said with a giggle.

"I don't know how much rest a wedding is," Paula said. "But yes, we believe that your furlough should be spent being ministered to, not fundraising. That said, obviously we can't fund everyone who applies."

Jane's mouth went dry.

"So far, you three are the ones we are most interested in, but to be honest, with the economy the way it is, we only have enough support available for one new missionary."

Jane closed her eyes. The Lord giveth, the Lord taketh away.

"So our time together over the next year is really important. It will help us determine who we will be funding. We wish we could fund all three of you, really we do. But we can't."

"We totally understand." Kaitlyn nodded her head, a bit overenthusiastically, in Jane's opinion. Of course Kaitlyn understood. They'd almost have to pick her, since they already funded her future husband for the same mission.

"The one thing most field missionaries wish their new recruits had is solid experience in leading small groups. It's such a simple thing to do, but sometimes sending churches forget to let their future missionaries lead in the church."

"Oh, I know what you mean." Kaitlyn flipped her blond hair over her shoulder with her prosthetic hand. "They almost sent Spencer home after his first month. They thought he was useless."

Paula smiled.

Jane squirmed. It was wrong to dislike someone with a missing hand, but the way Kaitlyn said "Spencer" and was so completely sure of what she was going to do with her life irritated Jane. She popped a quick prayer up, for forgiveness and grace, and tried to remember that her work-stress was the problem, not Kaitlyn. It kind of helped.

"The other thing new recruits need is strong teamwork skills, so I'd like to ask the three of you to start up a new small group together."

Jane looked at her new teammates out of the corner of her eye. If she had to guess, Valerie would plan everything, Kaitlyn would get all of the attention for it, and Jane would do all of the work.

Jane passed her hand over her forehead. Her heart was not in the right place, not even remotely. If her future were to be based on today's attitude, she wouldn't send herself to the foreign mission field, either.

"Why don't we all grab some coffee and dessert, and you ladies can get to know each other and talk a little about the kind of small group you'd like to lead.

Desserts were spread across the breakfast bar in the kitchen behind Paula. The aroma of freshly brewed coffee wrapped Jane in a comforting embrace.

"Come on in and help yourself."

Valerie got up first, with a little grunt. "I won't be shy. I have to admit those desserts have been tormenting me since I got here."

Paula laughed. "No need to be shy here. We're family."

From the relaxed smile on Paula's face, Jane knew she meant it. She saw the three potential missionaries as family.

Jane stepped into the hall to compose herself. When she felt half-way normal again, she joined the others in the kitchen. She poured herself a cup of coffee, hoping it was decaf.

"So, Jane, I hear Isaac Daniels brought you to Columbia River, is that right?" Paula asked.

"Yes…" Jane took a sip of her coffee.

"How does he feel about missions?" Paula passed a strawberry topped cupcake to Jane.

Jane's hand shook as she picked up the cupcake. That was the million dollar question.

Jane kept her eyes glued to her bright red berry set into the creamy pink frosting.

"Whoops! Excuse me." Paula patted her pocket. "My phone." She pulled out her cell phone and padded into the hall.

Jane's second narrow escape of the day. She pealed the sliced strawberry from the frosted cupcake and bit it. She wasn't sure which was scarier: finding out how Isaac truly felt about missions, or facing Caramel and the missing diamond in the morning.

Jane took her cupcake to the dining room table where Valerie and Kaitlyn were chatting.

Kaitlyn turned her one hundred watt smile to Jane. "So what kind of small groups do you like?"

"Bible studies are good." Jane licked a dab of frosting from her thumb.

"We're all single ladies—for now anyway," Valerie said. "Maybe we could offer a Bible study for single career women."

"Sure…" Kaitlyn said, her voice trailing off in an unconvinced tone. "That's a possibility. But what about single moms, instead? That's a really needy group."

"We could do that." Valerie sucked in her cheeks. "We'd have to get babysitters lined up, but it is a needy group."

Jane set her cup down. Nothing wrong with single women— or single moms—as far as an outreach was concerned, but they were going about this backwards. "Do we have a list of small groups that Columbia River already offers?"

"Oh, I am pretty sure I know all of them already," Kaitlyn said.

"Okay." Jane nodded, but found the claim difficult to believe. "Why don't we make a list of what we know is going on and see if we could identify an unmet need."

Kaitlyn pulled her tablet from her purse. She stroked it and poked it. "All right, here's the list from the website."

Before Kaitlyn could start reading it, Paula came back into the room. Her face was paper white. She gripped the back of Valerie's chair, her arms shaking.

"Ladies, I…" She choked on the word. "I need to ask you to leave. There's been an accident." Fat tears welled up from Paula's eyes, and rolled down her cheeks.

Kaitlyn jumped up, and put an arm around Paula's back. She pulled out a chair. "You need to sit."

Paula collapsed into the seat.

"What happened? How we can help?" Kaitlyn knelt down beside Paula so they were at about eye level.

"It's Marcus." Paula covered her face with both hands. "They found him… He was on his way home." She shook her head.

Jane reached across the table for Paula's hand. "What happened?"

"They said it was a hit and run." She took a deep, ragged breath.

"Paula, what do you need us to do for you?" Kaitlyn asked, her young voice business-like.

"He's at the hospital. Providence."

For a moment, Jane's heart lightened. Marcus would be okay.

"They need me to come identify his body." Paula crumpled forward, laying her head on the table, her shoulders shaking as she wept.

Kaitlyn stayed next to her, the prosthetic hand resting

CHAPTER 3

KAITLYN DROVE PAULA TO THE HOSPITAL, and Valerie followed with the Ehlers' car. Jane had stood on the periphery, watching their careful handling of the mission coordinator, whom they had known for years and loved. Jane wanted to step in and help, too, but Kaitlyn had already thought of everything.

Jane had hugged the grieving woman and both of her new teammates. She would pray for Paula, but until some new task needed doing, she would attempt to get a handle on the issue of the missing diamond ring.

First thing she did when she got back to her own, small, crowded apartment, was call Holly.

"Listen," she said, after exchanging greetings, "I desperately need you tomorrow at the Swanson house."

"I'm free. What's up?" Holly said.

Jane explained the trouble with the ring.

"She really thinks you found it in the drain and stole it?"

"I can't know what she really thinks, but that is basically what she said. If I had enough money, I'd hire a plumber to come out, and I'd stand back and let him do the work."

"Why don't you?"

"Like I said, I don't have the money."

"You can bill her, can't you? It's not like you all agreed up front what tomorrow would cost."

Jane toyed with the idea before answering. It struck her as less than aboveboard. "There could be trouble if she decided not to pay, that's all. The last thing I need is for a plumber to take me to court for an unpaid bill." Jane scratched "call Holly" off her to do list.

"Oh well. You can count on me. Seven in the morning?"

"Yup, bright and early." Jane looked out the window. The sun hovered on the horizon, the long, slow summer sunset clinging to the edge of the Earth.

"Bet you wish Isaac was home."

"You bet I do." Calling Isaac was next on her list. Every time she pictured him in his jungle seminary her heart skipped a beat.

"Then I'll say goodbye so you can get hold of him. You know he'll have some great way to get you out of this unscathed."

"Bye, Holly, and thanks." Jane hung up. Holly had been a good find. She had come on the recommendation of Isaac's mom as well, but unlike Caramel Swanson, Jane was glad to have connected with Holly.

Jane started with a text, because phone reception was so patchy at Isaac's school. But before she knew it, she had added the tale of Marcus Ehlers' death to the message. Not only would the message be a pain to read, and ridiculously expensive, it was a terrible way to find out someone had died. Jane erased it, and dialed Isaac's number to call him.

The phone rang, and rang, but no one answered.

She turned it off.

The lesson, if she was forced to find one, was that in times of crisis like this, she was supposed to turn to God, and not her boyfriend. She curled up on her couch with a glass of ice water. You couldn't pray too much over a crisis, even if you were out of new things to say.

The next morning was bright and warm. A great day to spend on the lake, relaxing. Instead, Jane met Holly at the Swanson house. Holly wore her "Plain Jane's Good Clean Houses" T-shirt, and a determined grimace.

"Don't worry, Holly. Her bark has to be worse than her bite." After her long evening of prayer and meditation, the situation with the missing wedding ring had been put in its proper perspective. Caramel was being unreasonable and unrealistic. Showing up this morning to help look for the ring would prove her innocence. After giving the hunt the old college try, everyone could move on. Jane fully expected to be fired as replacement housekeeper, and that was fine, too.

Holly tried to smile.

"I mean it. This is no big deal." Jane rang the doorbell and waited.

Before the door was answered, a white panel wagon with "Trusty Plumbers" painted on the side drove up.

"This is great news!" Jane gave Holly a big grin. "Now all we will have to do is go fishing in drain gunk. The professionals can take them apart and put them back together."

The plumber joined them on the front step with his toolbox. He wore faded but clean overalls and looked about Jane's dad's age.

"You the little lady who lost the ring?" he asked.

"I am the housekeeper, Jane." Jane pinned her smile in place, but wondered what story Caramel had told the plumbers.

An older, white-haired man in crisp slacks and a golf shirt answered the door. "Come in, come in." He waved them into the house. "Caramel isn't down yet."

Douglas wasn't expected back yet, according to Caramel, so who was this guy?

The plumber set his toolbox down on the marble floor. "Where do you want me to start?"

"Caramel said to start in the mud room. Follow me." The man padded down the hall in his sock feet. He opened the door to a bright, airy mud room with a large, deep, utility sink in the corner. "Go ahead and rip into that one first. I'd like to talk to the ladies." He winked at Jane.

It had to be Mr. Swanson.

He led Jane and Holly into the kitchen.

"Mr. Swanson, I just want to let you know that I didn't see the ring yesterday. I tore the sink completely apart, and it just wasn't there."

"Call me Douglas." Douglas leaned against the wall, propped up on his elbow. His feet were crossed at the ankle. He looked Holly up and down like a new car, then turned his gaze to Jane. "Your friend there is sure a young one."

Jane frowned. "Holly is my employee, and she is young, just seventeen." She straightened up and crossed her arms over her chest. She was beginning to understand the reason behind Caramel's distrust of her husband.

Douglas sized up Jane, his eyes lingering just above her crossed arms. "How long have you been in business, darlin'?"

Jane caught Holly's eye. Holly was wide eyed and looked confused.

"I've been running Good Clean Houses for three years now."

"You'll never make me believe you are old enough for that!" Douglas let out a deep chuckle. "Have you had any coffee yet? Can I get you some? Maybe with a dash of Hawaii in it?" He gestured to a selection of bottles on the counter near a short refrigerator. Jane saw "Kahlua" on one of the labels.

"No thank you, Mr. Swanson." Jane held her ground. With her whole heart, which was beating like a dub-step flash mob, she wished she could run to the mudroom with the plumber, but she could tell her reputation was at stake. One wrong move and she could be held responsible for the missing half-million-dollar ring. "What would Caramel like us to do today?"

"Caramel is… embarrassed." The corners of his mouth hinted at a smirk. "Today she says she dropped 'something' but can't be sure that it was her ring. Here, sit down, girls." He waved to the bar stools at the kitchen island.

"She found the ring?" Jane didn't move.

"Not yet. She's not the brightest bulb in the box, to be frank. She called the plumber to find whatever it is she lost."

"Then can we go?" Holly had inched her way to the kitchen door.

"Yes, of course. Why don't you run along?" Douglas nodded in Holly's direction without looking at her.

"Wait a sec." Jane held Holly's gaze until Holly nodded.

Douglas moved closer to Jane. "We don't need your friend, Jane." He cocked an eyebrow. "Let her go so we can get to know each other a little better."

Jane shook her head, speechless. She'd rather be accused of stealing a priceless diamond than spend one minute alone with this man. "I have another meeting to get to by eight. If you no longer need us, we'll be leaving."

"Are you sure about that?" Douglas's voice was a low purr.

Holly was shaking in the doorway, and Jane was about to holler for help, the tension in the room was so thick, when the silence was broken by the sharp clacks of high heels on marble.

"I see you've met the help." Caramel entered the room in a swish and swirl of satiny fabric, some kind of thin night gown wrapped around her. She planted a red kiss on Douglas's cheek, and squeezed past Jane.

Caramel held up her hand, a huge diamond sparkling in the bright kitchen lights. "Well, you had a close call, didn't you?" Caramel looked from her ring to Jane, and then over to Douglas. "Two close calls, I'd say." Caramel poured herself a cup of coffee. "I'd rather you not come again when my husband is home." She sipped her hot drink.

Holly nodded so hard her glasses slipped to the end of her nose.

"Did you find your ring, sugar?" Douglas sidled up to his wife. He pulled down the bottle of Kahlua and opened it up.

"I bought a new one, baby." Caramel smiled like the Cheshire cat.

Douglas set the bottle on the counter, his body bristling. "You what?" His words were ice cold.

"I went to Joe, sweetie. Joe takes care of me."

Douglas inhaled deeply through his nose. His face grew red, but he pulled a smile into place. "Joe is her brother."

Jane had the feeling Douglas was reminding himself, rather than telling her and Holly.

Douglas lifted Caramel's hand and examined the new bauble. "It had better not be real." He dropped her hand and stalked out of the room.

Caramel picked up the abandoned Kahlua bottle and splashed a little into her mug. "You all can leave now."

"Of course." Jane crossed to where Holly stood, very near their exit.

"It is real," Caramel said, her dark black eyelashes at half-mast, as she stared at the girls.

Jane and Holly inched their way to the door.

"Of course," Jane said with a quick nod.

"Joe wants the best for me, always."

Holly and Jane turned and nearly ran out of the house.

Once inside her car, Jane stopped to catch her breath.

"I wouldn't want to get stuck in an elevator with that man," Holly said as she clipped her seat belt.

"Me neither." Jane pulled out of the driveway, wondering what was behind Caramel's story of the missing ring. Had the ring ever been missing? Had the whole thing been a ruse to get her to the house while Douglas, the philandering spouse was home? If so, was the missing ring a trap set for Douglas or for Jane?

Jane worried over it the whole drive home, yet again wishing that Isaac wasn't all the way in Costa Rica when she needed him.

CHAPTER 4

AFTER FINISHING UP HER EIGHT O'CLOCK CLIENT'S HOME, Jane met Kaitlyn at the food court of the mall.

Kaitlyn wore her Bubble-Bubble Tea uniform. Her shiny blonde hair was pulled back into a high ponytail. Jane noted that she wasn't totally fixated by Kaitlyn's hand any longer, but a wave a guilt washed the feeling away. Obviously, she *was* still unnaturally fixated on it if she noticed how little she noticed it. Jane sipped her bubble tea, the tapioca "bubbles" rolling over her tongue. It was… different.

"Valerie had to work today, but she gave me permission to try and make a plan."

"Great." Jane took another sip. It made sense to turn to Valerie as group leader, since she was the oldest. It would be much easier following her lead than Kaitlyn's.

Kaitlyn whipped a small notepad out of the front pocket of her Bubble-Bubble smock. "First off, I think we need to arrange meals."

"Shouldn't we decide who we are trying to serve first?" Jane stirred her drink with her straw. She didn't want to attempt another drink.

"We have to serve Paula." Kaitlyn frowned. "We need to put aside our personal goals right now and just help her."

"Yes, of course." Jane's cheeks burned, as a wave of embarrassment rolled over her. She had been wanting to do something for Paula herself, but of course, Kaitlyn brought it up before she did.

"I think that Valerie, you, and I should arrange meals, help around the house, and also help with anything funeral related she might need."

"I'd be happy to offer to clean for her." Visions of the Crawford funeral rushed in. She could arrange a funeral and serve food, if push came to shove, but folding laundry and taking out the trash sounded simpler.

"Don't worry about that. I ran over this morning and did some chores. She's really holding up pretty well. She said I could come back later this week and do a deep clean before the funeral."

"I could help. I'm a housecleaner." She was aware that she was begging to do housework, which just seemed wrong. But why should Kaitlyn get to do it, when it was really her "thing"?

"Uh-huh. I know." Kaitlyn tilted her head. "Do you feel like you would do a better job?"

Jane hated the combative feeling that welled up in her. What had Kaitlyn ever done wrong? Nothing. Until last night they had not exchanged more than hellos. Jane needed to relax. They were teammates, not adversaries. "No, I don't think that. It's just what I do, so it felt natural." Jane kept her eyes steady on Kaitlyn's nose, a trick she had learned in business school. Focused on the speaker without freaking them out.

"It might be a good idea to stretch yourself." Kaitlyn's smile was warm, and Jane begged herself to believe it wasn't condescending.

Jane took a deep breath. "Would you like me to arrange meals?"

"You really don't know anyone at Columbia River yet, do you? I mean, it might be hard for you to do that."

"It would be a stretch for sure."

"Valerie has volunteered to arrange meals, which I think is super, because that's a major priority, in my opinion."

"So I can't clean and I can't arrange meals. What *do* you want me to do?" Jane straightened up. Her defensive reaction was in high gear, and her inner monologue wasn't helping. She attempted to turn it into a prayer. She hoped that it had been her encounter with Douglas that had set her on edge, because the idea that she might be this defensive around Kaitlyn while they tried to plan a Bible study together was horrible.

"I was hoping you could tell me." Kaitlyn sat back in her seat and crossed her arms over her chest. She continued to smile.

Jane's eyes drifted to the prosthetic hand. She couldn't help feeling that Kaitlyn was used to being the center of everyone's attention. A pretty blonde girl with a romantic injury. Jane hated that she jumped to the idea that Kaitlyn was self-centered, but this meeting wasn't helping change her opinion.

"I could go visit Paula and ask her what she would find helpful." Jane took a big drink of bubble tea. She stifled her gag reflex.

"You could do that."

"It seems like a good idea." Jane tried to guess what Kaitlyn was thinking. *Jane Adler is useless? Jane Adler doesn't have a creative bone in her body? Bubble Tea is super yummy?* The last one was unfair. She had no reason to believe Kaitlyn was thinking vapid thoughts.

"Are you free to go over there tonight?" Kaitlyn appeared to be looking over Jane's shoulder. It was all Jane could do to not turn and look behind her.

"Yeah, I am. I could call Paula and see if it is good for her."

"Uh-huh." Kaitlyn's over-the-shoulder gaze suddenly focused. "Hey!" She stood and careened around the table.

Jane swung in her seat.

Kaitlyn had a chubby boy, about twelve years old, by the collar of his shirt. "Look at me!" Her voice was calm, but forceful. "Don't ever let me see you treating someone like that ever again, do you hear?"

The boy was shaking, but he spit, missing Kaitlyn and hitting the ground. "You're not my mom, you gimp." His voice shook, too, despite his big words.

A younger boy with a black eye scooted away from the scene.

Jane stood up, but hesitated. Would Kaitlyn get in trouble if she ran for a security guard?

"You don't mean that." Kaitlyn's voice went lower. "Those are the words of a scared kid." She dropped his collar, but stood, arms crossed, in front of him, blocking his access to the younger boy. "You bully because you are scared, but you have to stop. Two wrongs make the world an awful place."

The bully's face flushed. "I'm not scared of you." His eye was trained on Kaitlyn's hand.

Jane felt sick to her stomach. She was no better than a prepubescent little boy, focusing on Kaitlyn's difference. She joined Kaitlyn. "Would you like me to get security?"

"Nah." Kaitlyn pulled a bright blue tract from her pocket. The cover said, "Where is God When You are Scared?" "Take this, sit down and read it, and I won't call security."

The boy grabbed the tract. He looked around the food court, only a couple of the dozen or so shoppers had looked their direction. The boy sat down. "Terrorizing someone weaker than you won't make you stronger."

Kaitlyn caught the boy's eye. He shrugged and scowled.

Kaitlyn led Jane back to their table. "I hate bullies," she said. "It's tempting to knock them upside the head with my bionic hand. It is pretty heavy." She held her hand up and smiled. "But two wrongs really do just make the world a rotten place, you know?"

"Do you know that kid?" Jane's smile stretched from cheek to cheek. Bionic hand. She had a feeling that "breaking the ice" about the hand thing was something Kaitlyn had to constantly do.

"Nah. But I see a lot of little boys trying to be big here. You'd be amazed at how little these big kids really are on the inside."

Jane turned her paper cup of bubble tea around in a circle, an idea brewing. "They're a pretty needy bunch, hey?"

"You got that right."

"A pretty needy *mission field*?" Jane asked.

"Ooh, I think I like what you are thinking." Kaitlyn's eyes sparkled. It was pretty clear the kids who loitered around the mall causing trouble had been on her heart for a while.

"Let's get Paula squared away and then we can meet with Valerie again. If we do want to reach out to these kids, we've got our work cut out for us."

"True that. Preadolescent bullies at the mall are a very specific target, and not at all an easy one to reach out to."

Kaitlyn and Jane exchanged a grin. "All the more reason to try," Jane said.

Kaitlyn checked her watch. "Break over. Call me if you need anything."

"Will do." Jane gathered her backpack and jacket. It was a pity that Kaitlyn had such pretty hair and freckles across her nose. Cuteness made people—made Jane—make unfair assumptions.

Jane popped into the mall library and found a comfy chair. She pulled out her phone and sent a quick text to Isaac. Just a "miss you" message. When he had a chance to call her she'd fill in the details.

She stared at the phone willing Isaac to reply to her message, but nothing happened. After her return from exile in Phoenix was over, the summer after she graduated from Bible School, she and Isaac had been inseparable. This Costa Rica teaching gig was their first real trial as an official couple. Jane loved that he was there, in theory. Every day she expected to hear him say that he had changed his mind and wanted to be a missionary. The strain of waiting for that was getting to her.

No text from Isaac came through, so Jane called Paula.

Paula invited her over immediately. They sat together in Paula's kitchen with steaming cups of tea. The sink was full of coffee mugs, and there was a pan on the stove. There was a smattering of crumbs on the counter by the toaster. Jane tried not to notice, but it was hard. Paula looked as undone as her kitchen. She had deep shadows under her eyes, and her hair hung limply around her face.

"It was very kind of you to call, Jane." Even Paula's voice sounded defeated.

"Can I do anything to help? Anything at all?" Jane felt awkward, like her elbows went too far out and she was going to knock over the mantle decorations even though they were all the way across the room. She tried to take a deep breath without being noticed. It didn't work.

"I spent many years overseas before I was married." Paula's eyes lost their absent look. "And one of the things I learned was important to people in the third world is the ability to be together with someone in their grief." Her voice choked on the last word. Her eyes were mournful, but they held Jane's gaze. "It would be good for you to sit here with me."

Jane opened her mouth to speak, but stopped. She needed to just sit quietly, so she nodded instead. She tried to smile, but it felt wrong. She let her smile morph into a sympathetic frown, but that felt condescending.

Paula made the same sympathetic frowning face—or at least, she successfully made the face Jane was trying for.

"I've known many young widows." Paula's voice had a thoughtful, faraway quality. "In some countries they wouldn't consider me a young widow, but Mark and I had barely been married two years." Her voice cracked. "So our marriage was young, even if I wasn't." Paula sniffled into her sleeve.

Jane jumped up. "Let me get you a tissue."

"No, sit down." Paula waved her hand. She dabbed under her eyes. "Sometimes sitting quietly will speak to people from other cultures about the peace of Christ."

Jane sat down.

"We can be peacemakers in the world, Jane. It's one of the beautiful jobs of the Church."

Jane wrapped the cuff of her sleeve around her fingers. "It sounds like a powerful experience."

"You're uncomfortable. I know." Paula's eyes were filled with tears, but she offered a comforting smile. "You don't have to stay."

"No, I want to." Jane's voice shook. She wanted to "help," whatever that would look like. She squeezed her fingers together. Quiet wasn't the problem, really. She could clean an empty house all by herself in the quiet. She could even deliver the silent treatment to people who were bothering her. But the sympathetic quiet... no. As far as she could tell, she was wired to work. She tapped her foot on the rung of her chair. Her whole body felt coiled to leap into the kitchen and attack the little pile of dishes.

Tears had spilled from Paula's brown eyes. She wiped them away. "Thank you." Her eyes turned to the picture above the mantle again.

It looked like a huge family picture, but the family was clearly not American.

"Why don't you come back tomorrow? I'll be home all day, so you can just come whenever you are free." Paula stood up. "I think I might be the one not ready to sit quietly together."

Jane tried for the sympathetic smile one more time, and it finally felt natural. "I will, Paula. I promise." She gave Paula a side hug and tried not to look like she was running out of the house.

The thing was, she was sure she could do this overseas. It was weird to sit quietly in America. In Kyrgyzstan or India it would feel perfectly normal. She was sure it would.

On the drive home, she prayed God would give Paula comfort—and give her the ability to relax at Paula's house.

CHAPTER 5

THE NEXT DAY JANE FOUND HERSELF back at Caramel's house. Rather than being fired, Jane had been offered an extra day of heavy cleaning. Douglas and Caramel were both missing in action, but there was a detailed message on Jane's voicemail that gave her at least three hours' worth of housework.

She started her day in the garage. From glossy white walls to the speckled floor, this five bay room was like a jewelry box for vintage cars, not a place people got dirty. Both of the Swansons' daily drivers were parked in the garage, so Jane guessed the two were out back on the property somewhere.

Though the room appeared spotless, Jane had directions to give it a deep clean.

Mopping the spotless garage floor was one of the weirder feelings Jane had had in her life—right up there with sitting quietly in Paula's house. A hot wave of embarrassment rolled over Jane as she remembered her failed attempt to offer comfort to Paula. She ought to have better people skills. After all, she was twenty-two now, and had been doing this "grown up" thing for a long time.

Clear water ran out of the mop every time she twisted it in the mop bucket. How like Caramel to make the maid do something that didn't need to be done. Classic power trip.

Jane ran the mop under the new Mini Cooper—Caramel's rather modest little daily driver.

At last the mop came back dirty. Jane felt a little thrill of pleasure. She let out a happy sigh and stuck the mop back under the car. When she was sure it was clean, she gave her mop a final rinse and dumped the mop water down the utility sink.

Since she was on the lower level, she ought to clean the hot tub room next. It was just down the hall from the garage, in the daylight basement, and had sweeping views of their vast lawns, but the hot tub room gave Jane the creeps. She paused at the door of the room—her least favorite in all of the homes she had ever cleaned.

The walls were papered in shimmery black with gold flecks and topped with a mirrored ceiling. Jane would have guessed this house was less than fifteen years old, but the hot tub room was straight from the 1980s—years before she was born.

A huge wet bar flanked one wall. A light made from wine bottles strung in a row hung over it. The bar stools were topped with leopard print cushions and the rug was a brilliant zebra print—brilliant because the white stripes glowed in the black light that was positioned over it.

Then there was the hot tub itself. It was the maid's job—therefore Jane's until the proper maid returned from vacation—to do the pH test and add chemicals as necessary. The tub was a beast. It looked as though it could seat twenty, and she had to climb a set of black marble—could it be real marble?—steps to get to the lid.

Every time she climbed the steps she felt like a missionary being led into the cauldron by cannibals. Cannibals aside, this hot tub water really was people-broth.

The hot tub room was warm and steamy. It smelled like a locker room. From the small pile of towels at the bottom step to the tub, Jane could tell it had been used recently. All lights but the black light were out, so the towels, the stripes on the rug, and the striations in the steps glowed. Jane crinkled her nose. She flipped the light on before she entered. It was better when the lights were on. Not great, but better.

Jane had the water testing kit in her pocket, so she went straight to the tub. Best to get the grossest bit out of the way first.

At the first step, she grabbed the pile of towels—still damp—and tossed them to the laundry hamper by the door. She missed.

Jane knelt at the top step and leaned over to get her water sample.

Something stringy slid through her fingers.

Hair? Short, gray hair that waved around in the water like sickly seaweed.

Jane wrenched her hand back. Her stomach heaved.

Douglas Swanson sat in the tub his face submerged just below the surface of the water.

Jane squeezed her eyes shut, and grabbed his head, trying to lift it from the water so she could find a pulse. Her fingers probed his bloated neck, but she couldn't do it. She couldn't hold his head, find a pulse, and not puke.

She turned her head to the side, and wretched.

Her guts were in a vice that wouldn't stop squeezing, but nothing came out. For the first time ever, she was glad she had skipped breakfast.

She tried again to lift him, so she could attempt CPR, but he was just too heavy. And, she was pretty sure he was dead.

She pulled her phone out of her apron pocket, but her hand was shaking so violently that she dropped it in the tub. She plunged her arm into the water up to her elbow, and the bobbing head butted against her arm as she fished for her phone. The phone lay on Douglas's knee. She pulled her arm out of the water and stumbled down the steps. She lunged for the door, but tripped on the tangle of wet towels and pitched into the door frame.

Her skull felt like a bell with her brain sounding against its hard sides. She wiped her forehead with her wet hand.

Blood. She was bleeding.

The room swirled around her. She stopped everything and sat down, legs crossed. She leaned forward, her head in her lap, and tried to breathe. "Dear Lord, dear Lord, dear Lord," she prayed over and over again, thankful that the Spirit would translate her panic into something useful.

When her body stilled she sat up. Her phone, resting on Douglas's knee, was the only phone she knew of in the house. In the three weeks she had been cleaning here, she hadn't seen a single land line. Should she run upstairs and search the rooms for one? Or was there a faster way to call the police?

She had seen a bright blue alarm system box in the garage.

With extreme caution, so as not to start the panic back up, Jane stood, and took the long walk back down the basement hall.

The alarm box was above the workbench.

Jane popped the cover and stared at the keys. Could she trip the alarm to make it call the police? Or was there an emergency button she could press?

She held her shaking finger in front of the keypad.

Maybe she should get a neighbor instead.

She turned her head toward the garage doors. The neighbors were so isolated on their acred lots. It would be faster to alert the police this way. If she could figure it out.

But wait.

Do you even call the police when a man drowns?

She pressed her fingertips to her forehead. She needed a phone to call 911.

But she didn't really need an ambulance, because Douglas was dead.

She looked up at the box again.

She chewed her lip.

How had that alarm gone off when she was a kid?

The switch box.

The switch box was near enough to the alarm box that she could reach it. She opened it up and began switching every one of them on and then off. Before she had done the whole box the alarm was sounding.

A shoulder-shaking sob escaped. She took a deep breath. Then another. Someone would come help her now.

Jane let herself out the garage door. She sat on the edge of the flower box nearest the garage and waited for help to arrive.

CHAPTER 6

CARAMEL SWANSON STORMED ACROSS HER DRIVEWAY. She was squeezed into a pair of curve-hugging jeans and shiny brown leather riding boots that were silent on the cobblestone parking circle.

"What is going on here?" Caramel held her phone in Jane's face like an accusation. "The alarm company just called me to see if I knew why our alarm was going off. I do not know why the alarm is going off."

Jane's whole body shook. Her mind told her to stand up and face Caramel, but her legs didn't agree. She wrapped her arms around her knees, trying to hold them still. She opened her mouth, but a garbled choke came out instead of words.

"Well? How did you trip the alarm? It wasn't even set." Caramel's face was violent red. "I was in the middle of something a little bit important."

Jane threw herself to her feet. She quivered top to bottom. "It's Douglas." Her voice matched her shaking body.

"What's that dirty dog done now?" Caramel pulled her phone back. Her face wrinkled like she had a mouth full of vinegar.

"He's dead." Jane's voice was barely above a whisper.

Caramel's eyes bulged out of her head. "What?"

"In the hot tub." Jane kept her eyes trained on Caramel's face.

Caramel's angry red face had bleached white. She looked Jane up and down, then frowned. "What do you mean he's dead in the hot tub?"

Jane just nodded.

"You mean Douglas is dead? In the hot tub?"

Jane nodded again. If she opened her mouth, all of her fear would come out in great hiccoughy sobs, and she couldn't do that in front of Caramel.

"What are you doing just sitting here? Call the ambulance!" Caramel's voice rose to a shriek that sent shivers up and down Jane's arms.

Jane gulped. "I dropped my phone. In the hot tub." She flinched.

Caramel waved her phone in Jane's face. "You are the most inept, useless person I have met in all of my life! Get inside the house and call the ambulance, you fool! They might have been able to save my husband!"

Jane wavered, looking from the door to the phone in Caramel's hand. "Is there a phone inside?"

"Oh, never mind!" Caramel stabbed her cell phone with a long, red, fingernail. "911? 911? There's been a death!"

The blare of sirens made Jane's skin crawl. She stood against the brick wall of the garage door, shaking with fear. When the paramedics poured out of the ambulance, Caramel swooped on them and led them to the hot tub room.

Jane considered running—just running down the street as far away as her feet could carry her. She could always run back again to talk to the police. But an officer reached her before she could will her feet to move.

The officer was a short woman with cropped brown hair and a deeply lined face. She frowned at Jane. "Caramel Swanson?"

"No, ma'am. Jane Adler, the maid." Jane bit her lip.

The officer looked her up and down as though recording her height and weight.

"You discovered the body?"

"Yes." Jane gripped her fingers together to keep them from shaking.

"Why didn't you call the police?"

Jane opened her mouth to answer, but she choked on a sob. She clamped her mouth shut and just nodded.

"It's okay." The officer lowered her voice, and looked over Jane's shoulder. "Take your time."

Jane nodded again. She blinked away the tears that were burning in her eyes. "I was going to call, but I was shaking so hard I dropped my phone in the water." Her words began to spill out. "I thought I was all alone here, and I didn't know what to do, so I set off the alarm. But they called Caramel's cell phone, and so Caramel came up here and then she called you."

The officer narrowed her eyes. "You're the regular housekeeper?"

"No. I'm just filling in while their maid is on vacation."

"So you didn't know where Caramel was or where the phones were?"

"I panicked. I couldn't remember seeing a phone, but there might be one upstairs in the office." Jane rubbed her lips together hoping to make her jaw stop trembling.

"So your cell phone is in the hot tub with the deceased?"

"Yes." Jane looked at her feet.

"I need you to remain outside now. Two officers are staying out here, and you cannot leave the property. Do you understand?"

Jane nodded. This time the tears spilled down her face.

The officer looked her up and down again. Her eyebrows lifted a tiny bit. "Go ahead and sit down." The officer indicated the ground.

Jane slid to her seat. She wrapped her arms around her knees and laid her head on them. She had been alone in the house with Douglas, and now he was dead, and she wasn't allowed to leave the property, and her cell phone was in the hot tub. They were going to arrest her. She pinched her eyes shut and prayed the prayer of a desperately scared kid. "Dear God," she whispered, "I want my mommy."

Jane kept her head down and her eyes shut until she heard the paramedics exiting the house. She opened her eyes, but didn't lift her head. Two paramedics carried the stretcher off to the ambulance. Douglas Swanson was zipped in a body bag. Behind her somewhere, maybe still at the threshold of the door, Caramel was answering questions, her words mingled with deep, chesty sobs.

A man in a raincoat crouched beside Jane. "I'd like to ask you some questions. Do you mind stepping over here?"

Jane wiped her eyes, nodded, and followed the man to the front door of the house. They both sat on the stone benches that flanked the front door.

"I'm Detective Bryce. Are you Jane Adler?"

"Yes." Jane chewed on the side of her tongue. She would have given her own left hand to stop shaking. Kaitlyn's bionic hand popped into her head, and she almost smiled. She took a deep breath, slowly calming down.

"Can you tell me why you were in the basement of the Swanson house?"

"I'm their cleaner—just while their real maid is on vacation." Jane took another deep breath.

"Tell me about what you did today." The officer had a baby face, with big blue eyes and an easy smile. His words were slow, with a hint of the South. He seemed like the safe spot in a whirlpool of sharks. She couldn't pull her eyes away.

"I started in the garage, tidied the work bench, mopped up the floor. Then, since I was downstairs already, I went to the back room with the hot tub. I needed to clean it up."

"What happened next?" He leaned forward a little, as though she were telling a fascinating story.

"I wanted to check the pH on the tub—I do it every time I come. Balance the chemicals and all of that." Jane took another deep breath. "I dipped the little tester thing into the water, to get the sample, you know? And that's when I saw him in there." She squeezed her eyes shut for just a second, wishing she could see anything but the straggling hair floating at the surface of the water.

"And then what happened?"

"I had to call the ambulance, so I grabbed my phone, but I was shaking so hard—" Jane held out her hand, still quaking "—that I dropped it in the tub."

"What did you do then?" Detective Bryce had a surprised tone, like he hadn't already known that, though Jane thought surely he had.

"I didn't know what to do. I tried to think of where there was a phone in the house, but I couldn't remember, and the house is so big. I didn't want to waste time running around."

"You didn't try to get him out of the water and revive him?"

Bit her bottom lip. She had tried to pull him out, but he was so heavy. What if she should have tried harder? Her hard-won composure was gone again. He had just looked dead. He had looked hideously dead, lying there in the water. "He was too heavy…" Her voice trailed off.

"Do you have CPR training?"

Jane nodded. After the situation with Bob Crawford the previous year, she had gotten CPR training. But in spite of that she still hadn't been able to save Douglas.

"But you didn't try to resuscitate him?" Detective Bryce hadn't changed his tone of voice one bit; he still sounded interested and concerned. But Jane felt convicted.

"I couldn't get him out. And he just looked so dead." Jane pulled her eyes from the detective's face.

"What happened next?"

"I just tried to think of some way to get help, and the fastest thing I could think of was the house alarm."

"You didn't try and find Caramel?"

"I didn't know she was home."

The officer nodded. "Okay. So you set off the house alarm. Then what happened?"

"Caramel came and called the police." Jane was suddenly exhausted. She didn't want to relive every step of the last hour— the sloshing water, the moist towels, the frantically flipping switches at the electrical panel, or Caramel yelling at her while Douglas floated in the filthy water of his playboy tub.

"There's just one more thing I'd like you to do today. Do you think you are up for it?"

Jane frowned.

"I just need to get your contact information. Okay? No big deal. Later, we'll want to connect with you to get an official statement. You know, if this is just some kind of accident, it's no big deal at all, but depending on what the coroner says, we'll need to get in touch with you for a statement." Detective Bryce's voice was friendly, not condescending. It had a little up note at the end, like getting in touch for a statement was kind of the same as going out for coffee, or meeting at the library.

Jane gave him her address. "But… I have to get a new phone now, so I don't know. Should I call you when I have a new number? Or maybe I can have the phone people switch my number to a new phone?"

"Yes, you'd better give us the old number, and then try and have it moved. If worse comes to worst we'll just pop by. And as soon as you have a new phone, you can call us and confirm the number." Detective Bryce passed her a business card.

"Okay." Jane felt tongue tied.

"Wait here just a minute, all right?"

Jane nodded and watched the young detective go back to his car. He stood next to it and made a phone call.

He was back on the porch with her before she could decide what she should do next. He had a pad of paper and a pen.

"I had a quick chat with my boss, and he suggested since you might not be easy to reach, that you could write your statement out for us now." He handed her the pad, with a disarming smile. "Do you think you are up for it?"

Jane swallowed hard. What could it hurt? "Sure." She took the notepad with a shaking hand.

"Just write down everything you told me, and it will be perfect." He sat down on the bench across from her again.

Jane started to write. The words seemed to flow from her pen like water. She said everything she could think of from mopping the spotless garage to how she flipped the electric switches to set off the alarm. When she was done, she was exhausted.

"Good job!" Detective Bryce flipped the pages of his notebook. "Five pages! This might be a record." He turned it to the last page. "Just sign here for me, okay?"

Jane signed the notepad underneath her statement.

"I'd like you to remain up here for just a bit longer, in case we have any more questions. One of the officers will let you know when it's okay to leave."

Jane leaned back against the house and waited to be released from the scene... of the crime? Was Douglas murdered in his hot tub? She sincerely hoped not, and yet, murder seemed highly likely this time.

CHAPTER 7

JANE STOPPED AT THE STORE on the way home to buy a new phone. She grabbed a pay-as-you-go phone and a time card, and set it up before she drove away. Not that it was a real help, since it didn't have her phone numbers in it, and no one knew its number.

She charged it in her car as she drove home. It wasn't much use, but it was something to call her phone company from—and her parents, who paid the bill on their family plan—to replace her real phone.

When she got home and her phone was finally usable she called Isaac—one of the few numbers she knew by heart.

And he actually answered.

"Jane!"

A smile spread across Jane's face that started in her heart. His voice was a breath of fresh air. "Where have *you* been?"

"In the mountains. Very sketchy reception. You, my friend, would love it."

Jane exhaled slowly. His voice sounded so happy and confident. A gray shadow lifted from her picture of the future. Isaac was totally going to want to be a missionary after this.

"I've had a horrible week. Tell me something to take my mind off of it." Jane stretched out on her futon and kicked her shoes off.

"I can hear the ocean from my office."

"I thought you were in the mountains?"

"I was, but I'm back at the office now. I'm staring at a picture of the view from the ridge of the mountain we climbed and listening to the sound of the ocean from my office."

"Can you see the water?"

"Nah, there's a forest, a wildlife preserve, between here and there, but it's a short walk, and I can hear it."

"You can hear it with a forest in the way?" She wasn't sure if Isaac wasn't making any sense or if she was just having a hard time concentrating. Whenever he said ocean, the image of Douglas's head floating in the water came to mind. She wanted it to go away, but it wouldn't.

"It's not loud, but it's there."

"So location is perfect. Now, how is the work going?"

"Great. The students are serious. None of the slackers you get back home."

"You love it."

"That I do. But you had a horrible week? What happened?"

Jane paused. She wasn't ready to talk about Douglas yet. "Paula Ehlers—the mission coordinator at Columbia River? Her husband was killed in a hit and run."

"That's awful."

"She's a wreck. I feel so bad for her."

"You've got to step up, Jane. These are the moments God put you on Earth for."

Jane pictured the last time she had gone to Paula's house to help. "I want to help, but I don't think she needs me."

"Of course she needs you."

"Listen, that wasn't the worst of it."

"Mark Ehlers dying wasn't the worst?"

"It was bad, but not the worst. You know my new clients, the Swansons?"

"Wait—hold on a second."

Jane waited. The silence was killing her. Had the line been dropped?

"Okay, I'm here. Something was worse than Mark dying?" He had a distracted tone in his voice.

"Mr. Swanson, my client, died, too. They think it was murder."

"Get out."

"What?"

"Another murder? Are you kidding?"

"No, I'm not kidding in the least." Jane rolled onto her side, she needed a bit more than disbelief and distraction right now.

"No. I'm sorry. Of course you wouldn't, but you can see what I mean, can't you? It's a little unbelievable."

"Yeah, of course." Jane's heart was heavy and her whole body felt tired. She had waited ages to be able to talk to him and this was the support he offered?

"How did it happen?"

"I don't really know yet. I was cleaning the hot tub room and I found him, drowned in the tub."

"No way."

"Really."

"Hey, Jane. I hate to do this, but I've got to go. They need me outside. But I'll call, okay? Until then, see what you can do for Paula. This has got to be hard for her."

"Yeah. Of course."

The phone clicked off.

Jane traced the screen of her new phone with her finger. Had he just dismissed her troubles? Surely not. That wasn't his style. His teaching gig at the seminary in Costa Rica was just all consuming. She knew what that felt like. He would call her back when he had more time to talk about things. Probably.

Jane called her parents next to take care of the family plan phone thing.

Her mother answered on the first ring.

Jane rushed through the tale of how she found the body and lost her phone.

"Oh, Janey! Do you want to come home? You don't have to stay there after all of that. What a nightmare."

"No, Mom, I don't need to go back to Phoenix, which as you remember, is not my home."

"Honey, you want to be a missionary. You don't have a home."

"True. And I don't have a phone either. Or, not a permanent phone. What am I supposed to do now?"

"Just go buy lots of minutes for that one, sweetie. We'll call the phone company and fix the situation, but until they send you a new phone, you need some way to get a hold of people in an emergency."

"That makes sense. Thanks." Jane picked at the lint on her denim shorts. She was tempted to ask for a phone upgrade while she had her mom.

"I'm uncomfortable with this Swanson situation, honey. It sounds dangerous."

"I'll be fine, Mom. Don't worry." Jane changed her mind about a phone upgrade, and now just hoped to cut the call short.

"I just remember last time…"

"I live with Gemma now. Aunty Gail sends us casseroles. I'm not homeless, hungry, or anything. And I have lots of clients since school is out. Don't even worry."

"You go straight to Aunty Gail's if anything goes wrong. Promise?"

"I promise." Jane sighed.

"No attitude."

"Mom."

"Okay. I love you. Call your dad."

"As soon as I can. Bye, Mom."

"Bye, baby."

Jane hung up and flopped back on her bed. Calling her mom had been worse than calling Isaac, though she wasn't sure why. It hurt to think there were problems so bad in the world that her mom couldn't fix them just like that. Jane dialed Isaac's number again but didn't press send. Her heart was lonely, and she was scared. She just wished she had someone in Portland who loved her right now.

The next day was Sunday, and after church and lunch, Jane met her ministry team at the new Bean Me Up Scotty's coffee shop by the mall.

Jane sipped her iced mocha. Valerie was texting. Kaitlyn was late.

Jane wasn't sure how to propose their new idea to Valerie. Kids that hang out at the mall and get bullied. They exist, but were they a group? Did they have a self-identity that she and her teammates could tap into? The coffee shop was quiet, which was nice. If Valerie was going to laugh her head off at their dumb idea, at least the audience was small.

Valerie looked up at her phone and smiled. "I'll be just a sec."

Jane looked out the window. Kaitlyn was just pulling up in her shiny silver Jetta. She had a frazzled look about her that Jane had never seen before. Her hair was in a messy bun—but not the carefully messed up kind. In fact, patches of white showed through the bun—clear signs the mess on top of her head was supposed to be a big, sleek, "sock" bun and not a messy bun at all.

When Kaitlyn managed to pull up a chair at the table, it was obvious she wasn't herself. She took a deep breath. "I need prayer warriors, stat."

Valerie reached across the table for Kaitlyn's hand and bowed her head.

Jane took a hold of Kaitlyn's prosthetic and looked around the room. The barista wasn't watching.

"Oh, Lord, I need your strength now, more than ever."

Jane echoed the sentiment in her mind. She peeked at the barista again. This time the girl with the nose ring was watching. Jane shut her eyes.

"Today your enemies are trying to thwart your plans, but we trust in your strength, and your will, Lord God, but please help us trust."

Jane peeked at Kaitlyn. Kaitlyn's head was slightly bowed. Her eyes were squeezed shut and her brows drawn close together. She wasn't faking her stress, even if Jane thought the words were a bit melodramatic.

Kaitlyn closed with more of what Jane secretly considered church jargon, and then lifted her head, chin stuck out.

"Poor girl, what has happened?" Valerie kept her hold on Kaitlyn's hand.

"Yo-Heaven has just opened up at the mall food court."

"So?" It popped out before Jane could control herself. She hadn't meant to say it. But really. So?

Kaitlyn stuck her chin out a little further. She cast her big, sad blue eyes on Jane. "They are Bubble-Bubble's strongest competitors."

Jane wanted to say, "So?" again, but refrained. With effort she asked, "Tell me more about this problem."

"Yo-heaven is way more popular than Bubble-Bubble. It just is. And they opened up in the empty spot right next to me. I don't know how I can take this."

Valerie made some soothing sounds but caught Jane's eye. She shrugged lightly.

"Are you concerned the Yo-Heaven is going to affect your job?"

"I'll lose my job. We won't last a week next to Yo-Heaven. But even if we do, I won't get to stay on. I've only been there a month."

"But you'll land on your feet, won't you? I mean, don't you live with your parents still?"

Kaitlyn nodded. "I moved back home to save money for the wedding and for moving to the Philippines. But I can't save any money if I don't have a job."

On the one hand, Jane could sympathize, but on the other... all of Kaitlyn's immediate needs were met. "I'll keep you in my prayers."

"I need thirty thousand dollars in the bank before the wedding."

Val dropped Kaitlyn's hand. "Why on Earth do you 'need' that much money Kaitlyn?"

Kaitlyn held up her prosthetic. "This." She set it down again with a thud. "The organization Spencer serves with won't take me on board if I'm not self-insured. I need to have enough money for a round trip ticket back to America, a hospital stay, and a new prosthetic if anything should happen to this one."

"That costs thirty thousand dollars?" Jane tried to hide her disbelief.

"It's a really handy hand." Kaitlyn flexed the fingers on her fake hand. "Plus, I have a special one for swimming. And anyway, a hospital stay could easily eat up that much money in a day."

"I see," Jane lied.

"So your job is very important to you right now." Valerie had a sweet, cooing tone to her voice. Jane knew it was what Kaitlyn needed, so she attempted to adjust her own attitude.

"Yes." Kaitlyn sniffed. She dabbed at her nose with Jane's napkin.

"But there's really no way you could save up $30,000 in—what, a year?—working at Bubble-Bubble Tea."

Kaitlyn nodded, chewing on her lip. "I sell Bible studies I write on Amazon too."

"I can see how stressful this is for you." Jane's first attitude adjustment hadn't helped, so she tried again. "Let's keep optimistic. You haven't lost your job yet."

"That's right, sweetie," Valerie said. "Let's not jump the gun, okay?"

"I just know that whenever we get really close to doing a good work for God, the enemy comes in and tries his best to blast it all to pieces. And, Jane, we have a great idea for a good work, yeah? My job at the mall is a key piece to that."

Jane had her eye on the barista, who appeared to be laughing. A second barista, a good-looking man with graying hair and black plastic glasses, flicked the laughing one with his towel. "I'm sure your job there could be very useful." The black eye-glasses barista caught Jane's eye and mouthed, "I'm sorry." Jane looked away.

"It's a great idea. Let's focus on that right now," Valerie said.

Kaitlyn nodded, still sniffling. "We've just got to trust God, right?"

"Right." Valerie nodded her head, curls bobbing as she offered reassurance.

From the corner of her eye, Jane glimpsed the glasses-wearing barista watching their table. He seemed to have his eye on Valerie, and he was smiling.

The idea tickled Jane. She'd have to make sure they had more meetings at this very coffee shop.

While Jane distracted herself from her annoyed feelings with matchmaking schemes, the glasses-wearing, gray-haired barista himself joined the table.

He set a tray of pastries down. "You all looked like you could use a little cheering up." He addressed them all, but his eyes were only for Valerie.

Valerie blushed, just a little.

"Thank you." Kaitlyn offered him a small, sad smile.

"Anytime." He went back to his work station, stumbling a little on the way.

"Why don't you all tell me about what your new idea for ministry is?" Valerie kept her eyes on Jane, and not the handsome barista who, as far as Jane could tell, still hadn't taken his eyes off of her.

Kaitlyn leaned forward. "We want to reach out to victims of bullying."

Valerie drew her eyebrows together. "How?"

"We want to get them together at the mall where I see them suffering. We can give these little guys a taste of God's love." Her face did the beatified thing that Jane found a bit over the top. But considering the rest of the hyperbole Kaitlyn had delivered, she figured a little wide-eyed passion wasn't going to kill her.

"But how? Victims of bullying are a pretty non-specific group. How are you going to identify them and connect with them?"

"I was thinking it might even be too specific," Jane said.

"Either way, it's the wrong kind of specific. No one wants to join a group where their identity is tied up with being victimized."

"We could base it around an interest, like some game kids are playing these days." Jane racked her brain to think of something kids were into, but failed.

"How would you keep the bullies themselves from taking over the group?" Valerie asked.

"That's easy. We'd pick something they weren't into."

Valerie pursed her lips. "I don't know, girls. I think this one needs quite a bit more prayer and thought. Why don't we put it aside for now and brainstorm some other ideas."

Kaitlyn crossed her arms. "I think Jane and I feel strong about this one, don't you, Jane?"

Jane looked from Valerie to Kaitlyn. Kaitlyn had offered her boundless enthusiasm and support for the idea she had hatched at the mall, but it wasn't like she was married to the idea. And with today's display of job-related panic, Jane wasn't sure she wanted to hitch her wagon to Kaitlyn.

This must be why missionaries needed practice. They hadn't started the work yet, and it was already hard.

"I don't think it would hurt to pray over it more," Jane said.

Valerie nodded and smiled. "It never hurts to pray more. Listen, girls, I have to get to work, but I'm glad we had a chance to reconnect. Email me with your thoughts on this." She excused herself from the table. Jane watched closely, but Valerie didn't offer a passing glance to the employees behind the counter.

"Jane!" Kaitlyn's big eyes looked hurt. "You totally just threw me under the bus."

"What? No. Not at all."

"You should have my back on this. You know God is calling us to this thing. Why else would I be under such a direct attack right now?"

"From the Yo-Heaven?"

"Yes, from the Yo-Heaven. Bubble-Bubble Tea has been absolutely fabulous. Everything has been going so smoothly. Why would my job be threatened by the competition, all of a sudden, if it weren't a direct attack from the devil?"

"I don't know the answer to that, Kaitlyn. I'm sorry. But if one of our teammates isn't on board, what I say can't make a difference. All we can do is pray."

Kaitlyn stood up with a huff. "Oh, I'll be praying, all right." She flipped her hair over her shoulder and stormed out of the café.

Jane picked at a raspberry Danish sitting on the still-full tray of pastries. If this little team was meant to prove to Paula that the three of them were ready for prime time, it was failing.

CHAPTER 8

JANE PRAYED THE MATTER OVER, and determined that the first thing she should do on behalf of Kaitlyn was check out the lay of the land, so the next day when she was done with her clients, she headed to the mall.

How close was this Yo-Heaven to Bubble-Bubble Tea? How many customers did it have during the peak frothy-beverage-drinking hours? How many kids could she find hanging out at the mall without their parents, who also appeared downtrodden, and in need of some kind of undefined activity?

Jane stuck her earbuds in and walked the mall slowly, pretending to listen to music.

Little knots and tangles of high-schoolers jostled and flirted at the corners of the mall. But they were older than the kids she and Kaitlyn had in mind.

The arcade next to the food court was quiet. Just a few boys were playing games inside, but they didn't look particularly downtrodden. A couple of women with really nice hair were drinking coffee at a table next to the arcade entrance. The game-playing boys' moms perhaps?

She scanned the food court. The fattening aroma of cinnamon rolls floated through the air. People milled about, reading the menus that hung from the walls. She spied Kaitlyn's golden head holding court over the cash register at Bubble-Bubble Tea. Three teenage girls appeared to be placing an order.

Yo-Heaven, the popular yogurt smoothie and salad shop, was in the small restaurant space right next to Bubble-Bubble Tea.

While Jane could understand why that might make Kaitlyn nervous, it didn't strike her as an impossible co-existence. Bubble-Bubble had shared the food court with Frosty Maids just fine for a few years now. Jane meandered toward the line. She counted twelve kids in the food courts, four of whom looked a bit downtrodden, socially speaking, but all of whom were with their families.

"Vanilla mango, small."

"Hey, Jane." Kaitlyn's bright smile faded. "I'm trying to hold it together, but this has been the quietest morning in forever."

"Have faith, friend." Jane passed her debit card to Kaitlyn. Kaitlyn's forever was around a month. Jane had a feeling the slow morning and Yo-Heaven might not be related. "God's hand is in this, somewhere."

Kaitlyn shook her head. "I wish I were sure." She turned and mixed up a tapioca-based smoothie for Jane.

Jane scanned the food court again while she waited. It was getting a little busier as the lunch crowd filtered in. There were more teens, more families.

"Jane! You never called!"

Jane spun around in a circle. She knew that voice.

"Over here, Jane!" Jake Crawford leaned over the counter of the Yo-Heaven.

"Why didn't you call?"

"Call? When?" Jane went hot, then cold.

"All year, that's when. You didn't call me all year."

Kaitlyn put her hand out with the bubble tea in it.

"You're not drinking that bilge, are you, Jane? Where's your loyalty?"

Jane took the drink.

"Don't harass my customers," Kaitlyn snapped.

"Your customer?" Jake leaned on his elbow. "In the grand scheme of things, is Jane more your customer or my muse?"

Jane took a big suck on her drink. She gagged, just a little. "Jake—" Jane stopped. What was the point in arguing with him when you could just ignore him? She stepped closer to Kaitlyn's counter.

"I've been checking out the ministry potential here at the mall," Jane said in a low voice.

Kaitlyn eyed Jake warily, but answered Jane. "See anything good?"

"Not yet, but I plan on hanging out all afternoon. I want to see how the crowd changes over the course of the day." Jane checked Jake out of the corner of her eye. He was taking orders. In the few seconds Jane had been talking a line had formed for yogurt smoothies. She checked behind her. No one in line for the bubble tea.

"I'm off at two," Kaitlyn said. "Will you still be around?"

Jane checked her watch. 11:45. "Yeah, I think I can manage to stick around that long."

"Okay. I've got to get back to work, but if you meet me here at two, we can compare notes." Kaitlyn's face was dead serious.

Jane stifled the urge to snicker. "Sounds good. I'll be back." She turned to go, but Jake called out to her again.

"Cut in line real fast, Jane. Let me make you something to eat." His voice had a little pleading quality to it that Jane was very familiar with. He wanted to wheedle something out of her, but she had no idea what it would be, as he wasn't exaggerating when he said they hadn't seen, or heard, from each other in over a year.

Jane sidled over to Jake's counter. "What's up?"

"Just really fast, why didn't you call me? I mean, it was a whole year."

Jane licked her lips. "I didn't know you wanted me to call you."

"Really?" Jake's voice was low so the people in line couldn't hear him. Not that it would have been easy, with the noise of the blenders, shakers, and yogurt machines whirring behind him. Jane noticed two tall redheads whipping together drinks for the people in line. "I'm not kidding. After what we went through together you really didn't think I wanted you to call me?"

Jane looked at her hands. Then she looked back up. "You didn't call me either." She lifted her eyebrow and tried to laugh. "It's not like you were waiting around all year to hear from me."

"Yes, I did call you, and yes, I was waiting." Jake drew his eyebrows together over his gray-blue eyes. "I called two weeks after the funeral, and you never called back."

Jane bit her lip. She remembered that call. She remembered ignoring that call. "I'm sorry."

"Good. Make it up to me, but not right now. I'm totally swamped. Your timing is atrocious, but I know you'll call me. Tonight, okay? Call tonight sometime." He flashed her a grin and then turned to the redhead at the cash register.

Jane stared at him. What was his game this time?

She pulled her eyes away, and meandered slowly into the mall lunch crowd. She couldn't call him tonight. His number was stored in the waterlogged phone being held as evidence in the murder of Douglas Swanson.

After her mall recon and meet-up with Kaitlyn, Jane popped over to Paula's house. She still wanted to find a way she could serve the woman who had given her whole life to missionary work. She had yet to figure out what it was Paula wanted or needed, but she was determined to keep trying.

At the house, Paula led Jane into the kitchen. "How are the plans for your small group ministry going?"

Jane accepted a cup of coffee. "Slowly."

"Care to elaborate?"

"I think our idea is… complicated." Jane took a sip of coffee and watched Paula's eyes. While Paula was looking in Jane's general direction, she had a distant, almost vacant look on her face. She wasn't truly in the moment. "Kaitlyn wants to do something pretty unique, Valerie isn't convinced it's a good idea, and I can't quite tell how it would work, even though I came up with it."

"Do you think it is worth attempting?"

"Yes? Maybe? I mean, it's certainly a noble idea."

"Noble is good. Perhaps you three have stumbled onto something entirely new. New can be hard for people to wrap their minds around."

But was reaching out to youth new? Jane pondered that. Sunday school was invented to reach out to children who weren't being brought to church. Then there was AWANA. And the Boys and Girls clubs were around to connect with kids at loose ends. Not to mention all the variations of scouting programs available. And youth groups—the most obvious outreach to teenagers of all. Was there really anything new to what Kaitlyn was proposing?

"You're quiet… what are you thinking?"

"I'm just wondering if the idea is truly new. Maybe it's an old idea that we are making harder than it needs to be."

"How much time have you all spent praying over it together?"

Jane looked down at her cup. "None."

"No wonder the job seems too big." Paula took her coffee cup to the sink. "If you don't mind my giving you a little advice, I recommend getting together for prayer. No planning, no brainstorming, just prayer."

Jane chewed on her lip. "You're right."

"You are wondering how you can manage it, aren't you?"

Jane looked up, her eyebrow lifted.

Paula chuckled. "You're a bit like me, I think. You don't feel like a leader when you share responsibilities with noisier personalities. But I think if you put yourself forward—not as 'group leader' per se—but as the person trying to keep the job grounded in the Spirit, you will find the others follow you readily."

"Do you think so?"

"Yup. There is a quiet strength to your personality that is very persuasive. I'll say this, if there wasn't, I wouldn't have you in this group of candidates."

Jane's heart fell to the pit of her stomach. "Really?"

"You're young and not very well connected. You seem to have rather vague notions about what you want to do on the mission field. But… there is something in you that makes me want to see what you do with yourself." Despite the distant, sad look in Paula's eyes, her smile indicated a warmth of feeling.

Jane swallowed her disappointment. "Thank you." Her voice was weak, but how could it not be? Rather than being part of an elite group of future missionaries sent by Columbia River Community Church, she was… What was she? Entertainment? A third wheel?

Jane stood up, cradling her coffee mug in her hands. "I was wondering if there was anything I could do for you. I know you must be…" She trailed off. Paula gazed out the window, one hand resting on the faucet. She looked far away from the little house in East Portland.

"Between the three of you, I'd almost think I was your outreach project." Paula turned her eyes to Jane. "But no, I'm taken care of right now. Thank you."

"If there is anything at all I can do… Make a meal, come by and clean." Jane ran her eyes over the almost spotless kitchen.

"I'm doing okay. What would really bless me is to hear back from you after you've gotten the girls together to pray about your outreach. Will you give me a call as soon as you've met with them?"

"Yes, of course." Jane set her mug on the kitchen counter. "Thank you for giving me this chance. I really do appreciate it."

"I know you do, kiddo. That's half the reason you are here." Paula walked Jane to the door. Don't forget to call me after you all get together next time, okay?"

"Of course."

Jane drove home with a sick stomach. She had failed to find a way to serve Paula, which wouldn't make Kaitlyn or Isaac happy. And yet again, just when she thought she was making headway on her future, she found herself all at sea.

CHAPTER 9

JANE COULDN'T WALLOW IN HER DISAPPOINTMENT TOO LONG. She had a house waiting to be cleaned. Frida and Joe Walker were ER doctors who liked Jane to come by twice a month in the evening while they were at the hospital. She hadn't been to their house since the tragedy at the Swansons'.

The Walker house was a three story Victorian near Good Sam Hospital in downtown Portland. It had been in the middle of renovations for over a year. Jane was fairly sure she could plaster her whole apartment with the construction dust she had vacuumed up in the short time she had been their cleaner.

While she swept the newest layer of white dust into the newly installed toe board vacuum under the sink in the kitchen (a rather cool contraption that Jane wished more houses had) her phone rang.

"Janey!"

It was Isaac. A tingle of pleasure swept her whole body. "Hey!"

"What's with the new phone number? I went to call you, but no one answered your old number. So I checked the last time you called and it was a new number."

Jane detected shades of Mr. Daniels—Isaac's dad, the judge—in the interrogation.

"I dropped my old phone." While she wanted to tell him all of the details of the phone-in-the-hot tub, she just couldn't bring herself to do it. Not after the way he acted when she called him last time.

"Bummer. So I was thinking about your troubles."

Jane smiled. "Thank you."

"I think you should step up and maybe take over the house cleaning for Paula. I know you're pretty busy, but since school is out, you could take on another client, right?"

Jane put the broom back in the closet. She took the duster with the telescoping handle out of her cleaning caddy and clicked the pole out to its fullest extension and swept the corners of the dining room ceiling for cobwebs.

"Are you there? Did I lose you?" Isaac asked.

"No, I'm here. I offered to clean her house, but she declined."

"Then you should make her some meals. Something she can freeze."

Though Jane had offered the same thing herself, she wondered if ramen noodles froze well, since that was about all she could afford to feed herself. "She said no thanks for that too."

"Maybe it would do her good if you went by just to sit and listen. After all her years overseas, that might mean the most to her." Isaac's phone crackled while he spoke, as though he were moving in and out of cell reception.

"I have done. I hope it helped, but what do I know?" Jane jabbed the corner with the duster, in an attempt to kill a fast little spider.

"Glad to hear it. How's everything else going?"

"Fine. I haven't heard from the police yet, so I guess they don't need me for anything else."

"The police? What happened?"

"I discovered a body, Isaac. Don't you remember? Scene of the crime? Witness? Does this ring any bells for you?" Jane whacked the spider so hard that the plastic duster handle broke. The microfiber duster head fell to the floor with a dull thump. The little black spider scuttled away.

"Don't bite my head off, please. I'm just trying to help."

"Did you forget that I found a dead body floating in a hot tub?"

"Sorry."

Jane let out a long, slow breath and waited for him to say something else.

He didn't.

"The cops said they'd be getting in touch with me later, and they haven't yet, so that's kind of a relief. Maybe Douglas's death was just an accident."

"Why wouldn't it have been?"

"I don't know why. But grown men don't drown in their hot tubs every day." Jane tossed her broken duster in the cleaning caddy. She grabbed a rag and sprinkled a little lemon oil on it. She rubbed wide circles on the top of the cherry wood dining table.

"Did it look like a murder to you?"

Jane closed her eyes and pictured the scene. The room had been steamy, like the jets of the tub had been going recently. There had been damp towels on the floor, as though someone had been in and out of the water. Had Caramel taken a dip in the tub with her husband that morning? If so... had she left the body there for Jane to discover? Jane shuddered. "How should I know?"

"You were there. You know more than I do."

Jane knelt down to oil the legs of the table.

"I'll call back later. You don't seem to be in the mood to talk right now."

Jane chewed on her cheek. Isaac was the one in a weird mood, not her. "Fine."

"Talk to you later, love."

"Thanks." Jane hung up before Isaac could say anything else.

After eliminating the dust of two weeks' worth of construction and making every antique surface in the house shine, Jane went home and went to bed. She had an early cleaning scheduled for the Swanson house. She would have loved to talk it over with Isaac, but barring that, at least she could have a good night's sleep beforehand.

The next morning, all was quiet at the Swanson house. Jane ran the Swiffer over the wood floors and wondered how Caramel was holding up. From the little she knew of the family, Caramel was a newer wife, like Paula, but not at all like Paula at the same time.

Jane Swiffered over to the big, brick fireplace. Caramel and Douglas's wedding portrait hung above it, framed in glossy black. Caramel looked about the same, but that didn't help date the picture much, considering the effectiveness of Botox. Douglas hadn't aged much since the picture either. And from the crease between his eyes and the many smile lines, Jane guessed he wasn't Botoxing.

She ran a finger across the mantle. After the construction dust of last night, this house felt spotless. And empty. She hadn't made it upstairs to the bedrooms, or downstairs to the garage yet, but as far as she could tell, the house was unoccupied. She leaned on the handle of the lightweight dust mop. Had Caramel fled a murder charge or was she just out getting her roots done? Was she a cold-hearted killer or just a heartless widow? For some reason, Jane couldn't picture Caramel as anything else.

Jane and her Swiffer moved on to the office. She started at the top of the room, and dusted her way down. The desk was a mess. Jane straightened the piles, keeping everything together and in the same spot. A stack of photos dominated the mess. She picked them up carefully, keeping her fingerprints off of their glossy fronts. She didn't want to pry, but couldn't help noticing that the pictures were all of Douglas. Perhaps something for the funeral. A thin blonde woman shared space in most of the photos. It didn't look like Caramel.

Jane slid one out from the others and stared at it. Douglas and the lady were at the beach, the waves tossing behind them. From the palm trees in the distance, it was obviously not the Oregon coast.

The lady in the picture seemed younger than Caramel. She had a clear face and the small chest and thin lips of someone who had never been to a plastic surgeon. Douglas had his arm around the lady's waist and was laughing, his eyes directed away from the person taking the picture. Jane squinted. The lady was wearing a bikini, and though she was no expert, Jane would guess it was not still in style. So... an old picture?

Jane scanned the rest of the photos from the stack. Almost all of them were Douglas and this lady, and they all seemed a little old. Jane set them down. It must be Douglas's ex-wife. Perhaps Caramel was sorting through the old pictures for Douglas's kids.

Jane dusted around and under the piles, and then cleaned the floor. Caramel might be more thoughtful than Jane had given her credit for, but she still wanted to get out of the house before Caramel showed up.

Jane finished the lower level and moved up to the bedrooms. She didn't want to make a side business of cleaning up homes where someone had recently died, but she did seem to have a knack for it. Something about the loss made her want to work harder, leave the house better than normal.

When everything upstairs that could possibly be done was done, Jane made her way back down to the basement. The garage would need sweeping, the halls needed to be vacuumed. The hot tub room would need to be cleaned. As long as she was allowed to clean it, at any rate.

The basement was dark, but unbarred. There was no police tape or guards indicating she shouldn't be down there.

She was disappointed.

The idea of seeing the hot tub made her stomach turn. But rather than put it off, she went there first. She flipped on all of the lights and stormed right up to the tub. She hefted the lid off and looked down at it, facing her fears.

Empty.

No one was in the pool.

She took a deep breath, enjoying a brief moment of relief. Dusting, vacuuming, and shining all the mirrors she could… she could do that, But dipping her hand into the water to check the pH? She'd just have to make herself do it.

When the whole room had been dealt with, she cleaned her way back to the garage. Get in, get it clean, get out. That's all she needed to do at the Swanson house. She'd dust, Swiffer, mop, vacuum, whatever, and then get the heck out of Dodge—and maybe, if she could work up her nerve, she'd make this day her last day at the Swanson house.

When the garage was as clean as an already-clean garage could get, Jane dumped her mop water in the utility sink. She turned the water on and rinsed out the head of the sponge mop. She had been the only person in the house the whole time she was cleaning, and yet, all three of the Swanson cars were parked in the garage. Perhaps Caramel had gone out with a friend? Not that it mattered, Jane reminded herself.

"When you are done with that, I want to see you in the kitchen."

Jane jumped and dropped the sponge. She turned, the water still running behind her.

Caramel stood in the doorway. Her hair was pulled back in a severe ponytail, but her clothes were as bright and tight as any other time Jane had seen her.

"Yes, ma'am." Jane mentally kicked herself for mopping the spotless floor. If she had skipped that step she could have been long gone by now. She turned off the faucet, wiped down the water that had splashed when she dropped the mop head, and wished she could think of one more really big, really long job to do before she went up to the kitchen, but she couldn't so she followed Caramel upstairs, determined to get it over with (whatever it was).

"You are probably aware that the death of Douglas was a complete surprise to me, and to all of us." Caramel bit her lip and looked up, to the left. The doe-eyed thing didn't work for her.

"Of course, it was clearly a tragic accident of some sort."

Caramel parted her lips and exhaled slowly. "Do you think so?"

"I-I couldn't really say. But it seems like it must have been some kind of surprise or accident."

"That is how it would seem, isn't it?" Caramel opened the pantry door. "With the ongoing investigation into his death and the arrangements for his funeral and getting his estate in order, I'm completely overwhelmed." Caramel affected a sad face again. "I could use someone to come in each morning and set us up for the day." She waved to a shelf full of coffee bags. "Would you be able to do that until our maid returns from vacation?"

"What kind of time commitment are you talking about?"

"Every morning, seven days a week—it shouldn't take more than an hour. I won't always be here, but I don't want the house to look vacant. I just need someone to come in and start the place up." A look of confusion crossed Caramel's face. She shut the pantry door.

"Do you mean like turning lights on, watering plants, making coffee, that kind of thing?"

"Yes, yes, that kind of thing. I can make a list for you."

Jane saw her freedom slip out of her fingers "It would have to be pretty early. I have other clients in the morning."

"So long as you're quiet, that's not a problem."

"And this is at my regular hourly rate."

"Fine. Just be here tomorrow."

Jane put out her hand to shake on it, but Caramel walked out of the room instead, her heels clacking on the hardwood floor.

Jane looked at her empty hand, hanging there. Had she really just sold herself down the river?

Jane spotted Caramel on the back patio, talking on her phone, as she left. As Jane loaded her cleaning supplies in the car, she listened in.

"Can we make it tomorrow, Joey? I'm just exhausted today." Her voice cracked.

Jane felt for her. What would life for Caramel be like without Douglas? Not the same, that's for sure.

"Fine then, if you come by here. But if I were you, I'd stay away for a while longer."

Jane shut the door of her car, cutting off her access to the conversation. Joey was probably the brother who sold her the expensive ring, which would explain why he wasn't welcome at the house.

Except Douglas was dead, so Joe should be more than welcome. Broken families broke Jane's heart. How sad for Caramel that at a time like this she thought her brother shouldn't come around.

CHAPTER 10

THIS TIME JANE WENT TO PAULA EHLERS' HOUSE
UNANNOUNCED. She rang the doorbell and hoped her hunch was right. If Paula, who had spent her whole life serving others, was ever going to accept help from a kid like herself, she couldn't have advanced warning.

Paula opened the door in her bathrobe. Her eyes were bloodshot, and her nose was swollen and red. Her cheeks were tear-streaked. She waved Jane in.

Jane went straight to the kitchen without a word. She filled the sink with hot water and soap. "Ignore me, Paula. I just really want to be here for you in some way."

Paula crumpled into her leather armchair and blew her nose.

Jane washed out the breakfast dishes. "Have you had lunch yet?"

Paula didn't answer. Her face was buried in her hands, but her body was perfectly still.

Jane put the kettle on. She didn't know if Paula was a hugger. It seemed like she would be if the culture she had served in all those years had been a demonstrative one, but Jane wasn't sure. It didn't look like Paula wanted a hug.

Paula was curled up in the leather chair, her face hidden behind her hands, her bare feet hanging off the edge of the seat.

Jane finished all of the dishes, and then wiped down the counters. She found a tea pot and made one cup of Tetley. She sat down on the couch across from Paula and waited in silence, the tea cup on the table between them. She had been there for almost a half an hour, but the time didn't seem wasted.

Eventually Paula sat up. She wiped her cheeks with her sleeve. "I'm sorry." Her voice was a choked whisper.

"Please don't be sorry. You need to cry."

Paula nodded.

They sat quietly together for another ten minutes in silence, but again, they weren't long minutes to Jane. She prayed as she waited with Paula, and every few moments she stole a glance at her mentor. Paula's posture began to relax. Her head lifted, and her face, which had been twisted in agony, was relaxed now, like the storm had passed.

"Thank you, Jane, for coming here and just being with me." She reached over and patted Jane's hand. "You have a very comforting presence."

"Thank you." A warm glow spread over Jane. She had almost given up hope of pleasing Paula.

"I need to pull myself together and get some work done today." Paula stood up and stretched. "But I'm really glad you came over for a spell."

Jane followed Paula's lead. "Thank you for letting me stay for a little while."

Paula opened the front door for Jane. "Come back again, okay?" Her eyes were terribly sad, but they had the light of a potential smile, something Jane hadn't seen since they had received the terrible news.

The next morning, Jane went to the Swanson's to open it up for the day. She got in with no problem, and found her directions on the kitchen counter. It looked like all she had to do was open all the curtains on the main floor, make a pot of coffee, and turn on all of the office equipment. And clean all of the bathrooms. From the scratchy tangle of letters that made up that line item, Jane guessed Caramel had added it at the last minute to make the job worth paying for.

But why? It was Caramel's house and Caramel's money. She could spend it on a maid to boot up the computer if she wanted to.

It was rather nice to picture Caramel getting up late, stumbling into the office with a mug of coffee, and getting straight to work, whatever that might be.

Jane started with the coffee. Five was early, even though early was normal. Jane leaned on the kitchen counter while the pot was brewing. She stared out the kitchen window. The Swanson land rolled off into the distance, green, green lawns with white horse fence. Far down the hills and off to the side somewhere was a stable full of horses. She wondered if the horses noticed Douglas was gone now. When the coffee was down, Jane poured herself a mug, and slipped off to open windows.

The sunshine poured into each room she unveiled. The day was brilliant and her heart was easy. She might have felt differently if she had wandered into the hot tub room, but the absence of Douglas and his insinuations and the untrustworthy gleam she had seen in his eye was a relief. It's not that she was glad he was dead… but she had to admit, she breathed easier knowing he wasn't about to pop around the corner.

The office wasn't as big a mess as it had been last time she was in it, but it had the dusty, unused smell of a classroom opened up after summer break. The stack of photos was gone from the desk, and the room looked emptier. Jane bent down to turn on the surge protector that had the computers plugged in. The carpet next to the desk was flattened, like something heavy had been on it. She really hadn't been cleaning the Swanson house for long, so it took a minute to remember that a tall cherry wood filing cabinet used to sit there. She got all of the machines turned on and then stepped back to look at the desk set-up. It looked off-centered with the filing cabinet gone, but that also explained why the room felt emptier. She turned around and ran the toe of her shoe across the carpet. There had been a bookshelf against that wall… she was almost sure of it.

She moved on to the bathroom cleaning. There were five of them, but Caramel was living alone now so it wouldn't be that hard to clean them all. Especially if Caramel was starting to unload Douglas's old furniture.

She was right. The bathrooms looked spotless. She ran a dust cloth across the horizontal surfaces and sprayed them all lightly with disinfectant. She swished the toilet brush and a little cleaner around the toilet, and then went to the master bedroom. She hesitated. Was Caramel still in bed? Had Caramel intended her to do the master bath when she had listed clean all the bathrooms?

Jane knocked lightly on the door. There was no answer, so she nudged it open and peeked. The room was huge, and the bed was against the far wall. She poked her head in and peeked. Caramel was still in bed.

Jane's heart leapt to her throat.

Caramel shifted in her sleep and let out a soft mutter.

Jane shut the door and leaned against it. She took a deep breath. It wasn't a repeat of the Crawford death. Caramel was still asleep, as she should be.

Jane left it at that. She wasn't going to risk waking up the sleeping widow.

She drove straight from the Swansons' to a very early meeting with her ministry team. She joined the other ladies at the mall food court, where Kaitlyn would be opening her Bubble-Bubble Tea shop in an hour.

"Thanks for meeting me at the mall again." Kaitlyn swept her blonde hair over her shoulder. The mall was opened for walkers, but none of the shops or restaurants were open yet.

Jane brought her own coffee with her—purchased from the Stumptown in the parking lot. They sat directly under an air return, so between the early hour, and the blast of cold, dusty smelling air, her paper cup of coffee was a welcome comfort.

"I think I figured out what we can use to connect with the kids." Kaitlyn pulled a stack of colorful, round pieces of cardboard from her purse.

"Pogs?" Jane leaned in and poked the stack.

"Pogs!" Kaitlyn beamed, her eyes and smile shining like the winner of a beauty pageant.

"But do kids still play with Pogs?" Jane poked the stack again. The little worn circles spilled across the table.

"What are Pogs?" Valerie swept an assortment of the cards over to herself and began to sort them by color.

"It's a game. I've got tons of these." Kaitlyn had a gleam in her eye that made Jane nervous. "But you can't buy them anymore, which means we have the monopoly."

"That's a good thing?" Valerie shuffled a stack of Pogs like they were poker cards.

"Yes! Because we can start a Pogs meet-up like they used to have when I was a kid. We'd be the only place in town where a kid could get their Pog fix. Totally proprietary. We could play and pray. It's perfect."

Valerie drew her eyebrows together. "But do kids still want to play with these? Wouldn't it be better to draw on something they are actually into right now?"

Kaitlyn looked undaunted. "The kids at Spencer's youth center love Pogs." She gathered all of her little round cards together. "Shall we review how the game works?"

Jane took a deep breath. She had come here to support Kaitlyn and to move forward with their idea… but… Pogs? "Kaitlyn… how do I say this? Spencer's youth center is in the Philippines."

"Yup." Kaitlyn began to pass out Pogs.

"And he mostly tries to connect with kids from the slums, right?"

Kaitlyn nodded. She was counting under her breath.

"And the kids from the slums don't have like, Nintendos or Playstations."

"Or Angry Birds," Valerie added.

"There really isn't any entertainment competition with that group. Pogs are in because…"

"Because that's all they have." Valerie's voice was completely matter of fact.

Kaitlyn laughed. "I had a Playstation, and a DS. We had the Internet and all that jazz, but we were wild for Pogs, too. It's a super fun game. Kids just love it."

Valerie put her hands on the table, palms down. "I feel like there are just too many unknowns with this plan, Kaitlyn. Help me see how you would make this work."

Kaitlyn exhaled. She was shivering with nervous energy. "We will start a once-a-week Pog meet-up at the mall. Games followed by Bible. It's a place and an activity that can help those who are being bullied build community with each other and begin a relationship with the One who will never reject them or humiliate them."

Jane caught Valerie's eye and offered a smile. "It's a good vision. Who do we talk to at the mall about getting permissions set up?"

Kaitlyn blinked. "Um…" She looked over Valerie's shoulder.

"You don't have that worked out yet?" Valerie took a drink of the coffee she had brought in with her, a tired look washing over her face.

"If we go to the management office, we can figure that out." Jane smiled again, nodding from Valerie to Kaitlyn, trying to get them to make eye contact with each other. "We have some logistics to work out, but we can get it done. No doors have been closed on us yet."

"I think we should just jump in with both feet." Kaitlyn lowered her voice and leaned forward. "I think we should start immediately—today, even. Once we've started and the kids love it, no one would make us stop."

Jane opened her mouth to speak, but nothing came out.

Jake Crawford was standing behind Kaitlyn grinning like the Cheshire Cat. He held a tray filled with sample cups filled with pastel yogurt smoothies.

"Good morning, ladies. Can I interest you in Portland's finest frosty breakfast beverage?" He lowered the tray and winked at Jane. "Three hot ladies like you need something cool to drink."

Valerie snorted softly, but took a pink cup.

"Excuse me?" Kaitlyn's face flushed.

"Thanks, Jake." Jane took a cup. The less said right now, the better. If Jake succeeded in getting a rise from them, he'd never stop.

"Hmmm, that is good." Valerie helped herself to a second sample.

"Yo-Heaven fruit and yogurt smoothies. What yogurt will be like in heaven."

Kaitlyn placed a hand over her stack of Pogs. "Will you excuse us? We're having a private meeting."

Jake leaned down, his mouth close to Kaitlyn's ear. "A private *Pogs* meeting?" Jake lingered by Kaitlyn's ear. He inhaled, a look of pleasure crossing his face.

Jane didn't miss the sarcastic edge to his voice.

Kaitlyn pulled away from Jake. "I'm engaged to be married!"

Jake straightened up and spun his tray, like a basketball, on his fingertips.

"Congrats. Have a drink on me."

Valerie pushed her chair out from the table and stood up, taking her time. "Thanks for the samples. Girls, I've got to get to work. Let's meet about this again on Friday night. Can you all meet me at the new Bean Me Up Scotty's at seven?" She eyed the Pogs hiding under Kaitlyn's protective hands. "I suggest we each bring an idea to the table and decide on our final plan then."

Kaitlyn's eyes filled with tears. "Jane and I believe in this ministry."

Jake's eyes were glued to Jane's face. Jane mouthed the words, "*Go away.*"

He held his hand up to his ear like a phone and whispered, "*Call me.*"

Jane nodded and then jerked her head in a way she hoped said "just go!"

Jake tipped back his telephone fingers like he was having a drink. "*You and me, yeah?*" His whisper was getting louder.

She nodded again.

He tipped an invisible hat.

She kept her eye on him as he sauntered back to his little restaurant. Kaitlyn frowned at Jane. "I thought you were in love with Isaac Daniels." Her voice was half accusatory, half concerned.

Jane took a deep breath. Kaitlyn didn't know everything Jake had gone through, or how much he had needed her last spring. "Jake has nothing to do with Isaac." From behind her, she thought she heard Valerie snort again.

"I'll see you both on Friday, at Scotty's." Jane left the food court like she was racing the Mommy Bootcamp ladies. She booked it to her car, arriving out of breath with a burning sensation close to her heart, that she hoped was related to the run she had just had.

She had been dating Isaac exclusively for almost a year. Some Bible School students were married well before their first year anniversary. She caught herself. She wasn't a sheltered Bible School student anymore. And neither were Isaac or Jake.

Jane sat in her car without starting the engine. Isaac had been gone for three weeks and instead of feeling like they were growing closer through his missionary activities, he was beginning to feel like a stranger.

Jake, on the other hand... she hadn't laid eyes on him once in the last year. But after seeing him only two times, he was proving to be as much a trial as ever.

CHAPTER 11

THE NEXT MORNING, Jane was less than inclined to go to the Swanson house. Her 4:30 alarm went off, and she really wished she had just said no. Wasn't that a thing these days? Knowing your limits was a virtue, wasn't it? "If a man punches you in the jaw, 'turn the other cheek' so he can punch that side, too." Jane pressed her face into her pillow, trying to muffle the memory of her old youth pastor's favorite paraphrase.

She lifted her head and glared at the clock. It was 4:40. She still had to get up, but now she had to rush, too.

Jane groped her way to her bathroom. Her roommate wasn't criminal, like last time, but she wasn't tidy either. And she was family. Jane couldn't easily unload her cousin Gemma for being a pig, or for being late on the rent. Plus, the apartment was Gemma's, so she'd have to accept her living conditions.

Jane kicked a pile of clothes out of her way. She stared at her face in the mirror. Tired, tired, tired. She had a feeling other girls her age looked bad in the morning because they had been out late having fun, not because they were up early to scrub toilets.

Cleaning clean toilets at that. She didn't need to understand her job to do it, but Caramel could have gotten the same job done by putting her lights on a timer.

Jane spit her toothpaste in the sink. What she needed was an interesting job to do while she opened the Swanson house every morning. For example... Jane rinsed her toothbrush and tried to dismiss the idea that was beginning to form. For example (the thought wouldn't be ignored), she could find out what exactly had happened to Douglas.

Jane threw on some clothes and went outside. She could have breakfast after she opened up the house for Caramel. And anyway—she knew what had happened to Douglas. He had drowned.

But how?

Maybe—she bartered with herself—maybe she could find out who the woman in the pictures with Douglas had been. If it really was the ex Mrs. Mayor Douglas Swanson, a quick Internet search would show as much.

And it might help her find out how or why Douglas had died.

Why had he died? As Jane drove to the house, she tried to remember as much as she could about Douglas. Former Mayor of Gresham, Oregon. Republican. Married twice. Acquainted with Isaac's parents. But how? The Daniels weren't very social people. Church and work was about all she ever heard from Isaac. And Mrs. Daniels (that's what she liked to be called) was one of the church secretaries, so she probably hadn't met Douglas at work.

Jane pulled around to the back of the Swanson house. She had only ever met Douglas once. She guessed he was about sixty. He had silver hair and a tan. He kept horses on his property and he had a couple of vintage cars.

None of this seemed related to drowning in a hot tub in the middle of the morning.

Jane let herself into the house and began opening it up. She started by making coffee. Then she pulled open the curtains. The rooms flooded with bright, cheerful, summer morning sunlight, just like last time. The perfect Oregon summers she loved so much were not the perfect background for murder mystery solving. Spring rains with their heavy black clouds and soaking, nonstop showers would have set the right mood.

She might not have the right mood-setting weather, but she did have a body. A man of about sixty, who looked to be in good shape, not overweight, not under.

His wife didn't trust him. And he was willing to hop in the hot tub first thing in the morning. Schmoozy old men in hot tubs... cocaine sprung to mind. An overdose, maybe? Jane ran the vacuum over the rugs. Pity the Swansons didn't have a kid they could send to get the autopsy report for her.

Jane stopped mid-pass with the vacuum and closed her eyes. She pictured the scene of the death. Were there any signs of drug use in the room—beyond the weird black light and fully stocked party bar? She had barely done anything in the room. She was just going in and was headed to test the water... She gagged a little as the image of Douglas's dead body filled her mind.

What about that fully stocked bar? Had alcohol played a part in his death? She couldn't remember seeing any cups on the marble steps that surrounded the tub. No tumblers or wine glasses. Not even coffee mugs. Surely no one else had cleaned up the drinks but left Douglas in the water... Or had they? If he had been alive when they left the tub, they might have cleared up for him.

Jane finished the floors and moved on to her bathroom cleaning. Today, she'd start in the basement and take a peek in the hot tub room while she was in the vicinity. Maybe seeing it again would trigger a memory.

It would be her second trip back to the room since she found the body, but that didn't seem to make the trip easier. Jane finished cleaning the unused and hardly even dusty bathroom, and stood outside the door to the room where Douglas had died.

She had to push the door open if she wanted to see the room again. But did she really want to? A herd of question marks thundered across her brain. She had to see that room again.

She popped the door open fast so she couldn't change her mind.

The black light was the only one on in the room and the white stripes of the zebra rug, the white veins of the black marble steps, and the bleached streaks in Caramel's hair glowed.

Caramel sat slumped in the hot tub, her head lolled to the side and her mouth gaping. Her arms stretched across the back of the hot tub seat, holding her body up.

Jane ran to her. She grabbed her wrist and pressed it, searching for a pulse. "Caramel? Caramel?" She was loud, but not screaming, surprised at her own lack of panic.

There it was, faint but real: a live pulse.

Jane dipped her hand in the water and splashed Caramel's face lightly.

Caramel flinched.

"Caramel?" Jane said again.

Caramel blinked her eyes open. "Mmm." She made a sound half way between a hum and clearing her throat.

"Caramel? Are you all right?"

Caramel wiped the water off her face. "I must have fallen asleep." She stretched her arms and looked around her. She locked eyes on Jane. "The maid?"

"I saw you in here, and I admit, it scared me." Jane rocked back on her heels.

"What are you doing in here?"

Jane lowered her eyes and noticed for the first time that Caramel wasn't wearing a bathing suit. "I'm so sorry. Let me get you a towel."

"Don't bother." Caramel stood up.

Jane averted her eyes almost in time. But not quite.

Caramel apparently used the hot tub and the tanning bed without her swimsuit on.

Jane kept her eyes glued to her feet, expecting to be reamed out for straying from her instructions.

Instead, Caramel padded down the marble steps, leaving behind a trail of wet foot prints.

"We liked to sit in the tub together after… in the morning. Douglas and I." Caramel paused at the door. "I miss him so much."

Jane managed to nod her head without looking up.

"Is there any coffee yet?" Caramel asked.

"Yes." Jane couldn't manage anything else.

Caramel left without another word. Her feet made soft but echoey noises as she went up the staircase. When the noise ended, Jane wished she had remembered to tell Caramel that she had already opened all of the curtains.

Jane wrapped her arms around her stomach and squeezed tight in a vain effort to suppress the nervous laughter that welled up inside. Was it hysteria or relief? Jane wasn't sure, but she had to pull herself together. Her very naked boss was upstairs having coffee, and Jane still had four bathrooms to clean.

Jane took the stairs two at a time. No use trying to hide from her work (or her boss). It was better to just get the rest of it over with as fast as she could.

She ducked around the kitchen—sneaky avoidance being an instinct after all—and hit the hall half-bath. She did the other two guest bathrooms in record time, too, but no matter how fast she finished those, she still had to contend with the master bath. But she would face it like a professional adult—with her eyes closed if she had to.

She rapped the master bedroom door with her knuckles. There was no reply so she pushed it open. "Caramel?" She attempted to sound relaxed and normal, but her nerves made her voice crack. Still no reply, so she made her way to the en suite. The door stood open. The room was empty.

A giddy wave of relief washed over Jane. Finding both the bedroom and bathroom empty was a bit of luck she hadn't counted on having. Just from her own sense of gratitude, she gave the bathroom an extra close clean.

Jane straightened the hundreds of make-up bottles and compacts and the mountain of hair stuff piled on Caramel's side of the vanity. Even the mirror was filthy on one side. The other side—Douglas's—was spotless.

In fact, there wasn't an old razor or bottle of aftershave to be seen. Nothing on the counter proved there had ever been a man in the bathroom. And it wasn't that Douglas had kept his stuff in some other bathroom. Jane had just cleaned them all. There were no razors, tweezers, or Old Spicy man stuff of any kind, anywhere.

Jane eased open the drawers on the "man" side of the double sink vanity. Empty except for a spare roll of toilet paper.

Caramel missed her husband so much that she had already cleaned out his bathroom, and his office, and had already resumed hot morning soaks in the tub where he had died.

Jane shuddered.

Jane had wanted her morning's work to be more interesting, but she hadn't bargained on it being *that* interesting. And she hadn't answered any of the questions she had about Douglas's death.

For example… how had he died? Heart attack? Overdose? Slipped and drowned? Head held under the water until he died?

Jane thought she ought to call the detective. She might be able to pump him for a little information.

She was back at her apartment munching a bagel and sipping a Yo-Heaven smoothie she had grabbed from a drive through. Kaitlyn would hate her drinking it. Jake would love it.

And Jake would probably be able to schmooze information out of the cops.

Or not. That cop had been a cute guy. A bit too old for her, but probably more likely to spill investigation secrets to her than to Jake.

She'd have to give the detective idea some thought. She wasn't a natural at weaseling information out of people, and she didn't have a good reason to call him—yet.

She did have a free hour or so and a nice fast Internet connection, so she began hunting for information on Douglas Swanson's first wife.

It took a few pages of digging, but she did find what she was looking for. An old article from the Gresham Report—about fifteen years old, in fact—with a big picture of Mayor Swanson and his wife Alexandra.

Alexandra was not the woman she had seen in the pictures. The woman in the pictures was a young, athletic-looking blonde. Maybe not natural blonde, but pretty close. The ex Mrs. Mayor Swanson was a petite woman with a frail look about her and dyed, red hair. Not fake looking like Caramel's blonde hair, but probably not her natural color either.

So if Alexandra wasn't in all of those pictures on the desk, who was? And why were they on the desk?

Jane wished the Swanson house had been a big old mansion with lots of fireplaces. She could have dug through the ashes to see if the pictures had been burnt. Lacking that, what could she do?

She could keep her eyes open. That was something anyway.

After cleaning two more clients, Jane went home for lunch.

She was certain the woman in the pictures with Douglas wasn't his wife, but it was clearly someone he was close to. A daughter, which wasn't likely, if she was remembering the body language correctly, or a lover, which seemed pretty icky but reasonable.

Douglas didn't seem like the kind of man to go bar-hopping, so his lover would have to come from some other part of his life—work, most likely. She pulled up every site she could find about Gresham politics. Her list of local officials, from the chief of police to school board, was long. Pictures were almost impossible to find for most of the names, so she had resorted to Facebook. One tab with Google results, the other with Facebook search results. So far, no matches, but Jane was sure she was on the right track.

In the middle of it, her Facebook instant messenger let off its annoying ding. She clicked over to the Facebook page.

It was Jake Crawford. His Facebook picture was of him in his Yo-Heaven uniform—complete with the lime green visor and little white nametag. He had embraced the call of healthy fast food, which was nice.

"Are you ever going to call me?"

"No." Jane wasn't sure why she typed it, besides it's being honest, and Facebook being the kind of place one wrote first and thought later.

"Thanks? Whatcha doing? Do you want to go out tonight?"

"Working. No."

"Do people pay you to clean their Facebook now?"

She lol'd, both in real life and on the private message box. She laughed so hard her side ached. For a moment, she considered what she could charge someone for popping into Facebook and cleaning up their newsfeed. Get rid of spam, ads, people who drink and post, anyone who makes a duck face. Not only could it be profitable, it would be satisfying.

"Want to go hear some live music?"

"No thanks." She tried to keep her eye on the task at hand, but Jake's messages were coming too fast. The beeps were driving her nuts.

"Just hang out at home then? Come by and see your old room? You could have a sleepover. Old time's sake."

Jane groaned. Then she typed, "*groan*" She wondered what had spurred Jake's recent interest in her. Just seeing her at the mall, perhaps? The food court couldn't be the most intellectually stimulating job ever.

"I could come by your place."

Jane didn't respond.

She thought she had a match for the blonde. The only trouble was that she couldn't remember exactly what the woman in the photo had looked like. This woman hit all the right notes though: trim build, natural look, blonde. She showed up on the Facebook page for the Gresham Mayor's office, and according to an old copy of the minutes of a meeting she had dug up in the online mayoral office archives, she was on staff back when Douglas had the job.

Jane squinted at the picture. Could Mary-Grace Hopkins be the mysterious lover? Jane tapped her toes. She had time to drive up to Gresham and pop into the mayor's office. Maybe chat someone up about their recent loss. A shiver of excitement ran up her spine. Did she have the nerve to do that? It wasn't any of her business, but it certainly passed the time.

Another message popped up from Jake. "Earth to Jane. I get the feeling you don't have time for me anymore..."

"Not right now, sorry!" The explanation point might have been overkill, but she didn't want to be rude.

"I'll call you."

Jane read the message twice.

It wasn't flirty, silly, or nonsense. Just a simple sentence. That worried her.

She didn't want to worry about Jake. She typed, "TTYL." She wasn't saying no, but she was resolutely non-committal. If Jake needed something badly enough, he'd call. She wasn't going to put herself out for it, though.

For one thing, she didn't want to talk to Jake. She wanted to talk to Isaac.

She stared at her phone, sitting quietly next to her laptop on the table. She thought for a moment it was going to burst into song, and that the call was going to determine her fate: Isaac or Jake.

But it was silent. Fate didn't get determined by a phone call, and before Isaac had left the country for his brief stay in Costa Rica, they had been seriously dating, with marriage as the long term goal.

Jake was just bored.

And so was Jane, which meant it was time to run to Gresham and have a chat with the staff of the mayor's office.

CHAPTER 12

AFTER FINDING THE GRESHAM CITY OFFICE BUILDING, Jane drove around the block to park and to try and come up with a reason for her visit. She'd love to walk in and ask for Mary-Grace, but she didn't have any reason to. She could go in and say she wanted to interview people about the former mayor for school or something but… that would be a lie. If she could think of something to ask that was both useful and true, she'd feel a lot better about it. But what did a housekeeper from Portland need from the Mayor of Gresham?

Jane drummed her fingers on her steering wheel. If only Caramel had sent her down for something—anything. Something for the funeral maybe.

Or something for herself? That wasn't a bad idea.

Jane smiled. Her boss was grieving. This could work.

Jane parked and went straight to the reception desk. Old industrial fluorescent bulbs flickered above the laminate desk, and a smell that reminded Jane of cleaning whiteboards at school hung in the air.

"Good morning." The receptionist was an older lady—curly white hair, wire-rim glasses on a chain. She had a sweet smile. The noises coming from her computer sounded a lot like Words with Friends.

"Good morning." Jane clenched her hands together to keep them from shaking. If she focused on her plan and just kept her eye out for Mary-Grace, she wouldn't be a liar. "I'm not entirely sure where to start, but I'm Douglas Swanson's maid."

The receptionist narrowed her eyes. "*You* are?"

"Yes, ma'am. Their regular maid is on vacation, and I'm kind of like the substitute."

"Ah." The receptionist relaxed, her smile coming back. "I thought you were a bit young for Doug."

"I was just thinking about Caramel and how sad she has been." A little lie, but maybe that was okay? "And I was thinking

that maybe if there was anything here from Mr. Swanson's days
as mayor, like, I don't know…" Jane froze. Like what? His desk?
Newspaper clippings? His red Swingline stapler?

"You were wanting to bring her something?"

Jane chewed her lip. "Bad idea?"

"Not at all." The receptionist stood up and reached a hand
out to Jane.

Jane accepted the warm, grandmotherly handshake. "It's a
kind idea, dear. A memento of an important man. I don't know
what we have around here from his days in office, but someone
might. Why don't you have a seat? I won't be a minute."

Jane sat on the edge of a threadbare, upholstered waiting
room chair. She took a deep breath and tried to gather her wits.
The receptionist had hinted that she had expected a different kind
of woman for the Swanson maid. It might be interesting to learn
something more about the woman she was substituting for. But
for the moment, she'd have to concentrate on phrasing her
sentences for the most impact. Bring up Douglas's social life if
she could. Mention Alexandra and the kids. See what kind of
reaction she could surprise out of the staffers, if any.

A thin young man in a golf shirt and khakis came out to the
waiting room with the receptionist.

Jane stood up and offered him her hand. "You don't look old
enough to have worked with Mayor Swanson."

The man, who had the slightly pimply jawline of a teenager,
laughed. "No, I'm not. I'm an intern. I probably wasn't even born
yet when he was mayor."

The receptionist swatted him on the elbow. "Of course you
were, Tad. You might have been in kindergarten, but you were
born."

Tad laughed. "When was he mayor again?"

"From 1989 to 1995."

"Ha! I was right, you were wrong." Tad squared his
shoulders, a grin spread across his face.

"Youth isn't something to brag about." The receptionist
chuckled, and then ambled back to her desk.

Jane smiled a little as well—she had been born in the middle
of Douglas's term as mayor.

"So, what did you need?"

"I was just wondering if there was anyone here who had worked with Douglas back then who could, I don't know…" Jane heard steps coming from the hall behind her. She turned a little. It wasn't the blonde.

"Someone who would remember him?"

"Yeah. Something like that. I really didn't have a firm idea. I just want to do something nice for his widow."

Tad checked his watch. "I wasn't here—obviously. But I can take you down to the morgue and let you dig a little."

Jane cringed. "The morgue?"

"The file morgue. All the outdated stuff." Tad shrugged. "I don't know that we have anything *that* old. But if we do, that's where it will be."

Jane followed Tad out of the reception room and down a staircase to a basement full of old tan filing cabinets. The same kind of fluorescent lights they still had upstairs flickered and buzzed to life when Tad flipped the switch. The room wasn't huge, but there were still more drawers than she could look through in a week. She tugged her ponytail and ran her fingers through her hair. How would she lay eyes on the blonde down here in the basement?

Tad wrenched a drawer open. "This is the kind of stuff interns get to do." He laughed. "But I don't mind. I get a little work experience, with very little real work involved." He began flipping through the file folders.

Jane looked back up the staircase. The door at the top was shut. She might as well dig, since she was here. She pulled open the drawer labeled "1993," in a cabinet next to the one Tad was using.

At the back of the drawer, almost last file, was a folder labeled "personnel." She slid to the floor and sat cross legged with the folder open on her lap. She hadn't come ready to do research—she didn't have scratch paper or a pen.

She yawned.

"No luck?" Tad slid his drawer shut. "I haven't found anything particularly memorable. Just meeting minutes and stuff."

"Me neither." Jane flipped to the next page in the file, but didn't look at it. "My idea was probably a dumb one. Thanks for looking anyway."

"No such thing as a dumb idea." Tad pulled open another file drawer.

"Isn't that supposed to be no such thing as a dumb question?"

"An idea is just a question you put to the test."

Jane scrunched her mouth up. Tad was clearly headed for political life. She turned back to her folder. This page was just a list of names and dates with no clue as to what the people did or what the dates indicated. She read them. None were familiar.

The next page was exactly the same. The only name that looked remotely familiar was Danae Monroe. She knew she had seen it somewhere before because the "ae" at the end of Danae and the "oe" at the end of Monroe had stood out.

"Tad, do you have any idea of what these lists are for?" She picked the page up and held it out for him.

Tad looked it up and down. "Looks like an end of month time sheet summary." He turned back to his own files. "Can't see how that would be something Mayor Swanson's widow would care about."

"Yeah…you're right." Danae Monroe 3/1/1993-3/30/1993, followed by a seemingly random list of numbers, though Jane guessed they were the days and times Danae Monroe had logged in to her time clock. If Danae Monroe was a name she had run across at the Swanson house, she might be the mysterious blonde in the picture.

"Hey, how about this?" Tad flapped a paper at Jane.

She grabbed it. "'Mt. Hood Community College Honors Alumnus, Mayor Swanson.' That looks good." The paper was a photocopy from the local college newspaper. Jane had no particular interest in it other than that it was a nice cover for her visit. "May I take it with me?"

Tad scratched his chin. "Let me copy it for you so I can put the original back."

"Fine by me."

They went back upstairs to a little nook in the back hall that housed a small office copy machine. Jane lingered by the door while Tad zapped a copy.

The very blonde she had been looking for—Mary-Grace Hopkins—walked past, and then stopped in an open doorway across the hall.

"Knock, knock." The blonde leaned into the office but didn't enter.

"Whatcha need?" The voice coming from the office was a bit muddled, but masculine.

"I'm making a coffee run. What do you want?" Mary-Grace stepped into the office.

A coffee run? Mary-Grace had been working in the mayor's office since the early 1990s—so almost twenty years—and she was still getting everyone else coffee? She was either exceptionally humble or lacked ambitions.

"Here you go." Tad tapped Jane's shoulder.

Jane accepted the paper with a smile. She wondered how Caramel would react if she offered her this outdated accolade as a "comfort."

"Tad, there you are."

Jane turned to the voice. Mary-Grace Hopkins was in the doorway to their little copy room now. "You and your friend can get the coffees, but don't take forever, got it?" Mary-Grace passed a piece of paper to Jane.

Jane handed it over to Tad, but not before she got a good look at the handwriting. Big, loopy letters with dark lines that looked like Mary-Grace had pressed hard when she wrote. Jane looked up and tried to memorize Mary-Grace's face. She couldn't tell if the difference in looks was because the Mary-Grace who stood before her was several pounds heavier than the lady in the pictures, or if it just wasn't the same woman.

"Hi, I'm Jane." Jane thrust her hand forward.

Mary-Grace accepted it and gave it a firm shake. "Mary-Grace. Can I help you with something?"

"Actually, I was looking for anyone who might have been in the office when Douglas Swanson was still mayor."

"Then you are barking up the wrong tree with Tad here! He wasn't even born yet." Mary-Grace let out a big laugh, almost a guffaw. Jane flinched, but plastered a smile on her face.

"Do you know anyone in the office who was here back then?" Of course, Jane knew that Mary-Grace had been, but she wanted to know what Mary-Grace would say about it.

"I just might be the last of us. Such a pity about his death." Mary-Grace frowned and shook her head.

Jane nodded. Now was her chance... But how? She looked over at Tad, he was inching his way out the door so Jane stepped aside to let him pass.

He slid between Mary-Grace and the door, then bolted down the hallway.

"Don't mind him," Mary-Grace said. "He knows he has to get that coffee pronto or we'll make his next hours a living nightmare. But what can I tell you about Doug?"

Jane licked her lips... What could she tell her? "To be honest, I'm not quite sure."

"Why don't you come to my desk? It's more comfortable." Mary-Grace led her to a large office space with several cubicles. She took a seat next to her desk, not behind it, and offered Jane the seat opposite.

"Are you from the school paper?" Mary-Grace asked, her eye on the paper in Jane's hand.

"No. I'm their housekeeper."

Mary-Grace narrowed her eyes. "You?"

"While the real housekeeper is on vacation." This was the second questionable response to such a simple statement. Third, if you counted how Caramel herself had acted early on.

"Ah." Mary-Grace relaxed.

"Mrs. Swanson is just so broken up. I thought a memento of Mr. Swanson's days as mayor might be a nice thing to bring her."

"That's very sweet." Mary-Grace rolled her chair back behind her desk. "But, I'm sorry to say, it was just so long ago nothing is left. If there had been any great memento, the Swansons already have it."

Jane nodded and chewed on her lip. Mary-Grace may have been a blonde lady who was around during Douglas's day, but she didn't seem to be at all broken up about his death. Sure, she had said the right thing, and even looked sincere, but she wasn't acting like someone who had spent the quality time with Douglas that those pictures had indicated.

"Thank you anyway." Jane stood up. "It was really nice of you to take a minute to talk to me."

Mary-Grace nodded the way people do when they are saying goodbye. "No problem. It was very kind of you to think of Mrs. Swanson. I'm sure she's lucky to have you filling in."

The emphasis on "filling in" made Jane pause. Why was Mrs. Swanson lucky? Because she had thought to do something nice, or because she was so young that even Douglas wouldn't make a pass at her? Or because there was something about the regular maid that no one liked?

"Wait a second." Mary-Grace looked up from her computer. "I almost forgot. Matt came by just about a month ago and cleared a bunch of old stuff out of the morgue. You should call him."

Jane paused by the fuzzy cubicle wall. "I'm afraid I don't know who you mean."

"Matt Swanson, Doug's son. He left with a carton of old papers. I'm sure he'd have something his stepmom might like." Mary-Grace looked over the tops of her tortoise-shell glasses, her eyes smiling, and then turned back to her computer.

Jane chewed on her bottom lip. Why had Doug's son cleaned out the old files so very close to the time of his father's death?

Jane's drive home from the Gresham mayor's offices took her past Paula's house. She wanted to stop in and say hi, but she didn't think she could pull off quiet, supportive listening at the moment.

She turned over all the little things she had picked up at the mayor's office. People seemed to have certain expectations of a Swanson maid. Either it was usually just a particular person or it was a certain "type." The name Danae Monroe from the time sheet had rung a bell. Perhaps Danae Monroe was both an employee at the city offices and Douglas's maid. It seemed unlikely, but what was really wrong with the idea? Danae Monroe could be the maid, the woman in all of the pictures, the woman from the mayor's office, and the reason Caramel held Douglas's head under the water that fateful morning.

Jane was stopped at a stop light, which was good since her mind was not on the road. Douglas had probably been murdered, but if it had been Caramel, Caramel would be in prison. She wouldn't still be wandering naked around her house. That was just silly. Someone else must have done it.

Maybe this Danae Monroe herself?

Whatever else she got done tomorrow at the Swanson house, she was determined to find out where she had seen that name before.

CHAPTER 13

BACK HOME, JANE TRIED TO GET HOLD OF ISAAC, but there was no answer. She called Holly, her employee, instead.

"Hey, Jane, listen to this," Holly said, after the initial greeting. "'Douglas Swanson, former Mayor of the City of Gresham's death has been declared a murder. Investigations are underway. The police are looking for an employee of his house. They have not released the employee's name.' Is that you, Jane? Are they looking for you?"

Jane's heart stopped for a beat. "But they can't be! I gave them my address, my name, everything. They have my phone number, even."

"But you dropped your phone in the hot tub."

"Oh, that's true. But they have everything else!"

Jane paced up and down the short hallway of her apartment, stepping over a pile of laundry in front of Gemma's bedroom.

"What if they think you lied when they interviewed you at the house? Do you think they could think that?"

"Of course not. Why would I lie?" Jane paused by her door, her hand hovering over the dingy brass doorknob.

"But what if you said something wrong, by accident? You know? Because you were scared. Just what if? Then they would think it was a lie. You didn't write anything down, did you?"

"Yes, of course I did. I signed a statement and everything. But I didn't lie." Jane sat down, right in the middle of her hall floor. "You don't really think they could be looking for me, do you?"

"I dunno, Jane. They might be."

"But what do your parents think?"

"Oh my gosh, Jane, I didn't tell them! If I told them you were wanted for murder, they'd never let me talk to you again."

"I'm not wanted for murder. Oh, Holly, you're all mixed up. This isn't about me at all." Jane stood up again, but leaned against her door, stretching her back out, trying to relax.

"The police are looking for an employee that works for their house, and you are the only one."

Danae Monroe.

The name popped into Jane's mind. Of course it had—it hadn't even been a half an hour since she had seen it on the paper. "Forget about it, Holly. I'm not lost. They must be looking for the real maid who is on vacation."

"Oh yeah! You've got a good memory, Jane."

"Thanks so much." Jane let out a long, slow breath she had been holding.

"But whatever happened to that ring?"

"The ring?"

"The diamond that Caramel thinks you stole."

"My gosh. I wonder how I forgot that. I don't know. I suppose bigger things are on her mind right now." Jane scratched the back of her neck. Caramel had either really thought Jane had stolen the ring, or had planned on framing Jane for the loss. Either way, it was smart to remember that Caramel wasn't on her side.

"I've gotta go, Jane. My mom is calling me."

"Okay." It wasn't really okay. Jane didn't want to end the call at all, not after Holly getting her all keyed up like that. She would far rather use up all of her nervous energy talking to someone. The girls of her ministry group came to mind but… they wouldn't do. They wouldn't get what she was up against at all.

Jane clicked her fingernails against each other. She could call Jake, just since there was no one else right now. She tapped the screen of her phone.

Then she stopped.

She could look into Mark Ehlers' unsolved hit and run case. It would be way better to catch that bad guy than to spend her time fussing over Douglas Swanson, who at his worst was a dirty old man, and at his best was a politician.

But how did one look into a hit and run? Jane went back to her room and set up her laptop. She could spend some time trying to learn what she'd need to know to even start the process. That would be something anyway.

She had gotten far enough into Google to realize that there was really no way to solve an unsolved hit and run as an amateur detective. All she could really do was sit and wait, hoping a witness would come forward.

A witness would be good for both deaths, frankly. A little someone who saw something that could be used to tie up the loose ends. Jane stared at a pocket police manual for writers, which had come up in her search. It had a perfunctory description of a crime scene, followed by the interview process. According to the menu at the top of the blog, there was also a standard format for arrest and trial tucked away on the site. But all the site did for her was make her nervous. Sure, the police were almost certainly looking for the real maid, who was probably Danae Monroe. But what if they were looking for her? She slammed her laptop shut without closing her programs. She would just have to go see Detective Bryce and make sure everything was okay.

She threw her door open and bumped right into Gemma.

"You're home?" Gemma stood in the hallway in her jammies and bunny slippers.

"Yeah, no clients left for the day."

Gemma yawned.

"You just getting up?" Jane drummed her fingers on her doorknob. She had to be polite to Gemma, who she really did like, even if she wanted to run right over the top of her to get to the police station.

Gemma yawned again. "I am. I pulled two fourteen-hour shifts in a row, and I was dead to the world."

"Lots of new babies?"

"Finally. It's nice to be off 'call,' but now I've got to go find a few more mommies-to-be."

"If you have any trouble, you could probably pick up a house or two with me." Jane stole a glance at her bedside clock, then reminded herself no one was expecting her at the police station.

Gemma smiled. "Sure, thanks. But you know, it's not the same. I like being a part of the miracle of birth. Nothing like it in the world." Gemma padded down the hall to the bathroom. "Don't go anywhere yet. We need to have a chat." She pulled the door shut and the lock clicked.

Jane stood still. Needed a chat? Now? Maybe not. Jane grabbed her purse from the hook by the door and left. Nothing her slovenly cousin-turned-roommate had to say could compare with making sure the police didn't think she had skipped town after murdering her boss.

Jane drove to the same police station where she had picked her dad up the year before, but when she got there, she stayed in her car, her courage completely gone. She dug through her wallet and found the card the detective gave her. She could call him first, and then go inside, if she was needed. Or if he didn't answer. Either option was better than going in and saying, "Here I am!"

She dialed half of the number and then stopped. The detective was an important man. He didn't need her bothering him. It would be much better to walk inside and talk to the person at the desk. Much, much better.

She got out of her car, shut the door, and stared at the police station. The low-slung concrete building didn't look scary. There was even a small lawn with a playground off to the side. As she hadn't done anything wrong, walking in and just saying she thought they might need to get in touch with her couldn't do any harm.

She walked to the big, heavy glass doors. She took a deep breath, and then pulled one open.

The waiting room wasn't empty, but it was quiet. Two people in crisp business clothes stood in front of the bullet proof glass partition, talking with the person at the front desk.

Four more ragged adults, one holding a squirming toddler on her knee, sat in the waiting area. The smell of cold cigarettes and dirty clothes hung over them all like a cloud.

Jane queued up behind the people in the business clothes.

Waiting gave her time to second guess what she was going to say again. "*Hi, I'm Jane. You might be looking for me in connection with the murder of Douglas Swanson, but then again, you might not.*" Or "*Hi, I'm Jane. I saw a little thing in the paper that made me think I should check in.*" But… she hadn't seen it and she was keen not to lie to the police. The people in business clothes brushed past her, and there she was, at the desk.

"Hi. I'm Jane Adler. I work for the Swanson family."

The man behind the bullet proof glass looked to be about Jane's age. His hair was buzz cut and he wore a policeman's uniform. "Can I help you with something?"

Jane chewed her lip. She leaned forward. "I feel really stupid right now, but I heard the police are trying to locate one of the Swanson family employees."

The officer's eyebrows shot up. He held a finger up to her. "Wait just a second." He grabbed his phone, pressed a few buttons, and then spoke in a low voice. "Sir, someone is here claiming to be an employee of the Swanson family." He looked up and smiled at Jane, but his eyes were wide, and excited. He said a few "Mmm hmms" and "Yessirs," and then hung up.

"Come along with me." He met Jane at a door next to his reception window and led her down the hall in the interior of the police station.

It reminded Jane of the emergency room, but cleaner and calmer.

The police officer knocked on a door that said "Detective Roberts" on a gold-colored name badge, then opened it. "Here she is, sir."

"Thanks." The man behind the desk was a tall, muscular man with silver hair and square, silver glasses. "Have a seat."

Jane sat.

"You work for the Swanson family in what capacity?"

"I'm the substitute maid, sir." Jane's voice and body shook like a kid waiting to get a tetanus shot.

The man looked over his glasses at Jane. "The same maid who found the body?"

"Yes, sir. Jane Adler, sir."

"Relax, Jane. You're not in trouble."

Jane took a deep breath, and held it. Not in trouble. Words she lived for.

"What brings you down here today?"

Jane chewed her lip. She felt twelve years old, and very foolish. "I just heard from a friend that the newspaper said you were looking for their employee, and that's me, so I came in. At least, I am pretty sure I'm their only employee."

The officer smiled, though his eyes looked tired. "You're not. Don't worry. It was good of you to come down, but you're not who we are looking for."

"But who else could it be?" Jane sat up straighter. They must be looking for Danae Monroe, like she was. If they would just tell her that before she left, it would make the trip worth it.

"Don't let that worry you right now." He slid a business card across his desk. "You can save yourself trouble by calling this number next time.

Jane accepted the card, but slid it into her pocket without looking at it. She could tell she was being dismissed, but she had to try again. "I didn't read the article in the paper myself, a friend read it to me over the phone. It did say household employee, didn't it? That's me until the other maid comes back from vacation."

The police officer stood up. "What newspapers say and what we do are not always the same thing. Thank you for coming in. It was very conscientious of you."

Jane considered keeping her seat, but she was more afraid of the Detective than she wanted to admit. "Okay. I'm sorry, I mean thank you. I, uh…"

"It's okay, Jane. You did the right thing."

Jane nodded, and left. Back at her car, she dialed the number for Detective Bryce.

The baby-faced detective who had taken her statement at the house that morning answered on the third ring. "Bryce."

"Detective Bryce? This is Jane Adler. I was the girl who found Douglas Swanson?" She kicked herself for sounding so insecure.

"Yes, of course. How can I help you?"

Jane kept her eye on the door to the police station. She didn't dare drive away while talking on her cell phone. "I was, um, just checking in. My new phone is hooked up and all of that. I hadn't let you know yet."

"Well, good. I'm glad to hear it." He waited a moment. "Is there anything else?"

"No, I don't think so. I just remembered I needed to let you know."

"Great." He paused again. "You know what? I did have a couple more questions for you. Do you have a minute to talk?"

"Of course." Jane's heart skipped a beat. If she could keep him on the phone maybe she could insert the name Danae Monroe into the conversation. "What do you need?"

"Can you meet me at the Swansons' house? It would be best to talk there, in person."

Jane stomach flipped. Meeting at the house sounded official. "When do you want to meet? I'm there every morning from 5:30 to 6:30."

"That will work. I can meet you there at 6:30 tomorrow morning."

"Okay. Is there anything I should do or something?" Jane's words and ideas were so tumbled together now she didn't know what she was asking.

"Nope. We'll just look at the room together and I'll ask you a few questions to clarify the statement you made. It's really no big deal, but I think it will help."

"Okay." Jane squeezed her eyes shut. What had she said wrong in her statement?

"See you tomorrow." Detective Bryce hung up.

Jane laid her phone down in the passenger seat. If she wanted to get any information from Detective Bryce, she'd have to pull herself together.

CHAPTER 14

WHEN SHE GOT BACK HOME SHE FOUND a scribbled note Gemma had pinned to her bedroom door. She pulled it off and read it in her room. "Will you be home tonight at 8:00? I really need to talk to you. Urgent."

She was disappointed to admit she'd be home. It was hard to take roommate-related criticism from someone who left piles of dirty clothes in the bathroom, and criticism was the only thing that came to Jane's mind.

That or Gemma needed help making rent, which was about as welcome as criticism. She'd probably propose taking a third roommate into their two bedroom place—again. Jane flopped back on her futon. Would she ever make enough to live on her own?

She rolled over. Probably not, since her whole future would be based on donations from nice people. But housing was cheaper overseas, and her roommates would be on the same team, so living together would be easier.

Speaking of the same team, she had a meeting with Kaitlyn and Valerie to prepare for. Did she want to stand 100% behind Kaitlyn and the Pogs or did she want to come up with her own idea for ministry?

By the time 8 o'clock rolled around, Jane's laundry was done, her missiology book was read, and dinner had been cooked and eaten, but she hadn't solved the problem of the outreach yet. Should she try and prove she had what it took to lead a group or try and prove she was a team player who would support the people she served with?

The apartment door swung open and Gemma pushed a wire basket on wheels through it. "Can you grab that for me?"

Jane rolled the cart into the kitchen for her.

Gemma followed with three canvas sacks full of produce. She dropped them on the floor next to her cart and then sat down. "I'm pooped."

"Did you have fun at the market?"

"Why didn't you wait for me? I thought we were going together."

"I had an urgent thing. I'm sorry." Jane fiddled with the hem of her T-shirt. She didn't remember making plans to go together.

"Whatever." Gemma rolled her back slowly down to the floor, her arms above her head.

"Farmers' market was open late," Jane said.

"I stayed for a concert."

"Well, it's eight, and I'm here now. What do you need?"

"I have a friend coming to town and she needs a place to stay."

"That's no big deal. I don't mind." Jane began to put the groceries into the cupboards. "I don't see why that was urgent."

"She's driving down from Seattle and will be here in about ten minutes."

"Ah. Well, that is a little urgent I guess. But still, no biggie. It's your place."

"She's got a bad back, and can't really sleep on the sofa."

"Okay." Jane didn't like the direction that the conversation was taking.

"I'd let her stay in my room, but you can understand, with all of my client files and stuff, I really can't."

Jane crinkled her nose. By client files, Gemma meant her huge, disastrous mess. "Do you think she's not trustworthy or something?"

Gemma sat up and smiled. "So she can have your room?"

"I would rather not." Jane let the cupboard door swing shut with a clap.

"She needs a really dark, quiet space and a firm mattress or she can't sleep."

"Because of her back?"

"Yeah. I forget what exactly is wrong, but she can't sleep just anywhere."

"How long is she staying?"

"I'm not sure." Gemma pulled an apple from her canvas tote and crunched it.

"You want me to give my room to your friend indefinitely?" Jane turned to her cousin. "Is she planning on paying rent for me?"

"It's not like that—she's coming for a couple of days, or a week or something. Not forever. She's thinking about moving back and just wants a place to crash for a few. It's not a biggie. She just called today."

"She can sleep in my room tonight, but after that, you need to make room for her in yours." Jane left the rest of the groceries and went to her room. She wanted to barricade the door to protect it from the random intruder, but barring that, she'd at least change the sheets and grab some clothes and blankets for herself.

While she was putting things in order, she heard the doorbell ring and Gemma greet the guest. Jane smoothed the blanket on her bed, and then picked up the stack of stuff she couldn't live without for the week.

Her door popped open. Gemma stood next to a short girl with puffy eyes and frizzy blonde hair. "Hi, Jane," the guest said. "I'm Steph. Thank you so much for letting me use your room for a little bit."

Jane was overcome with sympathy. The woman looked like she was in pain. Of course, she'd give a hurting person her bed. Obviously she would. "You're welcome to it."

Gemma caught Jane's eye and smiled.

"Let me just clear out some stuff. I get up really early for work and don't want to disturb you."

Stephanie and Gemma had stayed up talking in Jane's room until after midnight. How long after, Jane wasn't sure, because she had fallen asleep around then. And young though she was, as she showered and dressed the next morning, she didn't look forward to a full day of physical work on only four hours of sleep.

She didn't dare hope for an afternoon nap, unless she stole it in her car, since it looked like Stephanie wouldn't want to be traveling and Gemma didn't have any clients ready to deliver.

At the Swansons'—her first client every morning—Jane decided to beard the lion in her den. She went straight to the master bedroom.

It was empty and so was the bath, so Jane wiped the clean surfaces even cleaner and opened the curtains. Then she ran all the way down to the hot tub room, just to check. She didn't want to see "all" of Caramel again, but she'd rather be sure she knew what she was up against for the morning.

The hot tub room was empty as well. It looked like this time Caramel had made good on her promise of not being around at all some mornings.

The cleaning seemed to fly by. The machines were turned on, the house was opened, filled with light, the smell of coffee, and clean bathrooms, and Jane was done. She was early, so she let herself sit at the kitchen and enjoy a cup of coffee while she waited for the detective.

The doorbell rang, which jolted Jane out of her reverie. Detective Bryce was here. It was time to talk about murder.

While Jane went to let him in, she tried to remember the questions she was hoping to get answered. But, frankly, the idea of figuring out anything about Douglas's death was less interesting on four hours of sleep than it had been the day before.

She let the detective in.

"Why don't we go straight down to the hot tub room?" Detective Bryce cut to the chase. "Get us in *loco situ* and see what you can remember."

Jane led him downstairs and wondered if all detectives liked to toss around Latin, or if this was something Bryce did to make himself seem older. She remembered he had seemed young, but she didn't remember him seeming this young—or cute. Despite the thought of her distant boyfriend, she found it hard to look Detective Bryce in the eye when he talked to her. He was really cute.

"So, we don't usually take a statement like we did last time, right away. But with the difficulties we thought we'd have getting in touch with you, it seemed like a good idea."

"I understand." Jane kept her eye on the hot tub, though it wasn't a comforting sight.

"After the team was done with the scene, we compared our notes with your statement and found we had a few questions."

"Sure." Jane picked at her fingernail. She knew if she looked up she'd blush, which was so stupid. All of her monosyllabic, eye-contact avoidance was just going to make her look guilty of something.

"Just relax, and look around the room while we talk, okay? I want to see if you can remember what you saw that morning."

Jane nodded.

"What happened when you came into this room?"

"Um, I wanted to check the pH of the water, so I went to the hot tub."

"What did you see as you went there?"

"It was dark. I needed to turn on the lights. I always notice how the black light makes everything weird when I do that. That's what I noticed first."

"What happened next?"

"I went to the tub, and I reached in to get a sample, but I saw Douglas in it."

"What did you see between turning on the lights and finding Douglas? Anything out of the ordinary?"

Jane moved to the door. She flicked the lights on and off, and then walked to the hot tub. She leaned down. "The towels! There were some towels on the ground. Did I forget to write that on my statement?"

"No, you didn't forget that. What were the towels like?"

"They were heavy. Damp, or just plain wet, even. Thick white towels. I've had to replace them in the cupboard once before. I guess maybe they are the special towels for the hot tub."

"How many wet towels were there?"

"Two."

"Are you sure?"

"I picked them up and it seemed like two, but I didn't count them or anything."

"And what happened next?"

"What do you mean? With the towels?"

"Anything."

"I tossed the towels toward the hamper over there, but I missed." Jane pointed to the corner near the door. "Wait, where's the hamper?"

"That's what we were wondering."

Jane stared at the door. "The towels weren't in the room when you went in to get Douglas?" A shiver that started at the end of her spine swept over her whole body.

"No towels, no hamper. I've interviewed the guys who made the crime scene report. You are the only one who saw towels or a hamper." Detective Bryce stepped away from Jane.

A wave of frustration followed the shiver. "But why would someone remove them?" She stalked to the doorway. "You can see the scuff marks of the hamper here by the door." Jane pointed to the dull scratches on the tile.

Officer Bryce joined her at the door. He knelt by the marks on the floor. "Interesting."

Jane went back to the hot tub. "See this?" She pointed to the marble steps. "You can see a kind of foggy spot on the lower step. That's where the towels were sitting. It looks to me like they always drop their towels in the same spot."

"Could be."

"Right. It could be. Which would mean the person who dumped their towels there had done it before." Jane walked around the hot tub in a circle. "What else did you all find in here?"

Detective Bryce looked up at her and raised an eyebrow. "Are you sure the incident with the towels happened this time? It wasn't something that happened on another day and just sort of slipped in on accident?"

Jane's mouth opened.

He didn't believe her.

She crossed her arms over her chest and looked the detective up and down. He had an open look on his baby face. Even with the one raised eyebrow his eyes seemed clear and innocent. Either he really did think she was just confused or he wanted to think so. What was the alternative?

Jane moved back to the fuzzy spot on the marble. There were two alternatives. The first, someone removed the towels and hamper to make it look like Douglas had been alone. The second: she had added the details to the report to throw the suspicion away from herself.

Detective Bryce stood up. He smiled at her and nodded, as though he wanted her to answer his question.

Jane shook her head. "No. I really did pick up the towels." Jane touched the spot where she had hit her forehead on the door. The bump had shrunk significantly. "I even tripped on them on my way out. I hit my head on the door frame and got this bump."

Detective Bryce frowned. "Okay."

"Someone else was in the house."

The detective kept his eye on Jane.

"Caramel came to me from the front driveway. She could have come through the house out a back door, around and then up the driveway. But could she have removed the laundry basket and towels and still made that kind of long trip around the house so quickly?"

"Jane…"

"Or was she truly out back on the property? If so, there was a third person. Someone in the house with me the whole time, who knew about the towels and thought they might be evidence." Jane sat on the step. "But they would not have known that I was supposed to be there. They would have heard the alarm and panicked."

The detective opened his mouth, but he closed it again without saying anything. He narrowed his eyes at Jane.

"If there was a third person, where were they?" Jane looked around the room. "Two closets. Did they hear me coming down the hall and then hide in a closet? Then they could have jumped out, grabbed the evidence that they had been there, and then run out the back." Jane walked to the back door and stared at the green fields behind the house. "And then what? How did they get away?" The suburban acres swept down a hillside. Somewhere just behind the distant clump of trees were the outbuildings that turned the McMansion into horse property. Jane's heart thumped. The answer would be out there, far from the hot tub. It just had to be.

She turned back to the detective. "What did they find out in the stables?"

The detective smiled his disarming, easy-going smile and shrugged. "I can't discuss that."

Jane bit her tongue. Of course he couldn't say anything. She was ancillary to the situation. A witness at best, a suspect at worst.

"I picked up the wet towels, threw them to the hamper, and missed. Then I tripped on them as I tried to run from the room. I don't know what happened next." She tried to hold his gaze with confidence, but her eyes began to swim.

"Thanks for meeting me here." The detective offered her a gentle smile. "I'll get in touch with you again, I'm sure. Your account of finding the body is very important."

Jane chewed on her cheek to keep the tears from spilling over. His cool, calm delivery was so condescending.

The detective cleared his throat. "I think we're done here. You can go home now." Though dismissive, his tone was kind.

"If you find out what happened to the towels—"

"Then we'll find out what happened to Douglas." He lifted his eyebrow and smiled, one dimple popping out. "I had thought of that."

Jane drove away wondering if Detective Bryce's attitude was best described as gentle, condescending, or fake. Figuring out which one it was seemed almost as important as finding out what had become of the wet towels.

CHAPTER 15

JAKE TEXTED OVER LUNCH. "Call me, maybe?"

Jane sipped her coffee and considered it. If anyone would get how freaked out she was right now, it was him.

He sent another message on the heels of the first. This time it was a video of a goat "singing," if you could call it that, along with some old Crystal Gail. And yet, it wasn't exactly rude. Jane choked on a laugh. She should text him back.

She watched the video again. Jake, Jake, Jake. She took a bite of her sandwich and replied, "lol."

He responded again. "The song, or calling me?"

She shook her head at her phone. "Both."

Jane set her phone down and worked on her lunch and the little murder problem. Tomorrow morning she could run down to the stables. She had not been there yet, and it could be telling.

Or she could sit and visit with Caramel, if Caramel had clothes on.

Jane picked the seeds off the crust of her bread. She couldn't just "sit and visit" or pop into the outbuildings. She needed a plan.

It seemed clear to her that someone had been in the tub with Douglas. Otherwise there wouldn't have been wet towels on the step. The person had disappeared before she got into the room, so they had to have heard her coming. And they hadn't gone far, or the towels and laundry basket wouldn't have just disappeared. And if they had just stuck themselves back into the closet they would have been found by the cops. So the person and the basket and the towels had just gone outside. It was the only possibility.

Jane peeked at her phone. No new message. She checked again. Still, it was better. She didn't need Jake pestering her while she had so much important stuff to do.

She dialed Isaac's number. Yet again, no answer. She was disappointed—sort of.

Seven o'clock rolled around, and Jane, Kaitlyn, and Valerie were stationed on three sides of a small table in Bean Me Up Scotty's for their very important Friday meeting.

Jane's back was ramrod straight. She held her cup of decaf close to her mouth, but didn't sip.

Valerie frowned into her large cappuccino.

Kaitlyn sat like Jane, but with a thin line of tears glistening on one cheek. "I knew the cut was coming, but I didn't know it would hurt so bad."

Jane was torn. She had grown to like Kaitlyn, but the melodrama was exhausting.

"Can you get another part time job to help make up the loss?" Valerie's suggestion came in her matter of fact tone. Not cold hearted, but not easily moved either.

"It's the economy…" Kaitlyn wiped the tears away with her good hand.

"I meant it when I said I could offer you work cleaning." It would take some work, but Jane was fairly sure she could come up with a client or two for her friend.

Kaitlyn held up her prosthetic. "With this?" Her voice had a teary edge to it.

"Of course with that. What would that hurt?"

"The chemicals, the lifting. I don't know. I just don't think it would work." A thin silver bracelet with a diamond on the clasp slid back down her prosthetic wrist when she lowered her hand. The cuff of her crisp white button down had hidden it before.

"It's hard work, but I think you are up for it." Jane finally sipped her coffee. It was too hot still and burned the tip of her tongue. She rubbed her tongue across the back of her teeth.

"So far, you've only lost one shift a week. We will definitely keep you in our prayers, but I think we need to move on with our ministry plan." Valerie nodded while she spoke, as though trying to get the team to agree with her.

Jane nodded, but kept silent. The little murder she was wrapped up in had taken over all of her free time. She had nothing new to offer her team.

"I think it is clear that the church is looking for missionaries who can take on a task and complete it, so the task we choose should be in proportion to both the time we have available to work and our giftings." Valerie opened a burgundy suede folder. One side had a tablet and the other had a notepad covered in notes. She turned the tablet on and the Bible opened up.

"I think Paula is looking for innovative outreach." Kaitlyn caught Jane's eye as she spoke and nodded.

Jane scrunched her mouth.

"They want to see us try to touch the hearts of hard-to-reach places in our community. To really make an impact." Kaitlyn turned to Valerie and tried the nodding thing again.

Valerie frowned, and looked over her small round glasses. "Paula said she wanted to train us to successfully lead and mentor a small group. They want to build up our basic skills before sending us away."

Jane watched the coffee station over Valerie's shoulder. She hoped the gray-haired barista who had had an eye on Val was here tonight.

"Jane? Your opinion, please?" Kaitlyn attempted the level-headed tone that Valerie used.

"I think they want to see if we can work together to achieve a goal." Jane tilted her head. In fact, she was certain that's what this was about. "If they wanted to see us lead small groups, or do some crazy new thing, they wouldn't have put us all together." Jane took another sip of her coffee. "In fact, I am positive the only point in all of this is teamwork."

"You think that *who* is doing the job is more important to Paula than the job they are doing?" Kaitlyn's cheeks flushed.

"Yes." Valerie turned to a fresh page on her notepad. "I think Jane's right."

"The work is important, too…" Jane said. She smiled, but her heart wasn't in it.

"That's the problem with you, Jane." Kaitlyn narrowed her eyes. "You see 'good work' as an end in itself. Valerie and I have very specific jobs already lined up. Mission work we know we are going to do."

Jane set her cup down.

"Having a concrete goal really changes your perspective." Kaitlyn rested both of her hands on the table, her good hand toying with her silver bracelet.

"Don't put words in my mouth, please. I agree with Jane. This job is to show that we can work together—one of the specific skills that field missionaries asked the church to look for in candidates. Having a plan for our work in place doesn't change that we have to learn how to work together."

"I just don't know why Jane is even on this team." Kaitlyn looked down at the table.

Jane slumped. She didn't know, either, but that didn't mean she wanted Kaitlyn to say it.

"Jane is on this team because she is serious about missions." Valerie kept her matter-of-fact tone.

Jane only hoped she could be as imperturbable in twenty years.

"Jane, why don't you tell us what ideas you've come up with?"

Jane picked at her fingernail. Then she took a deep breath. "I… well…" She looked from face to face and couldn't do it. She couldn't talk about missions tonight. "Okay, this is the way it is. My boss was murdered. I found the body. The cops think I might have lied in my statement. I've been so wrapped up in this, I haven't really given any thought to our project. But I am perfectly willing to work hard at whatever decision we make as a team."

"Oh, child!" Valerie's voice held all the warm tones of a mother. She reached across the table for Jane's hand. "You poor thing. How can we help you?"

Jane let Valerie hold her hand. Tears sprung to her eyes. It was what her mom would have done and said, had she been in town, and exactly what Jane had been missing. She blinked the tears away. "I have to go back to the house where he died every morning to do some light cleaning. Tomorrow, I want to look around more, see if I can find any clues."

"But haven't the police already done that?" Kaitlyn's voice was excited, but her face had a weird, hard look on it, as though she were trying to suppress some emotion.

"Yeah, they have. But I don't know what else to do about it."

"You all keep telling me to just pray for my crisis. You should just pray about this one."

Jane looked hard at Kaitlyn. Was that envy in her voice? Because Jane's crisis was worse?

Kaitlyn's face was turning red. Her hand trembled. Her eyes sparkled.

No. Not envy. Kaitlyn was excited. She looked like she was trying to keep from smiling.

"I have definitely been praying, but I don't have any concrete plan from God, or even a strong sense of peace."

Kaitlyn leaned forward. She wasn't sympathetic, though; she was almost certainly excited. "Are you scared to look for clues alone?"

"I am, a little."

"Do you want someone there with you?"

Jane almost smiled. Kaitlyn was trying to get invited along. "I have to be there at 5:30 in the morning…"

"I can be there. Just tell me where."

Valerie let go of Jane's hand. "I think it is very admirable of you—"

"It's not admirable. She's my friend and she needs help." The hint of Kaitlyn's suppressed smile popped out in her dimples.

"Jane, have you had a chance to talk to Paula about all of this yet?" Valerie asked.

"She's got so much on her heart right now, I didn't want to bother her."

Valerie took a deep breath. "I'm glad you finally told us, but this is a very serious situation. I think you need to tell Paula so that she can allow you a little grace in our project."

"But I'm willing to work on it still."

"I know you are." Valerie tilted her head and smiled. "But you need freedom from this project until this trial has passed. Please don't underestimate this. Murder is very serious."

"But so is ministry. This thing, this murder is just a momentary trial, but the ministry we do can have an eternal impact on someone." Jane's heart was racing. She could tell she was being pushed out of the ministry team—out of the running for future funding. She didn't want Caramel and Douglas to do this to her. It wasn't fair.

"We can have eternal impact wherever we serve." Valerie turned her cup around in her hands. "I have been waiting twenty years to go overseas, but I had eternal impact here at home while I waited."

Kaitlyn waved her hand, brushing away Valerie's words. "This is a crisis, Jane. You'll still do ministry stuff. Right now, we have to clear your name. Get out your phone and text me the address, and I'll be there tomorrow, bright and early."

Jane looked at them both, Valerie with her motherly concerned face, Kaitlyn squirming like a toddler. What choice did she have, really? It's not like she had been contributing to the project. "But what does it mean to the team?"

"Just explain your circumstances to Paula and let her tell you what it means to the team," Valerie said softly.

Kaitlyn picked Jane's purse up from the floor. "Get your phone out and text me the number. You need someone by your side right now."

Jane pulled her phone out. Did she want Kaitlyn's help? Would it be wrong to text the wrong address? She sent the correct address, but wondered if she would regret it.

"First thing tomorrow, Jane. I won't let you down."

"And please, go see Paula as soon as you can."

CHAPTER 16

BY 6:00 IN THE MORNING, Jane was pretty sure Kaitlyn wasn't coming to the Swanson house.

When Jane finally heard a light knock on the back door, a wave of relief washed over her. She wasn't sure why, since having Kaitlyn there to snoop with her would blow her innocent, "I'm just cleaning up" or "I was looking for you" cover.

Despite the added danger, it was nicer to be together than alone. With a backwards glance down the hall, Jane opened the back door. She held a finger to her lips, and joined Kaitlyn on the patio. "I've got a horse blanket from the garage. It's been there since I started, but I thought we could carry it down to the stable."

Kaitlyn's eyes sparked. Her cheeks were flushed. "What's your reason?"

"Just tidying up."

"Who works down in the stables?"

Jane was taken aback. "I don't know. Don't you think they take care of the animals themselves?"

"Gosh, maybe? My parents hire someone, but then, we board our horses, so I don't know."

Jane shook her head. Of course Kaitlyn had horses. "Let's just mosey on down there. You can tell me if anything looks funky."

The Swanson property sloped away from the house, with the bulk of the land behind and to the side, sort of kidney shaped. A large field was bordered by white horse fence. A tree line stood toward the back, which seemed to be the only place outbuildings could be hiding.

"It's only about three acres of land." Kaitlyn shaded her eyes and looked from side to side. "They can't keep many horses."

"I think they just have the two." Jane kept her eyes on the ground, thinking that a solid idea of what the grassy land should look like would come in handy around the stable.

"What's that over there?" Kaitlyn pointed to the west side of the property.

Jane squinted. "A golf cart?"

"That's what I was thinking. But it's not like *that* much property, you know? Why did they need that?"

"Douglas was pretty old. Maybe he needed it to get around."

"Like seventy?"

"Not *that* old." Jane checked the grass for tire marks. It didn't look like the cart had driven over the soft grass.

"Watch out." Kaitlyn pushed Jane to the side. "Sprinklers."

The automatic sprinkler system shot to life. Jane was almost safe, but it soaked her from the knees down.

Kaitlyn was as well.

The girls hugged the fence line as they made their way to the trees. Jane had guessed right; there was a small stable tucked behind the trees. There were also a shed and two small garages.

"Do you hear anyone?" Jane asked.

"No. It's really quiet."

"I don't hear anything at all." Jane turned into the door of the stable. "Where are the horses?"

"Have they ever had horses here?" Kaitlyn ran the toe of her shoe across the dirt. "Where's the hay? Where's anything that shows a horse has been here?"

"It doesn't smell like horses, does it?" Jane walked into a clean, empty horse stall. "I thought Caramel had talked about her horses. I'm sure she had. But... was I wrong? Are they boarded somewhere else?"

"It looks like it." Kaitlyn walked to the back of the stable and then to the door again. "No tack. Nothing. She must not like to keep animals at the house."

"Which would explain why the horse blanket was in the garage, I guess. They drove it home from the stables where they keep the horses, but didn't have anywhere else to put it."

"Why did they bring it home?"

"Maybe she just took the horses somewhere else." Jane crouched down and pressed her fingertips into the dirt floor. "The ground is pretty hard packed. And it kind of looks like it was recently swept. It's been over a week since he died, and Caramel is kind of... impulsive."

"But everything?" Kaitlyn wrapped her hand around a tackle hook on the wall.

"How much stuff could it have been?"

"Maybe she's stuffed it all in the shed."

Kaitlyn pulled her eyebrows together and frowned. "I doubt it."

"Let's check anyway." Jane headed to the first shed.

It was padlocked.

She kicked the door.

Obviously, if there had been a pile of wet towels in the shed, the cops would have found them. She didn't have any special detective skills to make their trip out back worthwhile, but she didn't want to give up.

"Do you think these are the tracks from the golf cart?" Jane kicked a rock out of a bare patch of grass in front of the shed.

"What's in the other shed?" Kaitlyn ignored the track and went to the other shed. She rattled the door, but it was also padlocked.

Jane followed the track. Two tire lines veered toward the left, though they faded into the healthy grass of the well-watered field. Jane looked up and down the field, looking for something the golf cart might regularly travel to. She walked in an almost straight line toward the fence.

Jane climbed over the fence into an airy wood that smelled of hot leaves and damp soil. The branches were covered in their full summer foliage, and blackberry brambles tangled through the underbrush on either side of the trail, but overall, it was a pretty and light forest. Jane put out both arms, and tilted back and forth testing the width of the track. It seemed like a golf cart could get through.

The woods tapered out at the back of a neighbor's property. Jane was just a few yards ahead of some kind of pool house, or guest house.

She scanned the property. There was a pool adjacent to the little version of the big house. And to the left of it were some outbuildings, sheds perhaps. A fenced tennis court was just to the other side of the outbuildings. Trees behind the tennis court screened her view of the neighbor's field. If they had horses, Jane couldn't tell.

Jane went to the French doors of the little house and tried to peer through the sheer curtains. The lights were out, but sunlight shined in through dozens of windows. It looked like it was fully furnished.

Jane went back to the Swanson property. Kaitlyn was standing in the door to the stable, holding the horse blanket. And far off in the field, the golf cart was rolling.

Jane's heart leapt to her throat.

She ran to Kaitlyn.

Kaitlyn waved at her, a bright smile on her face.

Jane reached her, panting.

Kaitlyn's smile was plastered on her face. "Best to act natural," she said through clenched teeth. "Someone is driving that cart right to us."

Jane kept her back to the cart. "Wasn't it empty, and still, earlier?"

Kaitlyn shrugged and then laughed. "I didn't pay enough attention earlier."

The cart puttered up next to them.

A redhead Jane had never seen before was in it, her eyes on the horse blanket.

"Can I help you two?"

"I'm Jane, the maid." Jane's heart had settled down. Caramel wasn't in the cart, so she couldn't be in too much trouble. "This is my friend Kaitlyn. We were going to have breakfast, but she came down here with me first, just real fast."

"And then into the woods?" The redhead tilted her head toward the gate.

Jane chuckled softly. "It was so pretty, and I was done in the house, so I thought I'd just peek."

The redhead smiled. "It is really pretty. Can I have my horse blanket?"

Kaitlyn held the blanket out and the redhead took it. "I'm Amy, Douglas's daughter."

"I'm so sorry for your loss." Jane was glad to know who the driver was, but what was she doing at the house at 6:30 in the morning?

"I really miss the horses," Amy said.

"How long have they been gone?" Kaitlyn asked.

"Dad sold them around Christmas. Said he didn't want to bother with them anymore. He gave me the money, but I would have rather had my babies still."

"He sold your horses?" Jane noticed that Amy was showing a little gray in her roots, and had smile lines around her mouth, even though she wasn't smiling. She was probably about the same age as Caramel.

"Yeah. We talked about it, and I couldn't afford to keep them at my place, and I didn't want to board them. But I miss the girls." Amy patted the blanket. "I left this here last time I rode them. I'm surprised they didn't sell it with the rest of the stuff. I mean, they cleaned the stable out completely."

"It's the cleanest stable I've ever seen," Kaitlyn said.

"What brings you by this morning?" Jane was ready to get to the point. Amy clearly hadn't come for the blanket.

"Why am I driving around the property in a golf cart at six-thirty in the morning?" Amy laughed sadly. "I brought Caramel home. She stayed with us again. And then I just wanted to look at the place." Amy turned in her seat and took in the tree-lined property. "Dad just loved it here so much."

Jane's heart melted. This woman was kind and sad. She felt awful for lying to her.

"Thanks for the blanket." Amy revved the golf cart. "I guess I'd better go park my little toy."

Jane waved as Amy drove away.

"Close call?" Kaitlyn asked.

"I wonder what she'll tell Caramel about us." Jane swung the door to the stable shut. "But let's not be liars, if we can help it. Let's go get some breakfast."

"Even better, let's take breakfast to Paula so you can tell her about the trouble you are in."

They drove through McDonald's on their way to Paula's house.

Paula was up, but she wasn't looking well. Dark shadows haunted the hollows under her eyes. Her limp hair was unwashed. Jane reminded herself it had just turned seven, and they had surprised her, but her languid motions and threadbare bathrobe matched in sadness.

Kaitlyn and Jane sat at the table in the dining room. Kaitlyn dove into her breakfast while Jane caught Paula up on Douglas Swanson's death.

"Between Caramel and me, you really have your hands full."

Jane sipped her coffee and smiled. "I don't think the two of you can really be compared."

"Why not? We were both widowed this week by a tragic accident. She isn't handling it well, but neither am I." Paula spread her hands out, indicating her house, which was beginning to show signs of neglect.

"But what should she do?" Kaitlyn set her fork down. "Jane's got to clear her name, doesn't she?"

"That seems like police work. Jane just needs to get in there and serve."

"Like the Crawfords." Jane set her cup down. "I've been here before, with a grieving client. But that time, I was able to help catch the criminal."

"And now anything less feels like you aren't helping, right, Jane?" Kaitlyn said.

"I wouldn't go that far, but Detective Bryce made it sound like they were wondering about me. I mean, I really did find towels, and all of that, but no one knows where they are."

"I think you can scratch the towels off your to do list. As horrible as it is to imagine, I think whoever killed Douglas Swanson got rid of those forever."

"Did any cars drive away while you were waiting for the cops?" Kaitlyn asked.

"No. From the time I ran out of the garage to the time the cops showed up, no other cars drove on the Swansons' street."

"So, whoever it was knew the property and knew where they could hide while the cops looked for them."

Jane shivered. "That's what it looks like."

"Girls, I don't think this speculating is productive or healthy. We should pray about it before you go, but Jane, I think the best thing you can do right now is to serve faithfully. Work as hard as you can so that anyone who digs into your life will see the honest, hardworking life you lead. You've done nothing wrong, so you have no reason to be scared." Paula reached out, and they all joined hands.

She prayed that God give Jane strength and wisdom to bless Caramel in her time of need, and thanked God for bringing the girls into her life during her own time of need. Then she stood up. "I hate to rush you out of here, but I need to get ready for the day. I'm—" She choked on the words, then took a deep breath. "I'm meeting with the funeral director today."

The girls hugged Paula, and then let themselves out.

"Can you imagine? She waited sooo long to get married, and now he's gone." Kaitlyn looked down at the ring on her finger.

Jane opened her car door and shrugged. "It is sad. But I can kind of imagine. I'm not engaged yet, after all."

"But you will be." Kaitlyn leaned against her Jetta. "Absence is hard on relationships. That's why Spencer and I got engaged so quickly. He didn't want to lose me while he was away."

Jane snorted. "Isaac must be more confident, I guess. That, or less interested." She rested her elbows on the roof of her car and wondered for the millionth time why Isaac couldn't be home right now, when she needed him.

"Yeah, one or the other." Kaitlyn stretched her arms, hands in front of herself. The sparkle from the ring was impossible to miss.

Jane wanted to defend her boyfriend, but she had too many questions herself. Soccer games on the beach, mountain hikes, and teaching his seminary classes were all-consuming, once-in-a-lifetime opportunities, right? That's why he hadn't called in ages.

"Next week is our nine-month anniversary." Jane squinted into the bright summer morning sun.

"Awe. Dating anniversaries are so cute. What are you going to do?"

Jane shrugged again. "Nothing, unless he decides to come home from Costa Rica more than a month early."

"Maybe he'll have a ring for you when he comes home. Wouldn't that be rad?"

"Yeah. Fantastic."

"You do want to marry him, don't you?" Kaitlyn frowned.

"Only if he decides he'd like to be a missionary after this trip. Otherwise, I guess that's it." A small hurt developed in Jane's heart. He just *had* to want to be a missionary when he got back. That was all there was to it.

"Oh, Jane…"

The motherly tone in Kaitlyn's voice made the heart pain worse, so Jane dropped into her car seat. She called out, "I'll see you later," and started her car. From her side window she could see Kaitlyn admiring her engagement ring.

CHAPTER 17

BACK AT HER APARTMENT, Gemma and her guest Stephanie were lounging in their pajamas. The remains of a big breakfast were on the table.

Jane helped herself to a slice of bacon and a big mug of coffee. She stretched out on the floor next to her cousin. "I swear, the next time one of my clients dies, I am quitting the house cleaning business." She yawned and closed her eyes.

Stephanie chuckled. "Happen often?"

"Twice now, which is two times too often."

"Really?" Stephanie's voice pitched up a notch.

Jane opened her eyes. "Yeah, it seems odd to me, too, but I guess Portland is a big enough city to have two people I know die in a year."

Gemma yawned. "Don't quit yet. I am going to have to take you up on your offer to clean. Funds are precarious."

"Okay." Jane didn't want to think about finding new clients right now, but she had made the offer.

"But not yet," Stephanie added. "Because I want as much time with you as I can get before I have to go home. In fact, I can pitch in a little rent if it will help."

"You don't have to do that," Jane said automatically. Though on reflection, a little rent would be nice as Stephanie had taken over her bedroom.

"It's no problem, if you don't mind my staying a little longer."

What could she say to that? She'd quite like her own bed back sooner rather than later, but this was one of those no-way-out situations. In other words, she was pretty sure Jesus would say yes. "Of course." Jane couldn't pull off a bright smile, but she did her best. "While you are out here, I'm going to pop into my room for a minute."

Stephanie flinched, just a little.

"I won't be long." Jane sighed. If Steph pitched in some rent it would be worth it, but in either case, she needed to see this as the whole giving a coat to someone who stole her shirt; hard, but right. But hard.

Jane fell back on her bed and closed her eyes. Her brain was tired. If she didn't have the murder thing hanging over her, then maybe she could process her issues with Isaac. Or if future mission funding wasn't dangling before her, maybe she could focus on helping Caramel better. She rolled over and wrapped her arms around her pillow. Something inside the pillowcase crumpled.

Jane leaned on her elbow and pulled a piece of computer paper out of her pillowcase. A note was scribbled on it in black pen. It started "Dear Lover." Jane skimmed to the bottom. It was signed "D."

Jane shoved it back in her pillowcase. Stephanie's love life was none of her business. Of course, she would have a man whose name started with "D" while Jane was dealing with Dead Douglas, and her delinquent Isaac Daniels, but whatever. Jane pressed her face into her pillow. She really wanted this very nice-ish guest out of her bedroom.

Jane gave herself ten minutes to mope, but then she got up again. She had more houses to clean.

As Jane parked the car at her next client's house her phone rang.

Caramel.

Caramel pitched into her request without any formalities. "Jane—I have company coming late this evening. Family in town for the funeral. I'll be out all day, but the guest rooms aren't ready. I need you here by four, at the latest."

"I'll be there." A funny sort of excitement lit Jane. For the first time, she wasn't scared of Caramel, the cops, or the missing evidence. She wanted in the house so she could find that one clue everyone else had overlooked—whatever that might be.

When she ended her call with Caramel, she called Detective Bryce.

"Detective, this is Jane Adler, the Swansons' maid."

"Hey, Jane. How can I help you?"

"I was wondering… if the maid lets you into a house, can you search it without a warrant?"

"Nope." It sounded like the Detective was chewing. "But you have my ear. What are you concerned about?"

"The towels. The laundry basket. All of that. I'm going in to clean the house this afternoon, and Caramel will be gone. I was just thinking it might be a good opportunity for you to look for them."

There was silence on the end of the phone for a moment. "Sorry to disappoint you. You don't have authority to consent to a search of their house."

A thrill raced up Jane's spine. She'd be doing this alone.

"But… if you find anything interesting, you have every right to call and let me know about it. Then I can request a search warrant."

"Understood." Jane smiled. If she heard him right, she had unspoken permission to dig around the house. She was in control of her fate, a feeling she loved even though she knew it wasn't based on sound theology. "If I find anything, I'll call you."

"Jane…" Detective Bryce paused. "Be careful."

"Always. And thanks." Before he could caution her against her plan, she hung up. She'd be a real spy this afternoon, and not a victim of her circumstances.

The afternoon dragged on, but 4:00 came eventually.

Jane let herself into the Swanson house. First, she had to get two of the three guest bedrooms ready. That way, if Caramel showed up, she would have lots of evidence of having done her job, but have a reason to still be in the house. Fortunately, this job gave her every reason to dig around in the linen closet, laundry room, and the pantry. After all, welcoming guests the right way meant fresh everything, even bars of soap and bottles of shampoo in the Jack and Jill bathroom that two of the guest rooms shared.

Jane decided to save the bathrooms for last, so her snooping around the house could last as long as possible.

She ran the vacuum through the first two guest bedrooms, trying to keep her excitement from making her do a bad job. Then she stripped the first bed.

She tipped the double bed mattress on its side so she could take the bed skirt off and run it through the wash with the sheets. While shifting it off the bed and checking the care instructions (cotton-poly blend, wash with like colors, gentle dry), she also took a peek under the bed.

Completely clear. But that didn't mean all three of the bedrooms were completely clear.

Jane ran the sheets and bed skirt to the laundry room and put them in the machine. Of course, if Caramel had hidden the evidence that Douglas had not been alone in the tub in the guest bedrooms, then she wouldn't have asked Jane to make the rooms up. So if she found the laundry basket, then Caramel was off the hook.

Jane repeated her process in the second bedroom and added the bed skirt to the laundry. Nothing was hiding under the second guest bed, either. Jane checked her watch. She was flying through this, but if she wanted to look like she knew what she was doing she had better get the bed skirt from the third bed in the wash, too.

She stripped the bed, and tipped the mattress. The mattress hit the floor with a bang, followed by a soft thud. Jane scrambled to the floor to find whatever it was that had fallen. She patted the thick carpet blindly, until she hit on the smooth plastic rectangle that was most likely a phone.

Jane sat cross legged and licked her lips. She turned the phone over in her hands. It looked like a new model—small and shiny with a touch screen. It hadn't been used long before it was lost.

She turned it on and waited for the screen to come to life. Before the phone was lost, it had been both charged up and turned off, as though whomever it belonged to didn't expect phone calls while they were at the Swanson house, but planned on using it again right away.

She went straight to the pictures. There were only two. The newest was a close up of Douglas. He was on a bed, leaning on his elbow. He was wearing a white T-shirt and a big grin. Jane looked from the picture to the bed. The bedspread was the same. The next picture was Douglas shirtless, lying against a big, white bed pillow. He was grinning from ear to ear and flushed red. A bit of the headboard was in the picture, and it didn't match anything in the Swanson house.

Jane switched over to the address book. One phone number, saved as "Darcy."

Darcy? Not Danae? Jane pressed dial just to see who answered, but an automated voice chimed that the phone was out of minutes. Pay as you go—like Jane's new phone. Jane switched to messages received. There were only two, the first one was from the month before. It was just a date and time. It was from "Darcy."

Jane switched to messages sent. There were dozens. All sent to "Darcy." Jane read the most recent, which was sent two days before Douglas had died. "Pemberly, Baby?"

Darcy and Pemberly. Clearly pseudonyms.

Jane read the reply… which was the most recent text received. "No, the other place."

It seemed clear: Douglas the playboy had a lover who called him Darcy. If Pemberly was Darcy's house in *Pride and Prejudice*, then at least sometimes Douglas met his lover at his own house… That would explain why the phone had ended up behind the bed, which made Jane gag, just a little. But apparently, they only ever met one other place, which must be where the white pillow and unknown headboard belonged.

But according to the last text, the lovers were supposed to see each other next at the "other place" and not here, where the phone was lost.

Maybe they had changed plans via a voice call?

Or maybe they had met again, without making plans via the cell phone.

Or maybe the lover had surprised him.

And maybe the lover had killed him, too.

Jane set the phone down. She shivered. If only she hadn't smeared the screen with her own fingerprints.

Then again, she was very glad she had all the new information.

She left the phone on the floor and pulled the bed skirt off the box springs. She ran the linens to the laundry room and set the machine to a quick wash.

What if the lover had met Douglas at the "other place" as planned, and then waited and waited for him to make new plans? Then, perhaps she had surprised him at the house, where she had met him in the guest room and lost her phone.

Would she have come back a second uninvited time to see him, only to be rejected and kill him in a rage?

Jane returned to the bedroom to finish cleaning and looking for clues. Most likely, she had lost her phone and gotten a new one. Since it was pay-as-you-go, and had only one contact on it, it had to be her sneaking-away-with-Douglas phone.

While dusting the furniture, Jane opened all the drawers, but as with the first two bedrooms, all of the furniture was empty.

She checked the closet as well, but found nothing.

The laundry machine dinged, so she tossed the bed skirts in the dryer. She still had the Jack and Jill bathroom between the two bedrooms and the hall bath to take care of while she pondered the significance of the phone.

In the hall bath, she did a top-down clean, checking all of the drawers on the way down. But besides spare toilet paper, soap, and toothbrushes still in their packages, the drawers were empty. She gave the toilet a quick scrub, and then swept.

The hall bath did have a black rattan laundry hamper in the corner, but it was always there, as far as Jane knew. And apart from the white linen liner, it was empty.

The Jack and Jill bath was the same, right down to the hamper. But... Jane stared at the hamper. Could she be sure, really sure, that that hamper had always been there? She tipped it up and checked the tile floor. There were no signs of scuffing, to indicate the hamper had always sat there, but then, that could be because it had rubber feet.

She ran back to the hall bath and double checked, but the tile under that hamper had no signs of wear, either.

She just hadn't been cleaning the Swanson house long enough to be certain that things were exactly as they always had been.

But if she was Caramel, had taken a dip with her hubby, drowned him, and then hidden the towels, etc., she would have washed them and put them back in the closet by now, anyway.

Jane thought back to the incident.

Caramel had come up the front driveway. She had been fully dressed, without the slightest hint of having been wet recently. Jane shook her head. She couldn't have been the person who had jumped out of the hot tub, hidden in the closet, then removed the signs of having been there before the cops arrived. As threatening as Caramel seemed, she hadn't had enough time to hide the evidence, dry off, do her hair and makeup, and get dressed… and so couldn't be the killer.

Jane went to the linen closet and loaded up on bath towels and washcloths. She checked for the missing hamper, but the closet was strictly towels and sheets.

Jane stocked the shelves and debated her next move. Without any reason to truly suspect the lover, she decided not to report the phone to Detective Bryce. Instead, she cleaned it very carefully with Windex and a rag. Then holding it very carefully so that her fingers only went where they might go if they had picked up a phone they found under the bed, she set it on the dresser. That would let Caramel know she had found it.

Darcy and Pemberly. Did the lover call herself Elizabeth?

It had been a long time since Jane had read *Pride and Prejudice*. Wasn't there another potential lover for Darcy in the story? That didn't matter. She needed to think like a detective. In *loco situ*.

It was time to go back to the scene of the crime.

She ran to the basement taking the stairs two at a time.

She flipped on all the lights and took in the room. If she had drowned Douglas Swanson in the hot tub, what would she have done next?

Jane moved to the hot tub. Say she had been in the tub and heard someone coming down the hall. Jane scoped the room. Jane opened the closet door and stepped in.

The killer may have stayed in there until she heard Jane leave again. Maybe even until she heard the alarm go off. Then, she would have known she had to leave.

The killer would have looked to the door to see if anyone was coming, and seen the towels.

Jane went to the door and pantomimed dumping the towels in the hamper, and picking up the hamper. Then she ran to the sliding door, her arms still up like she had the hamper in them. She pushed the door open and stood on the patio.

There was a fenced-off square about four yards from the patio, where the garbage and recycling bins were stored. Jane went there... but no. It had a gate in addition to the lids on the bins. If the alarm was going off and the killer was in panic mode, she wouldn't have wanted to go through all of that. Where else could she have gone?

Jane scanned the property. The outbuildings were across the open field. The nearest house was on the other side of the white horse fence. No place to hide.

But there were landscaped plantings with bushes and trees scattered here and there between the Swanson house and the forested area on the other side. Was there enough cover to duck and run in that direction? Jane acted it out.

She made it in about three minutes.

She stopped at the fence. Once in the woods the killer would have been hidden, but if she had stayed there, the police would have found her.

Jane went back to the basement. When she was done putting the guest rooms together, she'd drive around to the street behind the Swanson property and see where the killer could have run to.

By the time the dryer buzzer went off, she had finished putting the bedrooms and bathrooms back together.

Jane stood by the back door, considering what she had gotten out of the day.

More information about Douglas's less-than-faithful love life.

A good idea on where the killer could have gone.

A strong sense of satisfaction for taking the situation in hand.

She could work with those things.

Jane texted a quick message to Caramel telling her the job was done, and then left to scope out the neighborhood for hidey holes where the killer could have stashed the hamper, or sally ports the killer could have escaped through.

The Swansons' neighborhood was pocked with small ponds and woods, but it was made up primarily of two to five-acre, suburban horse property parcels. An airy sense of open space was the primary feeling Jane had as she drove through.

Though on a regular day a person could wander the fields without being noticed, a wet person, likely in a bathing suit, running with a clothes hamper, and looked for—if the police had been looking, which Jane wasn't entirely sure—would have been easily spotted.

After driving around the community two times, Jane was sure that the killer had had to stay in the woods until dark.

Which meant the cops had not been in pursuit, despite the questionable nature of the death.

Which meant they thought that either she or Caramel had done it.

At least, that's the best idea she could come up with.

CHAPTER 18

JANE SAT AT A RED LIGHT. She exhaled. She needed to talk through the information she'd just gathered. She needed someone smart, but more than that, she needed someone who was interested in the case. Gemma was smart, but distracted by her guest. Holly was interested, but Jane doubted she had the kind of wits to draw the right conclusions. Paula had her own troubles to worry about.

Kaitlyn was sharp, fast, and invested in the cause. Jane turned left when the light changed and headed straight to the mall. Maybe she could catch Kaitlyn on a break.

Kaitlyn did take a break. She and Jane found a quiet table toward the back of the food court.

"I had the Swanson house to myself this afternoon, and I found a pay-as-you-go cell phone at Caramel's in one of the bedrooms. It had a couple pictures of Douglas on it, in bed of course, and a few texts about meeting places."

"Caramel's phone?"

"I think not. The pictures were of Douglas, but the texts came from someone called "Darcy" and the person responding to them asked if they were going to meet at "Pemberly." I think it belonged to his lover."

"Ew!" Kaitlyn scrunched up her mouth.

"I think she called him 'Darcy' on the phone because she was beneath him socially."

"Just like in the book." Kaitlyn sipped her bubble tea.

"Yup. I think he met this lady at work, for sure. And he was in charge of her ,one way or the other. So here's the thing. The phone wasn't dead, so it couldn't have been lying there for very long. Whoever dropped it, dropped it recently."

"Like recently enough to have been the killer?" Kaitlyn's eyes popped.

"It could be. I don't know what to make of it, but I know I need to keep it in mind." Jane sketched her ideas on a napkin as she spoke.

"So, if we can trace the phone, we can find the killer now, right?"

"We can't trace a phone but I do think it had to be this lover. It just had to be." Jane wrote The Maid on her napkin.

"Unless of course the murderer was Caramel," Kaitlyn said.

"The timing was all wrong; it couldn't have been her." Jane wrote No Wet Hair.

"Who else is there?"

"Danae Monroe, the maid. She has a long history with Douglas and could be the lover, but she's been on vacation. So she's got an alibi." Jane bit her lip. That vacation alibi was killing her. If she could prove Danae was in town, she could solve the case today.

"Then why mention her?"

"Because the cops are looking for her, but can't find her. If she was really on vacation like she's supposed to be, she'd be easy to find." Jane drew a fat question mark on the napkin. Where *was* Danae Monroe?

"She gets my vote for lover, since she's got a history with him and is beneath him socially, but how could the phone still be all charged up if she has been on vacation?" Kaitlyn set her paper cup on the table and leaned forward, her voice low. "Do you think he had two lovers?"

Jane frowned. "He could have, but he was kind of old... you know? But think about this... the phone was turned off when I found it. But it was pay-as-you-go and it still had plenty of days left on its account. It hadn't been there too long, but it was out of minutes, so if someone knew it was missing, they couldn't really call it to make it ring so they could find it."

"She might have bought one of those cards that keeps your phone active for a whole year." Kaitlyn was counting things off on her fingers as she spoke. "Then she would have had days on it, but no minutes left, and it could have been lying under the bed for any length of time."

"Except the most recent text was from right before the death. So I think the phone could easily belong to the killer. Unless it doesn't."

"In which case, we need to find out who was at odds with Douglas."

"And that makes me think of this Joe guy." Jane tapped her pen on the table.

"Who's Joe?"

"Caramel's brother. He sold her a big, shiny ring to replace the one she lost. Douglas was mad about it, and sounded like he didn't like him." Jane wrote Ring on the paper. The ring was one thing she hadn't resolved yet, but it seemed important. "The other day I heard Caramel on the phone with him, and she said he should stay away. Maybe he needs to stay away because he killed Douglas."

"Would Caramel protect the brother that killed her husband?" Kaitlyn sounded horrified.

"He was a cheating husband. Maybe she hired him to do it?"

"I have to get back to work, Jane. You have to get back to work, too. Find out why Joe should stay away from the house, and find out where this Danae has been."

"You make it sound so easy." Jane sucked in a breath. She wished she could do that. Just a quick search through a few private databases, putting a trail on a credit card. Following the calls from a cell phone. She'd have this case solved in a snap if she had some resources or some training.

"You'll figure out a way."

"Quick, before you go. Do you think Amy could have done it?" Jane folded her napkin and slipped it in her purse.

"Could have killed her dad? What a horrible thought."

"He divorced her mom, cheated on her stepmom, who she seems to like, and sold her horses. Maybe she was really, really mad?" Jane was on the edge of her seat, quivering with excitement.

Kaitlyn stopped. "Maybe she walked in on her dad and yet another lover and killed him in a fit of rage? She is a redhead."

Jane laughed. "Hair color is not a motive!"

"Ack, my break is over. I have got to go, like, five minutes ago. Call me though, okay?"

"Will do." Jane stood up. Tomorrow morning, she'd be back at the Swanson house again. Almost unlimited access to the house and family. If she could just figure out the right way to use her advantage, she could figure out who killed Douglas.

It had been several days since Jake had called, so when his text for grabbing some lunch came through, Jane took him up on it.

They met at the last Roly Burger in Portland, one Jane suspected that Jake owned. Her stomach was fluttery. Jake was a bit off limits—a friend, but a friend who threatened her composure more often than not.

A friend her absentee boyfriend might not want her to be eating with. She filled her paper cup with a caffeine-free soda. New murder suspects and lunch with Jake made her shaky enough.

"Don't you wonder where I've been?" Jake took a bite of his thick burger.

"No." Jane sipped her soda. "Once or twice, tops. I've been a little busy finishing my degree and working."

"How normal of you." Jake wiped his mouth with the back of his hand.

Jane passed him a napkin. "Now's where you tell me you joined the secret service and foiled an assassination attempt all by yourself?"

"Nope."

"Moved to Russia and studied ballet?"

Jake's eyes sparkled.

Jane's heart fluttered. It was a fun game, that's all. "You traveled with the circus?"

"Getting colder." Jake finished the last of his burger.

"You spent the whole year studying for your food handler's license?"

Jake tossed his burger wrapper into the garbage can across the room. "Nothin' but net."

"Okay. Where were you?"

Jake smirked. "There is no way you will ever guess."

"Then tell." The flutters abandoned Jane and were replaced by annoyance.

"Thailand."

Beaches, jungles, pineapples. Girls. Lots and lots of girls shopped around to the highest bidder. The heat drained from Jane's face. "Not really?" She pushed her drink cup away. "You wouldn't have."

"I did. It was a-maze-ing. You should have been there." Jake's smile was self-satisfied.

Jane looked at her watch. "I've got to go."

"Don't you want to hear about my time in paradise?"

"Not really."

"You would never believe the scene there. Seriously passionate."

"Please stop." Jane's stomach turned. She couldn't make eye contact with Jake.

"You would have loved it, Janey. I was there with ten great guys."

"Stop." Jane interrupted him.

"Will you just listen? Jeesh. You'd think I went kitten hunting or something." Jake's face was clear and happy still.

Jane sat back in her chair. He either felt no guilt, or had nothing to feel guilty about. She was curious which one it was.

"We started in the city, but ended up in this little village in the hills. There was a doctor there who would send us to the city for three nights at a time. We'd each try and find a girl and bring her back."

Jane's stomach turned. She looked down at her hands. She shouldn't have hoped for a good story, but why this?

Jake paused, a dreamy look taking over his face. "Sometimes they ran away again, but we saved ten girls last year. Can you imagine? Ten kids pulled out of the cities, safe from trafficking."

"Wait, what?" Jane leaned forward, her breath caught.

"A rescue mission. I would have stayed there forever if I could have."

"A rescue mission?"

"You're slow, Jane. I thought you had your finger on the pulse of missions."

"I do." Jane's voice rose in consternation.

"Ending trafficking. It's the new big thing."

"But this was a Christian mission thing?"

"Christian mission thing?" Jake raised an eyebrow. "You sound both surprised and confused."

"Did you just spend a year as a missionary, Jacob Crawford?" Jane's heart was going a mile a minute. She wanted to smack the smug look off his face, but not before he answered a few simple questions.

"Yes. Yes, I did. I spent a year with Daughters of Rahab. We bought girls for the night and snuck them back to a village that I can't name—not even to you—where the doctor got them all their shots, a teacher worked on their basic school stuff, and a few ladies taught them about Jesus. I want to go back forever, frankly."

Jane chewed her lip. This development had knocked her speechless.

"The 10/40 window is so yesterday. It's all about Thailand, now. And..." he lifted his eyebrow, and smiled, "the mission needs trained Bible teachers, like, yesterday."

Jane shook her head. "First of all, until poverty is eradicated in the two-thirds world, and the gospel is preached in all those Muslim countries, the "10/40 window" will be an urgent mission field."

"Yup. You're right. Second most urgent mission field in the world."

Jane shook her head. "But... I have to ask. Don't you have to apply, be accepted, and like, be a Christian to be a missionary?"

"That stings, Jane. It hurts right here." Jake patted his chest. "Did I not sit through chapel at Presbyterian Prep once a week for four years, just like you?"

"Not that I know of."

"I sat through most of them."

"But sitting through chapel doesn't make you saved." Jane furrowed her eyebrows. When she had last spent significant time with Jake, he had been in a perpetual hungover fog. Not the usual sign of someone who was hungry to preach the gospel.

"Jane." Jake frowned. The color rose in his face. "You really don't think I'm 'saved'?"

"I—" Jane stared at him. He was steaming. She shook her head. "Why should I think it?"

"I just spent a year in the Wild West doing things I never thought possible. I didn't know I had to come see you with a prepared testimony in hand."

"You don't. I just… I haven't seen you in a year, and when I last saw you, you weren't thinking about any of this."

"Because my parents had just been murdered."

"I know. But before that…"

"Not everyone leaps from their parents' head as a forty year old, Jane. I was a normal teenager. It doesn't mean I didn't love God."

"I'm sorry. I'm just so surprised."

"Your vote of confidence means the world to me." Jake looked away.

Jane opened her mouth to speak, but then shut it. What was there to say?

"Do you know what I thought the whole time I was gone?"

Jane shrugged.

"I thought, 'I would give my left arm to have Jane here with me.'"

"But why?"

He smiled just with the corner of his mouth.

"Jake…"

"Don't tell me you'd rather have Professor Boyfriend than a life with me, in the jungle, doing amazing things for God."

Jane watched his face carefully. He had this thing with his eyes; they were so sincere, but his smile was so teasing. She couldn't tell what was behind it. And for her own part? Nothing.

She felt nothing as she looked at him.

He was a smooth talker and could make her heart flutter. He was a flirt and, she admitted, so was she sometimes. But that was all.

"Don't look at me like that. Just, like, hang out with me tomorrow again. And the next day. You'll forget the Professor."

Jane looked away. More likely "The Professor" would forget her.

"He's never going to be a missionary, Jane, so I don't know why you are wasting your time with him."

"He might be." She twisted the end of her ponytail around her finger.

"Might be? Is that enough for you?"

"For now." Jane pulled the elastic out of her ponytail and let her hair fall through her fingers. It fell to her shoulders in a glossy sheet, shielding herself from Jake's sidelong glances. "It's not like I'm planning on getting married any time soon. I've got school, and work, and this murder to think of."

"Another murder, huh?"

"Yes." Jane flicked her hair over her shoulder and straightened up. The murder was a safe topic.

"You almost got kicked out of Bible school last time."

"That wasn't because of the murder."

"Right. That was Isaac's fault, wasn't it?" A knowing look played on Jake's full lips.

Jane took a deep breath. "Isaac is overseas right now, on mission work of his own. When he comes back, he and I will see what happens. I can't rush my life. I can only serve where I am, one day at a time. And right now..." Jane checked her watch again. "Right now, I really do have to focus on the murder. I'm a little bit invested."

"You don't *want* to be a missionary any more, do you?"

"I do!"

"No, you want to be a detective, because it's easier."

"It's not easier." Jane swept the crumbs from the table to her hand and let them fall onto the paper wrapper from her burger. She didn't look up.

"But you do want to be one." Jake took a deep breath. "Listen, maybe I spent the last year dreaming. I thought we had a thing, a spark, but it was probably just because you're hot. I can accept that, even though it sucks. But you... you need to figure yourself out."

"I just have to take life one day at a time, that's all."

"One case at a time." Jake stood up. "I've got to go. But I'll call, because I'm not fickle. You are hot, and as long as the sun still rises, hope lives." He leaned over and kissed her on top of her head. Then he left.

Just walked out the door.

Jane crumpled up the paper wrapper from her hamburger. Of course she wanted to be a detective.

Missionary.

She meant to say missionary.

CHAPTER 19

THIS TIME SHE HAD TO BE ON HER GUARD while she dug for clues at the Swanson house, since Caramel had said the guests would be there.

Jane noted two cars she had never seen before in the driveway, one of them from a rental company. Inside, she saw signs of life that had been missing in the last week; a coat left on the back of a chair, shoes kicked off by the front door. There was even a novel opened on the coffee table. It was funny how little things like that made a house feel warmer. Jane pulled open all of the first-story drapes. The sun shined through, a bright, happy sight at odds with the sad reason the company was at the house.

She made her coffee and turned on all of the office equipment. Knowing that it wasn't yet six in the morning, Jane cleaned the hall bathroom upstairs as quietly as she could. And she left the Jack and Jill bathroom alone completely, since she assumed someone was sleeping in the bedrooms on either side of it.

While she finished off all of the bathrooms, she tried to decide what she most wanted out of this morning. She couldn't land on anything more concrete than "information." She retied the pink bandana around her head and checked the time. The best way to get information was to ask questions. While she made the coffee, she came up with a few things she wanted to ask Caramel, if she got lucky enough to see her before she left.

Jane lingered in the kitchen. Making coffee was on her official morning to-do list, and if she could just wait it out until a little closer to seven, she might get a chance to talk to Caramel before she left.

The clock ticked impossibly slowly as she stood over the coffee bean grinder. She filled it with beans at 6:12. She put the lid on it and ground them at 6:24. She poured the grounds into the coffee filter at 6:35. She filled the pot with water at 6:50.

She hovered over the coffee pot, unwilling to press the start button until she heard the steps of people waking up above her. At 7:00 she couldn't delay any longer.

Just when she knew she had outstayed her welcome, Amy came down.

Her red hair was in a messy ponytail, and she wore running shorts and a tank top. "Oh, hey." She grabbed a bottle of water from the fridge.

"I was just leaving." Jane tried to think quick. Amy wasn't Caramel, but she could still be useful. "How is Caramel doing?"

Amy leaned back against the counter and drank her water. "She's holding up."

Jane took a quick inventory of Amy. While she came across as more wholesome than Caramel, it looked like she had a few of her own nips and tucks. Her lips were fuller than they had seemed before, and though her boobs were round and perky, the spaghetti straps of her tank top made it clear she wasn't wearing a bra, so they were definitely defying gravity.

"It must be sad to be widowed so young." Jane sighed and looked toward a picture of Douglas and Caramel that was magneted to the side of the fridge.

"I can't imagine it myself," Amy said. "And they'd only been married a few years."

"Were they happy?"

Amy shrugged. "Happy enough. She knew what my dad was like when I introduced them. But I was pretty sure she wouldn't mind."

Jane straightened up. "You introduced Caramel to your dad?"

"Yeah. And I feel so guilty about it now." Amy stretched her arms behind her head. Jane tried not to stare at her perfect chest.

"Guilty? But why?"

"Caramel was my sorority sister. We have a pledge to each other. If it weren't for me introducing them, she would be happily married to someone else right now, instead of a widow." Amy's eyes welled up with tears. She brushed them aside. "My mom thought I was crazy, but I knew she would make Dad happy, and that Dad would make her happy enough." Amy set her water bottle down. She wiped her eyes with the back of her hand. "I think they were happy, I really do. But now, she is so sad."

Jane had one shot at this. She had to ask something that would bring a useful answer. Something she could never find out on her own.

She took a deep breath. "So why do you think Caramel doesn't want her brother Joe to come by?"

Amy stiffened.

Jane waited.

"I think the restraining order is reason enough."

"She has a restraining order against her brother?" Jane tried to sound innocently surprised instead of shocked, which is how she really felt.

Amy looked toward the hall. She shifted her feet. "No, I do." She grabbed her water bottle and moved toward the kitchen door, but she paused, looking unsure of what she wanted to do next.

"But why? Isn't he your friend, too?" Jane blinked, hoping it made her look sweet like Holly.

Amy inhaled sharply. "No, he is not my friend." She almost walked away. "Jane, you're just a kid, but trust me, you don't always know someone like you think you do. Always, always take your drink straight from the bartender himself. Do you understand?"

Jane nodded. She felt sick. "Will he be at the funeral? I mean, Caramel is his sister..."

"If he shows his face at the funeral home or this house, he is going straight to prison." She spun on her heel and left before Jane could ask the question that was burning on her lips. Did Douglas know that Joe had assaulted his daughter? And had that knowledge led to a fight that ended in his death?

Jane slipped out the back door, no closer to knowing who had killed Douglas, and no closer to proving she hadn't invented the evidence that someone was in the hot tub with him. She was about to drive away when Amy knocked on her car window.

Jane unrolled it. "I'm so sorry..."

Amy waved her hand. "It was a long time ago, but that doesn't make it better."

Jane nodded.

"I want to you to do something for me, if you can."

"Sure." Jane left her hand on the stick shift, wiggling it back and forth a little in neutral.

"Caramel is a mess, but so is my mom. And my mom is coming by the house later today."

"She is?"

"I know, it seems weird. But I'm staying here with Caramel for a few days, while she pulls herself together. And Mom is just bringing some pictures and things by for the funeral. Stuff from when we were kids, and when he was a kid."

"What can I do?"

"Can you pick up my dry cleaning and bring it back here? I don't want to be gone when my mom gets here. But also, it would be nice to have an unrelated party at the house while Caramel and my mom are in the same building. So, do you think you could pick it up and bring it back around three?" Amy passed her a dry cleaning ticket. "Do you have the time?"

Jane clipped the ticket to her visor. "Of course. I can be here at three. I really do want to help."

"Thanks, Jane. You may be the first housekeeper who actually wanted to help this family." With that, Amy turned back to the house.

Jane went through the motions until it was time to get the dry cleaning. Houses were cleaned, clients paid her, she chatted with Gemma and Stephanie over lunch, but all she thought about the whole time was the dry cleaning that would let her be in on the showdown between the new, young wife and the ex-wife. She only wished the other maid, who had most likely been sleeping with Douglas during both marriages, could have been on hand as well. When it was time to go, she could hardly contain her excitement.

Jane folded the slippery dry cleaning bags over her arm. There were several heavy garments, each one just long enough to drag on the ground if she wasn't careful. Jane held her arm up at shoulder height and let herself into the Swansons' house by the back door.

Two cars she didn't recognize were parked out front. Perhaps Alexandra—the ex Mrs. Douglas Swanson—and Amy?

Jane heard the sounds of conversation coming from the front room, so she went there and stood quietly by the door.

Amy stood at the window, gazing out.

A petite redhead, who reminded Jane of Dr. Laura, stood next to the fireplace, in front of Caramel's wedding picture. She was speaking in a low voice to a man with thin blond hair and wire glasses, who sat on the white leather sofa.

Jane cleared her throat.

Amy looked toward her. "Thank you."

The older woman turned slowly toward Jane. "Ahh." Her thin lips formed the syllable and held themselves there for a moment. "You aren't Caramel."

Jane shook her head. "No, ma'am. I'm the substitute maid while the regular is on vacation." Jane wasn't going to make the mistake of appearing to be Douglas's current pretty young thing again.

Alexandra shrugged slightly.

Amy took the clothes from Jane. "She stopped off to get my things." Amy looked from the man on the couch to her mother again. "I think Caramel needs her this afternoon. Until then, um..." She appealed to Jane with her eyes.

The crisis hadn't occurred yet, and Amy looked desperate for Jane to stay. "Can I make you all some coffee?" Jane asked.

The man on the couch looked up at Jane, his face relaxing. "That would be nice."

Jane held out her hands for the clothes. "Let me take those to your room."

"No, it's okay." Amy pulled away from Jane's reach. The clothes slipped in her arms. Amy bent to gather them back up.

"It's not a bother." Jane reached for a blue dress that was draped on the floor.

Amy grabbed it with her fist and pulled it to her chest. "I said no!"

Jane stepped back. "I'll get the coffee, then."

Amy struggled with the slick plastic dry cleaning bags, until they all fell to the ground.

"For God's sake, let the maid do that," Alexandra snapped.

The man on the sofa stood up. "I'll grab them, sis."

"Matthew, you are worse than Amy."

Matthew ignored his mother and gathered the bags up. "Which room are you in?"

Amy lunged for the bags.

Matthew jerked his arms back, then laughed. "Sorry. Gut reaction. Sibling thing." He held the garments out for his sister.

Jane watched from the kitchen. Why didn't Amy want anyone to take the clothes? Couldn't be anything wrong with the clothes themselves. Jane had just taken them from the dry cleaners, at Amy's request. Was the problem in Amy's room? Someone or something in there that shouldn't be?

Jane took her time filling the coffeemaker with water.

Amy laughed, a tight, nervous sound. "Thanks." She pressed the clothes to her chest and left the room. Jane counted while she listened to the tread of Amy's feet upstairs. It sounded as though she stopped at the first guest bedroom.

Jane took out a tray and prepped the sugar, creamer, spoons, and such.

Alexandra's voice was too low to hear, but Matthew's wasn't. "She's not so bad, Mom."

Jane strained to hear Alexandra, but failed. She peeked around the corner to see what they were doing.

"That's not fair." Matthew was pacing. He was short like his father, thin like his mother, and older than Jane had expected. He looked like he was almost forty. "First of all, it was a very long time ago."

Alexandra's voice rose. "It doesn't seem long ago from my perspective."

The coffee had finished brewing so Jane filled the cups.

"Well, it was. It was almost twenty years ago."

"And here you are, all ready to offer comfort."

Jane stood in the kitchen door with her tray of coffee wondering exactly when the right time to break in would be.

Amy ran down the stairs, and into the living room. "Mom, don't be gross."

"He took her to prom." Alexandra spit the word out.

"Homecoming, Mom." Amy sat on the couch, and stretched her arms across the back. "And it was a group date."

"It is disgusting."

Matthew sat in a wingback chair across from his sister.

Jane went straight to Alexandra with her tray.

Alexandra waved her hand and turned away.

"Really, Mom. Stop and think. Twenty years ago, I went to my little sister's homecoming with a group of her sorority sisters. Five years ago, Dad married one of them. It's not as bad as you are making it sound."

"Mom, really. It's not that bad. Caramel isn't Matty's type anyway."

Jane held her tray up, standing to the side. She didn't want to stop the most interesting flow of conversation she had just stumbled into.

Alexandra looked up at the picture of the blonde, tan, full-figured Caramel in her slinky wedding dress. "Really?" She raised an eyebrow and shook her head.

"Matty has always preferred academic women."

Matthew's color rose until he was strawberry red. "My love life is no one's business." He stood up stiffly. "Mom, I can't stay here all day. Let me go get the stuff for the funeral, okay?"

"Fine." She sniffed, then reached for a mug from Jane's tray.

Matthew hurried out the front door.

Alexandra turned to Amy. "You and I both know your brother was in love with that girl."

"Caramel wasn't right for him. He would have been miserable."

"But she was right for your *father*?" The mug shook in Alexandra's hand. "And after what Joe did to you."

Amy sat up. Her jaw quivered as she spoke. "That wasn't Caramel's fault. Or Dad's. Or Matt's."

Alexandra sucked her lips in like a tight knot.

"Or *mine*." Amy stood up. Her big hazel eyes were full of tears. "My daddy just died, Mother. Do you realize that, or is this still all about you?"

Alexandra swept her silky scarf over her shoulder. "Is *she* going to stay upstairs the whole time I'm here?"

"It looks like it." Amy took a deep breath. "We'll get the boxes in, and then you and Matt can leave. How's that?"

Matthew entered with two plastic bins stacked up to his eyebrows. "Is this everything, Mom?"

"Yes, that's it. All I had left of your father."

"I'm surprised you didn't burn it," Amy said.

"I was tempted." Alexandra sat down. She pressed her hand to her forehead. "I'm sorry. I just can't wrap my mind around it. I can't believe he really is gone."

Amy held a tissue to her eyes. "Neither can I, Mom."

"He wasn't a great guy, but he had such a force of personality."

Matthew set the boxes on the floor next to the couch. "You were married to him for a long time, Mom."

Alexandra shook her head. "It was another lifetime."

Jane's arm was aching, but she didn't dare set the tray down. Could Matthew have killed his father to get to Caramel? Could Alexandra have killed Douglas out of a rage that had simmered all these years? And was Caramel hiding upstairs because of Alexandra or Matthew?

Matthew set the plastic containers down. "Let me take that for you." He took the tray of coffee and set it on the coffee table. Her cover gone, Jane slipped back into the kitchen.

She wished for a moment that the Swanson house wasn't so new. She would have loved to sneak up to the bedrooms via the servant's staircase, but there was no such thing. Jane emptied the coffee filter into the trash instead. Until Amy told her it was time to go, she could stay, even if she felt awkward just hanging around.

"Take what you need for the book, Matthew, and leave the rest for Caramel. I don't want any of it back."

"Thanks, Mom." Matthew's voice was husky, like he was holding back a sob.

"Let me go through it, too, will you?" Amy asked. "I mean, after you've gotten everything you need."

"Of course."

A book? Perhaps that's why Matthew had removed the files from the mayor's office.

Caramel, with a freshly sprayed tan, blonder hair, and higher heels than the last time Jane had seen her, descended the stairs and sauntered into the living room, her full lips pouting. Amy stood and gave her a hug. "How are you holding up?"

"I'm making it."

"Caramel." Matthew offered his hand.

Caramel smiled sadly. "Matthew," she drawled. She ignored his hand and gave him a hug. In her heels, she was several inches taller than him. "When did you make it in?" She lingered at his side, with her arm around his waist.

"Last night. I left the school as soon as I could get away." He patted her hand, and slipped out of her embrace.

"Alexandra." Caramel held out her hand.

Alexandra took it. She wrapped it in both of her hands. "Oh, child." Her voice broke, and she turned away.

Caramel sighed. "Can I get you anything?"

Alexandra waved her hand. "No, I can't stay. I brought the things you asked for. I really don't want them back."

"Of course." Caramel shifted her weight from foot to foot.

"Don't worry about it, Care. Matthew and I will take care of whatever you don't need."

Caramel swept her glossy hair out of her eyes. "Yes, thank you." Caramel helped herself to a cup of coffee. She turned toward the kitchen.

Jane stepped to the side, trying to keep out of eyesight.

Matthew picked up a white leather handbag. "Mom, are you ready?"

Alexandra gave her daughter a side hug.

"We'll see you at the funeral." Caramel gave Matthew another long embrace. From Jane's limited view, he looked like he was squirming to get away.

CHAPTER 20

WHEN MATTHEW AND ALEXANDRA WERE GONE, Caramel sat down. "Don't let the maid leave when you are done with her."

"She just brought over my laundry and stayed for a minute to help," Amy said with a tinny laugh.

"Well, I need her, so tell her to stay." Caramel sipped her coffee.

Amy sighed. "Of course."

She went straight to the kitchen. "I don't know what's on Caramel's mind, but she doesn't look well to me. She wants you to stay and help her with something. Your guess is as good as mine."

"I don't mind staying." Jane rinsed out the coffee mugs Amy had brought in with her. She especially didn't mind staying if it meant she could check out what Amy was hiding in her bedroom.

"I've got to get out of here." Amy chewed on her bottom lip. "Being a support to Caramel is all well and good in theory, but the woman is going to drive me mad."

Jane smiled and nodded, trying to hide her excitement. How much better to sneak around in the bedroom upstairs while Amy was gone.

"I can't guess what Caramel is going to ask of you, or when, so I suggest you sit back and make yourself comfortable." Amy pressed both of her hands on the marble counter and took a deep breath. "Best of luck to you."

"I don't mind, honest."

Amy left through the back door.

After about fifteen minutes of waiting in the kitchen, Caramel called for Jane. She was in the basement hall, near the garage.

"Jane, come help me with these boxes." Caramel stood in front of a short stack of cardboard moving boxes. "Stack them on the back seat of the golf cart."

Jane looked through the open door to the garage, no golf cart.

"It's by the back door."

Of course. The sliding door to the hot tub room. Jane hefted two boxes. They were small, but heavy.

"Douglas's law books. We're going to drive them down to the storage. His son can come get them later."

"You don't want them anymore?" Jane made her way to the stairs, but kept her face toward Caramel.

"They went to Matthew in the will, so it doesn't matter if I want them." There was an abused tone to Caramel's voice. Not so much grief as... exhaustion? Yes, Caramel sounded tired. Caramel lifted two boxes. "When he is ready to collect his things, every item listed under his name will be waiting in the shed." She pushed her way past Jane, and went down the stairs.

It only took two trips to the golf cart to get all of the boxes.

"Come on down with me." Caramel climbed into the driver's seat of the cart.

Jane got in next to her.

The little cart putted its way down the perfectly manicured lawn. About half way to the sheds Caramel stopped. She turned to Jane, her eyes narrowed.

"He would not have left me for the maid."

"Of course not." Jane tilted her head in sympathy. "He loved you."

"Ladies may have been his hobby." Caramel held the steering wheel in a white knuckled grip. "But I was his passion. From the day he met me, I was his passion."

"Of course." Jane tried to think of something comforting to add. "I'm sure everyone knew you were his true love."

Caramel let go of the wheel. She turned her whole body to face Jane.

Then she slapped her across the face.

Jane's head jerked to the side, and the sharp sting of the slap made Jane's ears ring. A flash of anger reverberated through her. How dare! How dare! Then she scooted to the edge of the seat, ready to jump and run. Caramel was unhinged, and Jane was ready.

Caramel snarled, and backhanded her across the other cheek.

Jane swayed, then tumbled backwards, flailing for the cart as she fell. Anger burned in her chest. She rolled to her knees and looked up at the cart. What was Caramel's game? Jane wasn't about to let herself be a punching bag for pent up emotions. A trickle of hot blood dripped down her face. Her cheek burned with pain. She pressed the palm of her hand against the gash in her cheek.

Caramel held her hand up, a huge diamond ring glinted in the sun. "They found the ring you stole, you nasty whore."

Jane scrambled to her feet and backed away from the cart. "I didn't!"

"Shoved down his throat." Caramel spun the golf cart around so that it faced Jane. "Did you do it because he wouldn't leave me? Is that why?"

Jane ran backwards, slipping on the damp grass. Her only thought was "run" and she tried.

The cart skittered toward her in awkward bursts.

Jane turned and ran as hard as she could toward the house.

The cart sped up. Caramel was at her heels.

Jane stepped to the side, her breath shallow in her chest.

The cart was next to her, so she grabbed the windshield frame and swung into the cart. "I only met your husband one time." Jane lunged for the steering wheel and wrestled it from Caramel. She pointed the cart toward the sheds.

"Liar." Caramel butted Jane with her shoulder.

Jane rocked in her seat, but held on to the wheel.

"It wasn't me, Caramel. I never touched him. I didn't kill him. I didn't even know him."

Caramel slammed the brakes. She spun in her seat and drove her elbow into Jane's chest.

Jane gasped, the wind knocked out of her, and skidded across the vinyl seat. She grabbed for the window frame again, but it slipped from her fingers. She thudded onto the ground and rolled away from the cart, letting momentum and gravity send her as far down the hill as they could. She was headed away from the house, where the guests who could help her were, but she still had her phone.

When she slowed, she pulled herself up and ran. She ran to the forest and climbed over the fence.

Caramel spun the cart around. She appeared to be driving it as fast as she could, but if Jane had to guess, the little cart wouldn't be able to crash through the gate. If Caramel wanted to chase her down, she'd have to get out of the vehicle.

Jane pushed her way through the brambles, on the side of the wide trail. When she was deep enough into the wooded part of the lot that she couldn't see Caramel, she pulled out her phone and dialed 911.

"Fire, ambulance, or police?"

"Police, please!"

"Okay, hold please."

The phone clicked over almost instantly to the police. "This is the police."

"My name is Jane Adler and I'm a maid and my boss hit me and is trying to run me over with her golf cart." She weaved her way through the trees.

"With her golf cart?"

"Yes, sir. It's Caramel Swanson; her husband just died. I think she's cracked." The trail came out near the neighbor's tennis court. Jane kept to the side of the court closest to the house, hoping she was in eyesight of someone inside.

"Are you in a safe place now?"

"Almost." Jane had made it to the front of the neighbor's house. "I see my car, just ahead." Jane ran to the little blue Mazda parked across the street.

"Do you see your boss anywhere?"

"No."

"Then get to your car, and lock yourself in. What is your location?"

Jane gave the address.

"We're sending an officer right over. If you think you aren't safe, come straight to the police station. Do you understand?"

"Yes!" Jane let herself into the car and locked all of the doors.

"Okay, stay on the line, until you see the police arrive."

Jane wrenched her bandana off of her head and pressed it to her cheek. Now that she was sitting and catching her breath the pain was almost unbearable.

Jane watched the minutes clicking past on her phone. If she hadn't been able to see them she would not have believed that only three minutes had passed before the police car pulled up.

She waved wildly, trying to get their attention.

One of the officers saw, and came to her window.

"Jane Adler?" The officer was a young guy with a receding hairline ,whose badge said McConnell.

"Yes, I'm Jane. I think Caramel is still out back." Jane took the blood-soaked bandana off of her cheek and refolded it.

Officer McConnell peered at Jane's cheek. "I think you need stitches for that."

Jane touched her cheek again. The gash was deep, and wide. It burned, as did her arms and legs from running through the brambles.

"Are you going to press charges?"

"I…" Jane paused. She had only called the police to make Caramel stop, not to get her arrested.

"This is assault, ma'am. It's a serious offense."

"I know. I just hadn't thought of that. Her husband just died, and she thinks I… well, I don't really know what she thinks, but she's mad and she took it out on me." If she had Caramel arrested, no one would let Jane come back to clean, and her search for clues would be over. Did she want to cut herself off from her investigation?

And when had she started considering it an investigation?

No. She did not want to cut herself off. She wanted to get to the bottom of this. Someone had killed Douglas, and it wasn't Jane. And despite Caramel's erratic violence, she didn't think it had been her, either.

"Do you want us to just give her a warning?"

"Maybe. Can you do that?" Jane let her breath out slowly. If she could negotiate this situation effectively, she could maintain access to the house.

"Did your boss have a weapon on her?" asked the other officer—a motherly woman with short gray hair and a name tag that said "Taylor."

"No, not that I saw."

"Do they keep guns in the house?"

Jane furrowed her brow. "I can't be certain, but I haven't seen any guns."

"Then why don't you come back with me, and we'll see if we can talk to her?"

"I think she needs mental help." Jane followed the officer into the house.

Caramel was seated on the edge of her white leather sofa speaking in clipped tones to the other officer.

"Why don't you tell us what's been going on?"

"The maid killed my husband." Caramel thrust her chin out.

Jane prayed hard, and silent. This might be her last chance to get information out of Caramel.

"Did you hit your maid?" Officer McConnell, asked.

"She stole my ring and shoved it down my husband's throat, after she drowned him."

"Did you hit your maid with your ring?" McConnell asked his question a little differently this time, and an irritated edge came into his voice.

Caramel looked down at her hand. "They won't give me back the ring she stole. It's evidence."

"Why do you think I did this, Caramel?" Jane stood beside the officer, liking the safety his presence offered.

"Douglas liked the maids. All of them." She grimaced.

"But not me. Remember? I'm dating your friend Mrs. Daniel's son Isaac. I only met your husband once."

Caramel's chin quivered. "She killed him and shoved my ring down his throat because he wouldn't leave me." She turned her eyes to the motherly officer Taylor. "He didn't leave his first wife, either. She left him. He wasn't faithful, but he was committed."

"But you don't really think it was this girl, do you?" Officer Taylor gestured to Jane. "She's just a kid." Her voice was warm and calming.

"But it couldn't have been Danae. She's out of the country."

Danae.

So Danae Monroe *was* their maid. And probably the employee the cops were looking for as well.

"Caramel." Officer McConnell's voice was even lower now. "The police are doing their best to find out what happened to your husband. And we don't think that this girl had anything to do with it."

Jane chewed her lip. Douglas was "committed." Had he been keeping up with the same "other woman" for all these years? A Danae Monroe from his old days as mayor who was currently his regular house maid? Jane's heart sped up. "Caramel, did Danae ever work for Douglas when he was mayor? Is she your regular maid?"

Caramel sniffed loudly. "Danae is just a cleaner. She cleans offices all over town. Maybe she used to clean that one, too."

"Mrs. Swanson, Jane said she doesn't want to press charges."

Caramel turned to Jane. Her face was dead and emotionless.

"I think you need to let her go. Okay? You should take a few days to relax, and then find a new maid." Officer Taylor continued to use her soothing voice, almost like she was clearing up a fight between two of her own children.

Jane flipped her gaze back and forth between Caramel and the officer, adrenaline rushing through her whole body. She didn't want the officer to make her quit. She wasn't ready to walk away from this yet. "I don't mind coming back. I mean, I don't think she'd do this again. She knows I didn't do anything. I could give it a few days, though, and just come back quietly, like on Wednesday?"

"That's not a good idea," McConnell said.

"I don't mind." Jane's heart was going a mile a minute. Not only didn't she mind, she was dying to get back into the house alone. She wanted to find out what was really in the boxes, and see if she could wrangle some more information about Danae Monroe out of Caramel.

"Why don't you go home now, Jane, and think it over?" the motherly officer said. "Go get your face stitched up and then decide if you really want to come back."

Caramel stood up. "I will decide if I want her to come back." Her words fell flat. If she had wanted to pull off an in-charge, imperious attitude, it had failed.

Jane walked herself to the front door without another word. Officer McConnell went with her. "Don't come back here. That woman is crazy."

"She's hurting." Jane put her hand on the doorknob. "And alone. I don't think she'll do it again."

The officer looked Jane up and down. He shook his head. "If you knew how many dead people said that same thing."

Jane looked at her sneakers. That was true. She sounded exactly like the kind of people that ended up dead. "I'll be careful."

Officer McConnell walked her to her car in silence. When she opened the door he spoke again. "I wouldn't let me wife go back to that house, even if we were about to be evicted. No amount of money is worth your life." He looked down at his hand.

Jane followed his glance and saw the dull gold band on his finger. "I won't come back alone."

The officer returned to his car, shaking his head as he walked.

Jane was coming back; that was 100% for sure. But she'd bring someone... Kaitlyn or Holly maybe, next time.

CHAPTER 21

FOR A FULL DAY, Jane toyed with the pieces of the very ugly puzzle before her. An ex-wife who was still hurting from the divorce, and possibly the death, though she wouldn't admit it.

A daughter who saw nothing wrong with her father marrying her sorority sister.

A son who might have been in love with the sorority sister.

A lover who left her phone behind.

A maid no one seemed to like.

A brother-in-law with a history of violence.

Jane thought it fairly obvious that the lover was the maid. As a maid, she was beneath him socially, like *Pride and Prejudice* code names on the phone would indicate. And if she had been both his maid at home and at work while he was the mayor, she was probably the reason Alexandra had left Douglas years ago.

But according to Jane's own work schedule, the maid was still away on her vacation, and quite possibly did not yet know that her long-time lover was dead.

Caramel's brother had done something ugly to Amy. From the hints Amy had dropped, Jane guessed date rape.

The one day she had met Douglas, he had made a comment... what was it? Something about the new ring not being too expensive... but he had said it in a disgusted voice. Douglas had not liked Joe, and for good reason. But had Joe hated Douglas?

But what about the evidence of the towels and the hamper? They pointed to someone being in the tub with Douglas, and still being in the house while Jane was there. Would Joe have been there that morning?

Would Joe have had a dip in the spa with his brother-in-law?

What about Amy? She seemed comfortable at her dad's house. Had she hopped in the tub with her dad for some fatherly chit-chat and then killed him? Why would she have? For selling the horses?

The people with motive didn't seem to have access to Douglas. The people with access didn't seem to want him dead.

Jane considered Alexandra again.

Had she come by to see her ex-husband? Perhaps they had rekindled their youthful love at some point? Maybe Alexandra had even pursued Douglas with the idea of killing him already in mind?

Jane drummed her fingers on her desk.

The most tantalizing clues were the towels and the phone. Had the lover snuck home early from her vacation? Had she killed Douglas and then made off with the clues that she had been there?

Jane had established, to her own liking, that Caramel couldn't have had a dip in the tub, then hidden in the closet, gotten rid of the evidence, and come back up the driveway dry and dressed. There just wasn't enough time between discovering the body and seeing Caramel for her to be the killer. But what about an ex-wife set on vengeance?

Alexandra could have done it. She was petite, so hiding in the closet and ducking around bushes and things as she ran away would have been easy.

Jane just needed proof. But first, she had to go clean another house. Groceries wouldn't buy themselves.

Her phone rang a few times while she drove home from cleaning her client's house, so she pulled over to see what was going on. The first message was a garbled mess from Gemma, but the gist was that Stephanie had found something weird.

While playing the second message her phone rang again.

"Gemma?"

"Jane—listen! You know how Caramel's ring has been missing?"

"Yes?" Jane squeezed the steering wheel.

"We think we found the matching bracelet."

"What do you mean?"

"It gets weird. Hold on to your hat. Stephanie was cleaning up a bit, and she found this bracelet… She was using your cleaning stuff—the bucket of stuff that's at the apartment."

Her work supplies. Wonderful. "What about the bracelet?"

"It's really fancy, thick gold with lots of diamonds. It's not mine, and it's not Stephanie's and I'm pretty sure it's not yours." Gemma poured the words out breathlessly.

"But why would Caramel's stuff be in my supplies? I have my cleaning caddy that I take from house to house with me. That one's just the refills." Jane had a sick feeling in her stomach She was sure the bracelet was Caramel's, as Gemma suggested, but the only way it could have made it into her things was too horrible to consider.

"I don't want you to freak out, but here's the rest of the story." Gemma paused for a breath. "Stephanie stripped the bed to do the laundry, and she found a letter in your pillow. I said it had to be from Isaac, but she said it couldn't be because it was signed 'D,' and I said Isaac's last name was Daniels, but she swears it could only be from Douglas, so... Now, don't freak out, but Stephanie's a little scared because you have this fancy bracelet, and she thinks you have a love letter from the dead guy."

"That's not my letter." Jane's jaw was tight. She was being set up.

"But it has to be; it was in your pillow."

"I saw it after Steph moved in and I thought it was hers. She was sleeping with it in the pillow, not me."

"I think that's why she was freaking, because she was sleeping on someone else's love letter. Not because you were doing anything wrong."

"It's not my letter."

"Okay, it's not. But the bracelet in your stuff... what do we do about that?"

Jane's head was pounding. She didn't want to think that Gemma's friend had set her up, but if not, then someone else had broken into their place and left behind stuff to frame her. An enemy she didn't know was even more horrifying than one sleeping in her bed. Jane took a deep breath before she spoke. "Gemma... how well do you know Stephanie?"

"What do you mean?" Gemma's voice was still high and excited.

"I mean, could she be a klepto? Could she have grabbed that bracelet somewhere and now just be blaming our unusual circumstances for it?" Jane crossed her fingers, hoping this simple answer would fix everything.

"Absolutely not, Jane. Don't be ridiculous."

If Stephanie wasn't an innocent kleptomaniac, then something much worse had just happened. Jane steeled herself for a confrontation. "Where are you? Can you meet me at the police station on Burnside?"

"We're just having lunch—we're not far from there."

"Then get here fast—both of you—and I'll meet you in the parking lot."

Gemma and Stephanie were so fast that they pulled in right behind Jane.

They went inside together, Jane leading the way to the front desk. "Excuse me?" Jane's voice cracked like a child's. She gritted her teeth and tried to steady her voice. "We had a weird incident at our apartment that we think might be related to the death of Douglas Swanson.

The receptionist narrowed her eyes at the girls. "Really? Can you elaborate?"

Stephanie pushed her way forward. "This!" She shoved the bracelet, wrapped in a handkerchief, through the slot in the bullet proof glass.

The receptionist lifted a corner of the handkerchief with her pencil point. "What is it?"

"I found that at our apartment, but it doesn't belong to any of us." Stephanie dropped her voice. "Jane is the Swanson's maid."

The receptionist pursed her lips. "Hmm. Why don't you all take a seat. I'll get right back with you."

They shuffled back to the waiting area. Jane kept her eye trained on the receptionist who made three phone calls in a row.

"What do you think they are going to do with us?" Stephanie sat on the edge of her seat, her legs shaking.

"Hopefully, they will get hold of Detective Bryce and interview us." Jane picked at a scratch on her phone case, but kept an eye on Stephanie.

"I think you need to let Jane do the talking, Steph." Gemma spoke low in the reassuring tone Jane had heard her use with her birth doula clients when they called in a panic.

"But Jane wasn't the one who found the stuff!" The color drained from Stephanie's face.

"Sit back and take a deep breath. Let me get you a glass of water. You are about to have a panic attack."

"We don't need that." Jane smiled at Stephanie and patted her leg. "I appreciate your help. I am sure we will all get a chance to say what we know."

Gemma was getting water when the receptionist called Jane and the girls back to the offices.

"Detective Bryce is in right now, and would very much like to hear what you have to say."

The young detective with the cute dimples was sitting at his desk, looking over a file folder when the receptionist opened the doors. He stood up and held out his hand to Jane. "Good to see you, Jane. What's up?"

Jane blushed, all attempts at feeling mature and in-control fleeing. Then she steeled herself for the job at hand. She wanted to lay the whole story in front of him before Stephanie had a chance to talk about the letter or jewelry.

"Why don't you all sit down and just start at the beginning." He indicated the chairs in front of his desk where the bracelet was lying. "So, Jane, why do you think this was related to the death of your boss?" The question, and the smile, were friendly, but there was a hard look in the detective's eye that made Jane shiver.

"Okay, so I've still been cleaning the house, and I've had my eye out for the missing towels and hamper."

Detective Bryce lifted an eyebrow. He smiled with just one side of his mouth, dimpling on that one side.

"I didn't find them."

"No? That's too bad."

"But I did find a funny phone in the guest bedroom."

"Go on."

"So, thinking I might have stumbled on something important, I turned it on and looked through it."

"Of course you did." Detective Bryce chuckled.

"It only had one phone number stored on it. It had pictures of Douglas in bed, and it had text messaged to 'Darcy' talking about meeting at 'Pemberly.'"

"Continue." Detective Bryce's face was mildly amused.

"That's all. It seemed like code to me. I assume it was his lover's phone."

"What did you do with it?"

"I left it on the dresser."

"To see if it would cause a stir?" His mildly amused smile turned into a mildly irritated frown.

"Well, yes. I guess so."

"Tell me about this." He lifted the bracelet with the end of his pencil.

"I found that! I found it in Jane's cleaning stuff!" Stephanie's blanched face was animated, her eyes bulging and jaw shaking. She sort of bounced on the edge of her seat like she was very anxious. "And I found this, too, in her bed." She pulled the crumpled paper out of her pocket and tossed it on the desk.

Detective Bryce looked at Jane with a lifted eyebrow.

"That's why we are here. It looks like someone has been planting evidence on me." Jane glanced at the gray wall covered in certificates and the metal filing cases that filled the room. Her body went cold, and her head felt light. "Frankly, I'm scared." Out of the corner of her eye she saw Stephanie, goggle eyed, shaking her head no.

Detective Bryce knit his eyebrows together. He looked directly at Stephanie. "What are you trying to tell me?"

Stephanie stopped, her mouth opened in a little o. "Nothing. Just. I mean, the letter, in her pillow. Signed "D" like Darcy or Douglas. I mean…" She glanced at Gemma, who stared at her, red faced.

"I'm glad you brought this here." He pulled the letter toward himself with a pencil. "I can have it dusted for fingerprints.

Jane shook her head. "I've read that letter. I found it in the pillow, so my fingerprints are on it."

"Then we will expect to see yours and… What's your name?"

"Stephanie Frances."

"We'll expect to see prints from both Stephanie and Jane. But we'll see what else we can find. On the bracelet as well. If I am correct, this bracelet was reported stolen not long ago."

Stephanie slumped back in her chair.

"Is there anything else?" He looked at each girl, one by one.

Gemma shook her head, and Stephanie chewed her bottom lip.

"That's it, sir. I just thought you should know." Jane sat on the edge of her seat with her hands pressing down hard on her knees.

Detective Bryce dimpled a little. "I don't like that these showed up in your apartment. I would like to send some officers over to take a look around."

"Oh!" Stephanie sat up.

"That would be so great," Gemma said. "I was a little bit thinking about staying at my parents' for a few nights."

"I'll have someone come by and check it out, and you guys need to have the landlord change your locks. And Jane, I strongly encourage you to stay away from the Swanson house."

"What if I only go when Amy is there?"

"Amy the daughter?"

"Yeah. She's very nice. If I keep popping in to clean like normal, but I always make sure she is there… that can't be bad, can it?"

Detective Bryce looked at the bracelet. "No. Don't do it."

Gemma leaned forward. "Where was the bracelet stolen from?"

"Joseph Dillon Jewelers."

"Caramel's brother Joe?" Jane leaned forward to look at it more closely. "Does this match the ring that Caramel lost?"

"I should say that that's privileged information." Detective Bryce chuckled again. "But it's not. It's even been in the news. Someone claiming to be Caramel's maid picked up a bracelet matching this description from the jewelry store where the missing ring was purchased. When Caramel came by to get it, they realized their mistake. But yes, both Caramel and the jeweler say they were part of the same design line."

"They said it was the maid?"

"Yes, but don't worry. You don't match the description at all."

"But the ring Caramel thought I stole was shoved down Douglas's throat." Jane shuddered. "So someone really did plant this on me to make me look like the murderer."

"You're not a suspect, Jane."

Jane tried to acknowledge him, but tears sprung to her eyes.

"Thanks for bringing all of this in." He rubbed his hands together. "We're getting very close to solving this one, I think. But please, by all means, keep your phone on all the time—all three of you—and the next time anything like this happens, call 911 immediately."

Stephanie gasped.

"I don't mean to scare you, but until we've got the killer behind bars, I don't want you taking any risks." He stood up and walked to the door.

Their interview was over.

"From the looks of this, I'm thinking the person we are looking for is looking for a little attention right now." He cleared his throat. "That's a good thing for me, but it makes me nervous for you."

Jane patted her pocket. "I'll have my phone with me and turned on at all times."

"Good girl."

CHAPTER 22

"SHOULD WE DROP BY THE JEWELRY STORE?" Jane asked before they all shut their car doors.

Stephanie's eyes went wide.

"I don't think so, Jane. You've never been there. You wouldn't want to show up now and get your DNA on stuff," Gemma said.

Jane fingered her stitches again. "No. I had better not."

Gemma started her car. "Whatever you do, be careful! We'll be home about five, and we'll stick around. Let's try to not leave each other alone, okay?"

"Sounds good." Jane sat in her car for a moment longer. Go back to the Swanson's house now or...? She didn't have a second option in mind, so she drove back to the Swanson's house.

She had almost reached the house when her phone rang. It was Kaitlyn.

"We need you at Bean Me Up Scotty's in ten minutes. This is the make-it or break-it meeting. Did you forget?"

Jane stared at her phone. "Forget? Was I ever told in the first place?"

"I texted. Valerie texted. Paula emailed. Something big is up with the funding. Paula called the meeting. I suggested Bean Me Up Scotty's—for Valerie's sake—good move, right?"

Jane squeezed her eyes shut and rubbed them. "Good move?" Jane pictured the coffee shop and came up with the barista with the glasses. "Yes, of course. Good move. But... I missed it all. Emails, texts. I saw nothing."

"I'm sure we sent them to you... Why wouldn't we have?" Kaitlyn's voice was leaning toward a whine. "Paula started it. She has big news about the mission mentoring and funding program, but she wouldn't let us know what it is."

Jane took a deep breath and then let it out slowly. From where she had pulled over, she could see the Swanson house.

Caramel's Mini Cooper was pulling out of the driveway. "I've got ten minutes?"

"Yes! You can make it, right?"

Jane chewed on her lip. She inched forward. Follow Caramel, or pin Amy down for a long talk?

"You can make it, *right*? Our outreach is massively on the line here. If we want to shine a light for bullied kids, we need to represent."

The front door of the Swanson house opened.

A head peeked out.

A blonde head.

Jane inched her car a little closer, but before she could get close enough to identify the woman, the door shut again.

"I'll be there!" Jane said. "But I've got to go!" She hung up before Kaitlyn could say anything else.

Had the owner of the phone come back for it?

Jane drove around the block and parked behind the Swanson property.

The house in back was dark, so Jane ran down the side driveway and didn't worry about being seen. She hopped their back fence into the wooded area that separated the properties from each other.

The stranger in the house could be a friend of Caramel's or Amy's as easily as not. She pushed her way through the brambles. She needed to find a spot where she could hide and still see into the huge back windows.

She hiked as close to the Swanson house as she could, but her angle and the angle of the sun were all wrong. The light glinted off the wall of windows, and she could see nothing. She pushed a little closer, hoping to snatch a view through the side windows.

Someone was moving around in the guest bedroom, but she couldn't make out much more than the silhouette. She took a few pictures, and then backed further into the woods so that she wouldn't be seen. She stopped when the masses of trees hid the house from her sight, and emailed herself the pictures she had taken.

She pushed through the woods and found herself, not in the back by her car but at the neighbor's pool house. The lights were out, but the door was ajar.

Jane stuffed her phone in her pocket, and slunk over to the door. From her limited experience in the neighborhood, she was pretty sure the folks who lived on this property were at work all day.

She pushed the door open and stepped inside.

Her heart pounded against her ribs. She knew the laundry hamper was in the pool house—knew it like she knew the Beatitudes.

Or that it had been in the pool house.

The police had searched the Swanson property from top to bottom, and this was the only building near enough to run to in the short time the killer had had.

The little pool house was dark inside. Jane left the lights off.

The building was one large room with two doors on the side. The floor was tiled in dark gray stone. The windows were all covered with airy, cheesecloth-like curtains. One wall had a small kitchen, and the center of the room was furnished with wicker that looked worn around the edges. Jane bent down and looked under the wicker couch where she found a pair of flip flops and a tank top. She tried to put them back in the same position she had found them in.

Jane opened the cupboard doors with a paper towel so she wouldn't leave her prints on the brushed nickel hardware.

The garbage can had recently used paper plates in it, but none of the cupboards were hiding the missing hamper.

Jane opened the first door with the same paper towel and found the closet. A duffel bag was squished inside. Jane dug through it. Pajamas. Underclothes. A toothbrush.

Was someone sleeping here? The sofa was loveseat sized, so if they were sleeping in the pool house, they weren't very comfortable.

Jane checked the bathroom next. Sink, mirror, toilet, shower. Nothing unexpected in a pool house. Except the sink was grimy, like someone had been spitting toothpaste into it.

If the neighbors had a guest in their pool house, it wasn't very likely that the murderer had run there to hide the dirty laundry.

Jane left the door ajar behind her, as it was when she went in. If the killer hadn't hidden the evidence in the pool house, where had she hid it? Jane flipped her phone over and over in her hand while she tried to think up options.

"Excuse me?"

Jane dropped her phone. "I'm sorry!" Standing right behind Jane was a petite, blonde woman in a sarong and swimming suit.

"What are you doing back here?" Her face was red from a fading sunburn, and her eyes were hidden behind huge, round sunglasses.

"I'm so sorry!" Jane stepped away from the pool house. She chose not to answer the question, to see what kind of question the lady would ask next.

"Why are you back here?" she repeated.

The woman stood between Jane and the woods. Had she come from the Swansons' house or this one?

"I was peeking in the house." Jane tried a little, innocent smile. "It's so cute."

The woman in the swimsuit's back stiffened. "You went inside?" Her words were sharp.

"Yes." The truth slipped out before Jane could decide if it was the safest choice.

The woman's jaw tensed. "Have you done this before?"

"No." Jane shook her head. "I spotted the house one other time, and peeked in the windows. But I've never been inside before."

"Why on EARTH would you go into my house?" The woman's voice was icy. She stepped forward, one long finger pointing at Jane.

"I am *so* sorry. It was such a jerky thing to do." Jane stepped backwards, too. Waves of shame rolled over her, making her face hot like a lamp.

"Yes, it was." The woman said. "I am sick and tired of everyone on earth thinking my backyard is theirs. Do you know how many people keep sneaking around back here?"

Jane stopped backing away. "The police, you mean? Because of Douglas?"

"I wish it were just the police. But every rubbernecker in town had been through these woods, and half of them stop at my pool house."

"Have you caught people inside before?"

"Not inside, but it was only a matter of time."

"Have you seen anyone really suspicious?" Jane tapped her foot, excited.

"Why do you want to know?" The woman narrowed her eyes.

"I-uh." Jane picked up her phone. "I guess I'm just a rubbernecker. I'll go."

"Do that, and don't come back."

Jane took a few slow steps toward the woods. "Have you called the police about the trespassing?"

The woman glared at Jane. "Yes. And I'll do it again, if you don't get off of my property."

Jane waved. "Again, I'm so sorry!" She ran through the woods trying to stick to the trail she had taken the first time. She had nabbed one more picture before she left. There was always a chance the woman in the swimming suit was the same woman who had peeked her head out of the Swansons' front door.

Jane headed home so she could try and make something out of her pictures, but on the way, she remembered her urgent meeting at the coffee shop. She was already twenty minutes late.

She switched gears and headed to the coffee shop. But she questioned her choice. Paula wasn't going to give her any money, which didn't matter anyway, since she didn't have anywhere to go. So why interrupt her current mission to listen in on Kaitlyn and Valerie's meeting? The only reason she could think of was commitment. She had made a commitment, so she went to the meeting.

She parked next to Kaitlyn's car and joined her team.

"Jane!" Kaitlyn grabbed Jane's hand and squeezed it. The Pogs were piled on the table in front of her. "Where have you been?"

Paula folded her hands in front of her on the table, but her face was relaxed. Valerie checked her watch.

"I was looking for clues to the murder." Jane pulled out a chair and sat down. "Things got very complicated this morning, and I had to take matters into my own hands."

"No matter. I'm glad you are here now. I won't go back over everything we've covered, but there are two important things for you to know," Paula said.

Jane held her pen at the ready.

"The annual Columbia River Community Church budget preview has been released to all departments of the church, and the missions' budget will not be increased for the coming fiscal year."

Jane glanced Kaitlyn's way. Her eyes were red.

"However, there has been a one-time, anonymous gift from one of our church families for a mission project."

"Like a short-term trip?" Jane scratched hash marks on her page. Had they been called together so they could be dismissed? The idea was a relief to Jane.

"It's up to us. My preference would be to help one of you make it overseas."

"But… if it's just a one time gift?" Jane wrote Compare Photos on her paper.

"If one of you really hustles and gets their funding in place, this one-time gift, spread out monthly, could be what pushes you into your 100% funding." Paula turned her hands palms up. "It's not perfect."

"No, it's not." Kaitlyn sniffed.

"What would you do the next year?" Jane wrote: Who lives in the house next door to the Swansons?

"Kaitlyn and Valerie would both be allowed to stay in their positions if they made it to 75% funding. I spoke with their sending organizations. If they could get say, 75-90% funded before they needed to leave, this one time gift would really help them start off strong."

"Mm-hmm." Jane wrote: Who is sleeping in the pool house?

"So now is the time to put the plans you have been making into action." Paula smiled, her eyes on the stack of Pogs. "If I want to convince the Missions Committee to release the funds to one of you, you are going to have to really show us what you are made of."

Jane tapped her pencil on her page. She was having a hard time organizing her thoughts while Paula talked.

"It's time to take a vote. We need to pick our ministry, pick our location, and pick our start date," Valerie said, in her matter of fact tone. "Are you ready?"

Jane circled photos on her list. If she could get to her computer and enlarge the photos she might be able to tell who the blonde woman at the Swansons' house was.

"Jane? Are you ready?" Paula repeated.

"What? I'm sorry." Jane shook her head. She needed to pull herself together and be present for her future as a missionary.

"I know this won't have as immediate an impact on you as it will on Valerie or Kaitlyn, but how you serve now will impact your future overseas."

Jane slumped. What future overseas? "Yes, of course." She set her pencil down. "I've had a really long day. Do you mind if I buy a cup of coffee first?"

Paula chuckled. "Not at all. We'll give you a minute to pull yourself together."

Jane caught Kaitlyn's eye. She tried to apologize with a smile, but didn't feel like it translated well. She went to the line to order a drink.

The man behind the counter seemed to have more attention for her team than she did. But wasn't that the way? He had every sign of being infatuated with Valerie, who had every intention of moving far, far away.

Jane ordered a mocha with whip cream on top. Comfort coffee.

When the barista handed her the coffee she stopped him. "Do you want to meet her?"

"What?" He smiled, innocently.

"Valerie, with the curly hair, do you want to meet her? I could introduce you."

"Nah." He glanced over to her table again and blushed.

"What's your name?" Jane sipped her coffee. The sweet whip cream laced drink burned her tongue.

"Anders."

"Okay, Anders, grab that plate of chocolate chip cookies—the one with four cookies on it—and come meet Valerie."

Jane waited.

Anders hesitated. Then he picked up the plate and came around the side of the coffee bar.

"Sorry that took so long." Jane sat down. "Paula, Kaitlyn, Valerie." Jane indicated each woman. "This is Anders."

"Hello." Paula shook his hand.

Valerie first looked at Jane with a small scowl, but then looked at Anders. Her face pinked, but she smiled.

Anders looked at her with wide-eyed admiration. He pushed his glasses up his nose and smiled. "Let me know if there's anything I can do for you."

Jane looked at the three women at the table. She knew, without at doubt, that this was her last get-together with them, and her last chance to do anything about Anders' obvious crush on Valerie. Her pulse had picked up, and she spun ideas of what to say next. "Hey, Anders, we all go to Columbia River Community Church. If you ever pop in say hey, okay?"

Anders stood up a little straighter. "Yeah, I know." His eyes were glued on Valerie. "I go there, too, but I don't think we've met."

Valerie looked at her napkin, her smile spreading.

"Hey wait, I know you." Kaitlyn beamed. "You run the sound booth at concerts."

"Yeah." Anders nodded, and looked down at the tray of cookies. "Well, see you around."

"Just a sec." Valerie sat up. She looked him straight in the eye. "Do you have a second?"

"Uh…" Anders turned back to the coffee bar. The other barista was poking at her phone. No one was in line. "Sure."

"Then sit down. We're trying to plan a new ministry, and since you're a part of the CRCC family, maybe you can help us." Valerie squared her shoulders and smiled at him, her eyes crinkling.

Anders sat down. "Sure. What are you trying to do?"

"Pogs." Kaitlyn pushed her stack of cardboard circles to him. "We want to reach out to kids and Pogs are the perfect medium."

Anders picked up a few Pogs and let them fall back to the table like a deck of cards.

"We're trying to decide who to reach out to, actually. Single women or troubled kids."

"There's a pretty significant difference between those two groups." Anders stacked the Pogs by color as Valerie had done.

Paula drummed her fingers on the table. "While I think there is value in asking for the opinions of other believers, I do think that it is important for you three to make this decision on your own."

Jane raised her eyebrow.

Paula nodded. "Even you, Jane." She folded her hands again. "If I can continue to meet with you despite my recent loss, I think you can keep working with us despite the complications in your work life."

Complications in her work life! Jane's hand moved up to her stitches again. Complications! A woman had tried to run her over. The police thought she had invented evidence. Someone was planting stolen things in her house. Complications! Jane opened her mouth to speak.

Anders stood up. "Hey, I really don't have a break right now, but if I were you guys, I'd work your strengths. Reach out to the folks you relate to the best." He pushed his chair in with a grating screech. "Sorry." He patted the back of the chair.

"Wait!" Valerie stood up. Her face was beet red now.

Anders stopped, his mouth slightly open.

Valerie chuckled. "Uh... see you Sunday?"

Anders smiled and nodded his head, the way men do when they have headphones on. "Yeah. Sounds good."

Valerie sat down and covered her face with her hands.

Kaitlyn giggled.

"May we get some of these issues sorted out now?" Paula's voice was stern, but the corners of her mouth twitched and her eyes sparkled.

Jane's phone buzzed in her pocket. She did not have time for Jake now, and as he seemed to be the only person who ever called her, she hesitated to check who the call was from.

But it kept buzzing, so, just in case it was important, she pulled it out.

Isaac.

It was Isaac.

Her heart flipped over.

Resolve her ministry situation to prove that she was serious about her future or take the call from her boyfriend?

Paula was still talking, but Jane couldn't track it. Her phone had stopped buzzing. Isaac had given up.

Jane's lips quivered. Had he given up on her entirely? Had she given up on him? What was God doing, making her want to go away forever, but letting her fall in love with Isaac?

"Earth to Jane, we are taking a vote." Kaitlyn waved her hands in front of Jane's face.

Jane flinched. "Sorry, guys. Important call just came in." She pushed her chair away from the table; every muscle she moved felt like it was in slow motion.

She heard Valerie as though through a fog, distant and just as slow as her own fingers as they tried to call Isaac back. She wanted to run from the room to be alone with her phone, but her feet felt like they were made of wet clay, heavy and sticking to the ground.

Isaac answered the call right away.

Jane had made it as far as an upholstered armchair by the door. She slumped into it and covered her ear with her hand so all she could hear was Isaac's voice.

"Hey, I just had to call."

"I'm so glad." Jane's heart was beating so hard that her chest hurt. She closed her eyes so she couldn't see if anyone was looking at her.

"It's just that, I had the best offer ever, and every time I have good news, you are the only one I want to share it with." His voice was slow; each word sounded thoughtful.

Hope flooded through Jane. If he had been offered a job at the seminary in Costa Rica, a full-time job... it wasn't the Kazak Mountains, but it was the mission field. Could she really have it all? She bit her lip to keep it from quivering.

"Jane?"

"What was the offer? I can't wait to hear."

"Full time, tenure track."

Jane's heart fell to her knees. Tenure track? That meant an American school. She pressed her cheek into the velvet chair back, the stitches stinging from the pressure. She didn't want to say good-bye to Isaac. Not ever again. She swallowed. "Where?"

Isaac didn't say anything. "First, can you be happy for me?"

"Of course."

"It's not a matter of course though, is it? You'll only be happy for me if it fits into your plan for the world."

"No, really. I will." Jane peeked around the back of her chair. Paula, Kaitlyn, and Valerie had their heads together and were talking fast, by the looks of it. "I just... I might be happy for you and sad for me."

"I wish we could have one conversation about the future that didn't revolve around you making me follow your dream."

Jane's eyes smarted with tears.

"I wish you would have just dropped me a long time ago. You let me fall in love with you, but you had no intention of ever being mine."

"That's not true." Her voice was a whisper. It was totally and completely true. She hadn't intended to love him until he changed to fit into her plans. And yet, somewhere these last few weeks while he had been gone, out of reach, and absent from her life, she had realized it was too late.

She was completely in love with him. Absolutely. "It's just that you had a plan, and I had a plan, and then we met. I didn't mean to screw up your life." Jane scrunched up as small as she could in her chair. She didn't want the whole coffee shop to hear her crying, but she couldn't move away. She could scarcely even breathe.

"If I said the new job was in Afghanistan, would you marry me?"

Jane pressed her lips together. This was not how he was supposed to propose. Not in the middle of a fight. Not like a challenge. "It's not in Afghanistan, so it doesn't matter."

"If it was, though, what would you say then?" His voice cracked—from emotion or from the phone reception, she couldn't tell.

Jane leaned forward, hoping it wasn't the phone reception. Fear that the call would drop right now squeezed at her heart. "I would say yes."

"You would say yes to Afghanistan, but would you say yes to *me*? Do you want to spend your life with me?"

Jane pictured the life she had always dreamed of: the imagined village full of people who had never heard of Jesus, the native clothes she would wear, the culture she would learn, the language. Her heart leapt to her throat. She wanted to learn their language. She could see herself in that life so clearly.

And she saw that she was lonely.

Then she pictured Isaac. Tall, dark, smart Isaac, and the lonely feeling in her heart intensified, because he wasn't sitting with her in the coffee shop.

She took a deep breath. "What about you? Do you want me, or do you want an accessory who looks and talks like me but always goes along with whatever you want to do?"

Isaac was silent for a moment. "The job is in Montreal. I start in September. I am as sure of this job as I am of you. I need you both in my life." Isaac cleared his throat. "But if you aren't sure of me—"

"I am." Jane interrupted him. She didn't want to hear the alternative. She didn't want to go to Canada, but she didn't want to imagine Isaac going without her. "It doesn't matter where. Not right now, not this minute. I am sure of you."

Isaac exhaled. "You're sure?"

"I'm sure."

"So…" Isaac cleared his throat again. "That wasn't my proposal. Just so you know. I'd never propose to you like that."

"Okay." Jane's head was spinning. He wanted her forever, but he wasn't asking her to marry him. He was moving to Canada, but she still had to finish school. But he loved her. And, at the back of her mind, the question of the blonde lady at the Swanson house was begging to be answered.

"I've got to go, Jane. Class starts in three minutes."

"Okay."

"I love you." He paused. "Don't just say okay again."

"Okay." Jane sighed, her body relaxing with the released breath. "I mean, I love you, too."

"I will call you the minute class is over, okay?"

"Yes! Please do."

"I love you!" Isaac laughed as he hung up.

Jane stared at her phone. What had just happened, and what had just changed? She didn't know, but she did know that she felt a thousand times happier than she had in weeks.

She turned to look at her team. Paula was speaking, but Kaitlyn was stealing glances at Jane. Jane made a tiny wave with her hand, and tilted her head to the exit door.

Kaitlyn frowned.

Jane shrugged. Then she left. The team needed to get on with it without her. She didn't know what it would mean for her future, but she did know it was the right thing for her present.

Jane went straight home, downloaded her pictures, and enlarged them. They were pretty fuzzy, as she didn't have any special software to use on them. But the blonde woman looked familiar. More than familiar. And yet, she couldn't place where she knew her from. She tried to get the image clearer; if the cops were coming soon to look around her house, she wanted to have the pictures ready.

The woman in the picture—the almost-clear picture she had nabbed through the side window of the house, had big, round, familiar eyes. Pale and pretty, but kind of buggy at the same time.

Jane flipped over to the website for the Gresham Mayor's office again, but Mary-Grace, the woman who wasn't the blonde from the pictures in Douglas's house, didn't have eyes like these.

Jane shifted in her seat. She had a prickly feeling in the back of her neck like someone was watching her. She turned, but the curtains were drawn and the apartment was empty. The stolen bracelet weighed on her mind. Was she or was she not safe at home? And was she in any more danger at the Swanson house?

Amy Swanson seemed reasonable, like someone she could talk to. Especially since she had a restraining order against Joe the jeweler. She wouldn't have stolen a bracelet from a man she went to the police to keep away from her. Jane tapped her foot on the rung of her chair. She could go talk to Amy right now, or she could wait until the following day and chat with her as she went about her regular cleaning duties.

After all, technically she hadn't been fired from the job. Knocked about a bit, sure, but not fired.

Jane scrolled through her phone pictures one more time to make sure she hadn't missed any. While doing so, it rang again.

It was Isaac.

"Hey." She tried to sound casual, but a wave of heat started in her stomach and washed over her. Even her toes tingled.

"I called as soon as class was out." Isaac sounded breathless. On the one hand, Jane wondered if he had fit in a quick game of soccer, but then again, maybe he had run out of class to call her. "I've been such a jerk all month."

"No…" Jane bit her lip. This morning she would have agreed.

"Yes, I really have. But the thing is, the whole time I've been here, I've been having one frustrating argument with God."

Jane frowned. "Really?" She moved to the sofa and curled up in the corner. She itched to have a conversation with Amy Swanson, but the urgency of the situation was fading.

"All month, He's been saying that I have to want His will more than my own, even if that meant I couldn't have you. I've been making a claim that the two of us could have it all, if God wanted us to."

"That sounds familiar."

"And I was getting mad about it—like God was on your side instead of mine—and I took it out on you. I'm sorry."

Jane rubbed her eyes. She didn't have the heart for a puzzle.

"I'm sorry I didn't take some of your calls, or call you back when I could have."

"Oh." The memory of many anxious moments waiting for his calls was still fresh.

"Don't say 'Oh.' Yell at me or something. I deserve it."

"I am too tired to yell at you." Her first flush of excitement was fading as the urgency to talk to Amy Swanson had. Maybe she did just need to go to bed. "I forgive you for not calling me back." She did a heart check. Still just tired. Not mad. "I understand what you've been feeling. I've been hard at it, too. I keep wrestling with why God made me want to serve him overseas but hasn't seen fit to use me yet."

"And why did he let me fall in love with you when we don't have the same plans for the future?" Isaac added. "I've been wondering for a long time if I was being a jerk dating you."

"You know what I like the least in all of this?" Jane released her hair from her ponytail and let it fall around her face. "I don't like that my mom will be right. She never believed I'd be a missionary."

Isaac laughed. "I'm sorry. It's not funny. But you're right. She never believed you would."

"So, what if I've been trying to be something God doesn't want me to be just to show my mom I was right?"

"Or what if God planted the seeds in you so you could get the training you need for a job he has in mind for you—in the future."

"That's what I console myself with." Jane combed through her hair with her fingers. "I scrub toilets now so I can spread the gospel later."

"I think that's pretty cool." Isaac's voice was relaxed, like life at his island seminary suited him.

"It's easy to admire when you aren't the one scrubbing."

"You won't have to scrub toilets in Montreal."

Jane smiled. Montreal was better than joining her parents in their early retirement life in Phoenix. "And after Montreal?"

"Who knows? Professors get sabbaticals and long summers and research trips to far off lands. Who knows how God could use this for us."

"You start this year?"

"Yup."

Jane sighed.

"You can transfer your credits there."

"One major conciliation at a time, okay? For the moment, let's imagine that I finish what I start." Jane rolled her neck from side to side. She was out of school for the summer, but that didn't mean she wanted to abandon her program to follow her man.

"Whatever you say. Now listen, this is important."

"Yes?" Jane sat up. It had better be life or death if it wanted to be considered important in light of her current goings on.

"You are in a crisis and I have been ignoring you. Please tell me everything that is going on with the Swanson situation and what I can do to help."

His words flooded her heart with relief and put a smile on her face. She lay back on the sofa and told him every last detail. Before they said goodnight, he had confirmed her plan to talk to Amy in the morning, but added his advice to not go alone.

Jane went to bed and squeezed her eyes shut like a child pretending to sleep. Her heart was racing, her mind was spinning. There wasn't one thing on her plate that made rational sense or fit into her own plan for her life. She tried to pray, to both calm her mind and to focus on what really mattered, but all she could say was "thank you" over and over again.

CHAPTER 23

THE NEXT MORNING, Jane served Gemma and Stephanie steaming cups of cappuccino, crisp, buttery English muffins, and yogurt.

"This is nice. Early, but nice." Gemma rubbed her eyes.

Jane tried not to stare at Stephanie. Somewhere in the middle of rejoicing over her newly not-engaged-but-basically-engaged status, she had realized where she had seen the eyes of the mystery blonde before.

Stephanie.

Stephanie wore black hipster glasses, but that didn't hide the pale blue, pop eyes that were behind them.

Jane had theorized the night before that Stephanie made liberal use of mascara, and/or fake lashes, and that was what had kept Jane from pinning the resemblance down immediately. She was using an early breakfast to try and catch her guest make-up free.

It worked.

If Stephanie was the key to the murder, she was a cool operator. From her natural relationship with Gemma, to her excitement over the stolen jewels, she seemed legitimate.

Jane needed to get under her skin, to up-end her complacency. From the phone to the letters, to the missing hamper, Jane knew she was being set up, and who better to do it than the girl sleeping in her bed? Her instinct was crying out to drag Stephanie to the Swansons' to see if Stephanie would crack under the pressure.

Gemma chuckled at something Stephanie had muttered under her breath. Jane chewed on the inside of her cheek. Gemma and Stephanie appeared to have a real friendship.

She could be wrong about Stephanie. Fortunately, nothing she had planned for the day would hurt Stephanie—if she was who she said she was.

Jane took a sip of her coffee. Then she looked at her watch. Then she coughed lightly, and fingered her stitches. As soon as

Stephanie and Gemma looked up she smiled conspiratorially. "So… Caramel has not told me to stop coming in in the mornings to open the house."

"Jane… what are you thinking? She tried to run you over." Gemma took a big crunchy bite of her English muffin.

"I'm thinking she's cracked, and if I go now, I might be able to find some crucial evidence to connect her to the murder." Jane sipped her coffee again. She made a discreet glance in Stephanie's direction. Stephanie appeared preoccupied with her phone.

"Breaking news on the Swanson case," Stephanie said, looking up for a second.

Jane leaned forward to see the screen. "Really?"

Stephanie held the phone out, but the screen was small. Jane thought she recognized the logo of the local paper, but couldn't read the text from across the table.

"Have they made an arrest?" Gemma asked.

"They announced the funeral."

Jane narrowed her eyes. "That's breaking news?"

"I'd say so. They wouldn't release the body for the funeral if there was still a suspect, right?" Stephanie shook her head while she spoke, a little quirk that made Jane doubt her words.

"That hasn't been my experience." Jane dusted the crumbs off of her hands. "So, can I ask you guys to join me at the Swansons' today? I just don't want to go alone." Jane widened her eyes, hoping it made her look vulnerable.

"Of course." Gemma smiled. "I don't know how much help we'll be, but if nothing else we can sit in the car, and you can call us in if you get scared."

"We could be the getaway drivers." Stephanie's face was shiny. Was she sweating?

"Oh no, I really can't go in the house alone. Couldn't you come with me? Since you want to take on some houses, I could say I was training you."

"And I can stick in the car and be the getaway driver. I'll wear my dark glasses and a wig, or at least a hat." Stephanie giggled a little.

"Honest, I'd be scared to leave you out there. Just come in with us, and we probably won't have to explain anything." Jane leaned forward and whispered, "What I really want to do is goad Caramel into saying something. I'll be so much more confident with you all in the house."

Gemma set down her cup. "I'm in. I know I owe you for all the times you spot the rent. And Steph, you owe her for that comfy bed. Let's get dressed and get this over with."

"Thank you soo much." Jane picked up her coffee cup and smiled.

Stephanie stretched, and popped her back. She chewed her lip, and looked over her shoulder. Jane marked each tiny movement. Were they evidence of her chronic pain issues or evidence that she was nervous about going to the Swansons'? Right now, it was anyone's guess.

A text came through from Isaac while the girls were getting dressed. "Just hi."

"Off to catch a killer." Jane read her note and then went to delete it, but hit send instead.

"WHAT!"

"Today's the day. I have a hunch. Pray!"

"Si!"

"& I love you." She bit her lip.

"I am PRAYING you don't get killed, because I love you!"

"I won't." She worked her jaw back and forth. She wasn't likely to get killed in a house full of people... was she?

Stephanie came back out, dressed in sweats, sneakers, and big, dark sunglasses.

Jane shoved her phone in her pocket. She forced a smile.

The drive to the Swansons' was tense. Jane was on her third cup of coffee, and her hands were shaking.

"Can you drive through Bean Me Up Scotty's really fast?" Stephanie pointed toward the coffee shop up the street.

"We can drink the Swanson's coffee. They don't mind." Jane merged to the left, keeping her distance from the coffee shop.

"My blood sugar is a little low..." Stephanie leaned her head against the window.

Gemma threw her a granola bar from the back seat. "Perk up. Jane needs us!" Gemma sat on the edge of her seat, straining the seat belt. "What's the game plan?"

Jane picked up her travel mug, but her hand was shaking so badly, she set it back down. "I need to play it by ear, sorry!" From the corner of her eye, Jane thought she saw Stephanie shiver.

At the house, Jane established Gemma and Stephanie in the kitchen. As a cover, she pulled a housecleaning blog up on her phone. Were a member of the household to enter the room, the two women were to appear to be reading the tips of the trade and could say they were there to be trained.

Jane went through the motions. She made coffee, opened the curtains, and went to the office to turn on the equipment. The room had changed again. This time, piles of books had been added to it, perhaps from Douglas's work office, wherever that might be. Jane whipped a rag out of her apron pocket and dusted the top of the nearest pile. Perhaps something stuck discretely into a book from his work office would reveal what she needed to know.

She knelt on the thick carpet and dusted the spines of the books, checking for any loose papers that might have been slipped between the covers.

The first stack was barren, but the second stack looked like it had some promise. The bottom of the stack was a leather-bound, three-ring binder, stuffed to overflowing.

"Whoops!" Jane knocked the stack down and looked over her shoulder.

She ignored the fallen books for a moment and opened the binder. The top pages were some kind of outline. Jane didn't read it, but scanned it and the other pages for handwritten notes, phone numbers, anything. Then she dug through the pockets pulling out every scrap that had been tucked inside. Most were just scribbles, but some had dates and names. Jane turned back to the first page of the outline and began comparing. If she had to guess, she'd say Douglas had been working on his autobiography.

"Excuse me?"

Jane flushed. "I knocked this stack of books over." Jane slid the pieces of paper into the pockets.

"And I watched you open that book up and read it. What are you doing?" Amy stood with her feet apart and her arms crossed over her chest.

"I'm just putting it away." Jane shut the book and stood up.

"What are you doing here?"

"Opening the house... I mean, I know it was rough last time I was here, but I really need my job." Jane heard something fall in the kitchen. She frowned. Now was not a good time for her friends to draw attention to themselves.

"I think you need to leave." Amy scowled. She had dark bags under her eyes, like she hadn't been sleeping well, and her thick red hair was pulled back in a scraggly bun.

"Do you think I can have my last paycheck first?" Jane pulled out the first reason she could think of to stay.

"You tried to have Caramel arrested." Amy held her position in the middle of the doorway.

"I really didn't. I was just scared." Jane let her hand drift to her face again, lightly touching her wound. "I don't want to lose my job."

Amy cleared her throat. "Listen, I don't not like you. But it was foolish to come here. Especially if you are just poking around in my family's business. If you leave now, I won't mention you were here." Amy took a step back into the hallway. "And I'll make sure you get paid. Okay?"

Jane shook her head. "I feel like I ought to at least finish the job." She bent down and picked up the notebook.

Amy flew forward and grabbed the book. "Let me have that." She pressed it to her chest and took a deep breath. "Go ahead and finish today's work. Just... make this the last day." She started down the hall, then stopped, and turned around. "Sorry about that."

"I understand." Jane straightened the rest of the books, mostly encyclopedias and biographies.

Jane turned on the computer, the whirring buzz as it came to life was drowned out by another crash from the kitchen. Jane ran for the door, but tripped over the stack of books. She scrambled back up and threw herself into the kitchen in time to see the back door swinging and a coffee mug in pieces on the floor. She could hear voices screaming.

She paused for a second and considered calling for help, but ran instead. She could see Gemma and Amy down the field a stretch, but where was Stephanie?

Gemma and Amy swung hard left, so Jane did, too, hoping to cut diagonal and catch up with the girls, who were only a couple of hundred feet ahead of her.

As soon as she was close enough she reached for Gemma's elbow.

A bang like a gun sounded and Gemma fell to the ground, her hands over her head.

Jane dropped, too. She threw herself on her cousin, as though she could protect her from what had just happened.

Jane felt Gemma's head for blood, daring to hope that she wouldn't find any. If Gemma died from this stunt...

Jane's heart stopped.

Her fingers had found a warm, wet spot on Gemma's temple. She held Gemma's head in her arms, desperate to keep it together.

"Get off of me!"

"But your head." Jane tried to keep her cousin pinned to the ground.

Gemma squirmed and shoved Jane to the side. "We've got to find her." She scrambled up and ran again.

Jane stared at her fingers, which were wet and warm and brown. She sniffed them. Dog doo. Wet, fresh, dog doo.

Jane wiped her hand on the grass and took a deep breath. She had to calm down. After all, she had no idea what was happening.

Jane shoved her hand in the pocket of her jeans, but her phone was still in the kitchen. Her heart was like a hammer in her chest, beating so hard it hurt.

Another reverberating bang broke the silence of the morning. Then a scream.

Jane got up and ran. She ran until her lungs burned. She ran until she passed Gemma. She ran into the woods, through the brambles that scratched lines of fire in her arms. She ran straight to the next-door neighbor's property line.

CHAPTER 24

JANE STOPPED AT THE EDGE OF THE WOODS and hid behind a large rhododendron. She knew Amy and Stephanie were just the other side of the bush, but her heart was beating so loudly she couldn't hear a sound. She took a slow deep breath. She couldn't burst onto the scene if there was a gun out there. She wanted to stop the violence, not die.

She gripped a thin branch and pulled it down so she could see. Stephanie was crouched behind a blue plastic canister.

Jane looked from side to side until she found Amy crouched behind a concrete urn full of roses. Amy's face was scared, but she didn't look like she was in pain. Jane turned her eyes back to Stephanie. Who had the gun? Her or Amy?

Stephanie narrowed her eyes, her thick lips pinched.

There was a whirr, then a piff.

A yellow ball shot out of the plastic tennis ball machine and hit the wall of the aluminum shed behind Amy with a noise so loud it made Jane's skull vibrate.

Amy rolled away from the planter and took shelter behind the shed. Then she poked her head out. "Stop it, Stephanie!"

Another ball rolled out and rammed into the shed.

Jane counted four dents, one for each "shot" she thought she had heard.

Stephanie wasn't talking.

Jane inched her way around the bush. If she could get Stephanie away from the machine, she could turn it off.

Jane heard Gemma behind her, panting. Jane turned, a finger to her lips, but she wasn't fast enough. Gemma burst through the bushes. "Stephanie! What's the matter?" she cried out.

Stephanie spun her machine. A ball flew out and hit Gemma in the shoulder. "Ouch!" Gemma fell to the ground. "What did you do that for?"

Jane picked her way through the edge of the woods until she was sure she could come out of them without Stephanie seeing her.

"My mother did not kill that man!" Stephanie spit the words out.

"Jeeze, Steph! No one said she did." Amy shouted from behind the shed.

Stephanie spun the machine again. This time the ball came out while she was turning. It flew through the window of the pool house with a great crash. A scream came from inside.

Jane froze. Who was in the pool house?

"Why would your mom kill someone?" Gemma stayed low, one hand holding her shoulder.

"She wouldn't." Stephanie pushed the machine closer to the shed.

"No one thinks your mom killed my dad." Amy poked her head from behind the shed again.

"Then why are the police looking for her? What did she ever do? She loved him, that's all!"

Amy let a long breath out through pursed lips.

Jane stepped onto the lawn, hoping Gemma wouldn't notice her.

"What are you afraid of, Steph?" Amy pulled her head back behind the shed before Stephanie could answer.

"I'm afraid that the police will be prejudiced against her because she loved him. It's always the lover, isn't it? It doesn't matter that they had been together for over twenty years. And it doesn't seem to matter he married a crazy lady. It will still look like my mom's fault, but it wasn't."

Gemma made eye contact with Jane. She opened her mouth as though to speak, but Jane shook her head. If Gemma revealed her…she flinched just thinking about what the tennis balls, shooting in close range, at one hundred and thirty miles an hour, could do to her cousin, to Amy, or to herself.

"No one thinks your mom did anything wrong, sweetie." Amy popped out from behind the shed again, but on her hands and knees so she'd be lower than the tennis balls. "We do want to find her and let her know what happened, but no one blames her."

Not so, Jane thought. If Stephanie's mom was Douglas's lover, the lover with the missing phone, then Jane thought there was a good chance she was the murderer.

"Well, she didn't do it. She's been in Cabo for a month. He was with her for most of it."

"She's *still* seeing him?" Amy crawled on her hands and knees to Gemma.

"Of course! Why would they break up when things have been going so well?"

"Because he's *married* to Caramel! You can't think it's okay for married men to have lovers."

Stephanie's jaw worked back and forth. Jane thought she must have turned the ball machine off, since it hadn't shot anything in a few minutes.

"Why not? She's always been his lover. She's been with him longer than either of his wives."

"But don't you want more for your mom?" Amy gently manipulated Gemma's shoulder. Gemma bit her lip and shook her head.

"It's a bit late for that now, isn't it?" Stephanie pushed on something on the back of her machine. Maybe it wasn't turned off, but out of balls.

Jane got around the other side of the pool house.

Stephanie had been staying with Jane, so she wasn't the one living in the pool house, but she had run straight there in a panic. Maybe her mom was the guest next door.

Jane tested the doorknob.

The door opened.

Jane stepped inside, trying to be quiet, but the blonde woman crouched under the broken window turned and looked at her. She had big, buggy blue eyes like Stephanie.

"I didn't do it, I swear." She pressed her back to the wall.

"Of course not." Jane dropped to a sitting position on the floor. The woman in front of her quivered, and her face was streaked with tears. "I don't know why Stephanie thinks I did. When she called me and told me what had happened, it broke me. It just broke me. Doug and I had come back from Mexico early, and I had just seen him. I couldn't believe what she was telling me…" She broke off, a sob choking out her words.

"Danae?" The woman looked up. "Are you Danae Monroe, the maid?"

She nodded, still sobbing great shoulder-racking sobs.

"Stephanie is just really, really scared. She needs you." Jane kept her distance and kept her words soft and warm.

Danae nodded her head.

"Just push open the door and step out. You can help her calm down."

Danae's body slowly stilled.

"Your baby needs you to be strong."

Danae opened the door and stepped out.

Jane crossed the room, but stayed in the little house with the wall between herself and Stephanie.

"Baby girl, what are you doing?"

"Don't come out, Mom!" Stephanie didn't turn. "Don't let them take you away."

Danae turned to Jane, her eyebrows pulled together in confusion.

Jane mouthed, "Keep going."

"I know you're scared, but you don't have to be. I've already seen the police. They know where I was. They don't think it was me." Danae placed her hand on Stephanie's shoulder.

"But the news keeps making it sound like they think it was you…" Stephanie turned slowly to face her mom. "I've been so scared!"

"Is that why you haven't come by to see me?"

Stephanie nodded. Her bottom lip trembled.

"Baby girl." Danae wrapped her arms around Stephanie.

Gemma and Amy rushed to the tennis ball machine and pulled it away. "Why did you bolt from the kitchen?" Gemma asked.

"I didn't want Amy to see me with you." She wiped her eyes. "She might tell Matthew."

Danae chewed her bottom lip.

"Why shouldn't I tell my brother that you came by here?"

Stephanie looked from Amy to Gemma and back to Amy.

Jane stepped out of the house, her pulse racing. "Stephanie, you planted that evidence on me, didn't you?"

Stephanie looked at her feet.

"You only came to my house to make me look like the killer." A strange peace fell over Jane as the pieces of the puzzle fell into place. She wasn't angry, or scared. She was in charge, and she was about to find all of the answers she had been looking for.

"No! I…"

"Stephanie, where is the laundry basket? Where are the towels?"

"I don't know! I wasn't there! I never saw those!" Stephanie's face drained of color. Her body shook. "I didn't want you to get arrested, Jane. I just wanted…" Her mouth hung open like a fish. Then she took a deep breath and straightened up. "My mom called. She told me that she had stopped by the house and seen Amy and Caramel. She mentioned some errands she had to do. I just went to the shop and said I was her. Joe wasn't in; the other guy let me pick it up. It was easy. Then I had it… and I could use it if I needed to. But, Jane… not to hurt you. Just to protect my mom."

"Oh, Stephanie…" Danae shook her head. "What did you think would happen to this poor girl?"

Stephanie's face flushed, and her eyes began to fill with tears. She ground her teeth together, a look of fierce determination fighting against the tears.

"But, Danae, if you weren't with Douglas that morning, and Caramel was out back on the property, who was in the tub with Douglas when he died?" Jane drummed her fingers on the wall. "Did he have a new girlfriend, Amy? What do you know?"

She shook her head. "I would swear that he doesn't." She paused. "Didn't. He was an old dog, and slowing down."

"Stephanie, do you want to come in and sit down?" Jane asked in slow, low tones, hoping to soothe Stephanie into telling them more. Her next question was about Matthew Swanson, but she didn't want to rush it. An idea had formed in her mind, so revolting that her stomach turned, but she was almost certain she had the key to the murder; maybe not the murderer, but definitely the motive.

"Yes, please."

Danae led her daughter into the pool house. "You're lucky Marion is letting me stay here still," she said. "I get to move back into the apartment next week."

"You popped into the big house to look for your phone, didn't you?"

Danae nodded. "Yes, once or twice."

"Amy, she was there the day that Alexandra and Matthew came over, wasn't she?"

"Yes, of course she was. But I certainly couldn't have my mother find out she was there."

Stephanie sat on the edge of the wicker sofa, her hands gripping the edge of the cushion.

"Would you have been embarrassed for Matthew to find you at the house?" Jane asked, still trying to lull Stephanie with a calm, low voice. Her whole body was tense with excitement, but if she could keep her voice calm, she could make it work.

"What would Matthew care about the housekeeper's kid?" Amy asked, her lip curled in distaste.

Danae rubbed Stephanie's back, but her face was awash with emotion, though she kept her mouth closed in a firm line.

"You didn't have a crush on him, did you?" Amy's face was clearly disgusted. "He's so old."

Danae stood up. "The important thing is we have all calmed down. If you all don't mind, could you just leave us alone? I'll clear everything up." She looked from Amy to Gemma to Jane, her eyes wild.

Jane was sure now, she was completely sure. "Danae, is Douglas Stephanie's father?"

"No!" Stephanie stood up, shaking. "My dad was a Marine! He died in Bosnia!"

Danae buried her face in her hands.

Amy closed her eyes, and rolled her head. "That's just brilliant. No wonder he hired you to work here after you had the baby."

"My *dad* is a war hero!" Stephanie spun, her eyes not stopping on any of them. "Douglas couldn't be my dad. Mom was married to a war hero!"

"My husband was gone a long time before he died." Danae's voice was a whisper.

"But Douglas took good care of you and the baby, didn't he?" Jane tried to match Danae's quiet tone.

"He always took very good care of us."

"Douglas is *not* my father." Stephanie's voice quivered with the sounds of doubt.

"You have a crush on your brother?" Amy's voice, while derisive and sarcastic, had just a hint of fear. Her own face had drained of all color, only her freckles standing out against her snow white skin.

"Amy…" Jane shook her head. She watched Stephanie as shock and horror flooded her features. As her mom failed to deny the accusation, Stephanie's rigid frame shook until her legs looked like they were going to buckle. She sat again, next to her mother, but not touching her.

It was Matthew.

Jane knew it now.

Danae still loved Douglas.

Stephanie had had no reason to hate her family benefactor.

But Matthew… Jane's mind spun as the pieces fell into place. His awkward posture and need to leave the house quickly. His absence from the house while Caramel sorted the things. His comment about his love life being no one's business.

"Did you tell him, Danae? When Stephanie started talking about her new relationship?"

"Yes." Danae inhaled deeply. "He was so much older than her, I never thought she'd need to know."

"Matthew can't be my brother," Stephanie whispered.

"Well, he is, obviously." Amy sat down on a footstool. "I guess we can all thank God he lived so far away."

"We weren't dating… yet," Stephanie said.

"But you were both in love, weren't you? He lived far away at some school, and you lived in Seattle. You emailed each other and talked on the phone and fell in love." Jane knew exactly what that felt like, and her heart broke for Stephanie. "But Danae, you got hold of Matthew and told him the truth."

"Yes, I had to. I could see how serious she was about him. Her heart was going to break, and it needed to happen fast." She rested her forehead on Stephanie's shoulder. "Oh, baby, I am so sorry. I should have told you the truth all along."

"Amy, how long has Matthew been in town?" Jane licked her lips.

Amy wiped a tear away.

"Amy…you see what I see, don't you?" Jane nodded toward Stephanie.

"He's a good guy, Jane." Amy held the cuff of her shirt under her nose. "He's a really good guy."

"But one phone call ruined his dreams, right?"

"Oh, Jane, he came home two days before Dad died! He didn't know I knew, but Caramel saw him in the garage with Dad, and she told me."

"And then one morning, he came by, and he talked your Dad into hopping into the hot tub with him, just to relax and hang out."

"I don't know. I don't think he would."

"He wouldn't have, he wouldn't have." Stephanie's voice was almost silent.

"Hello, I need the police." Gemma had her cell phone to her head.

"Please don't." Amy's words faded to nothing.

"We need to tell them what we know," Jane said. "The police can decide if we are right or not."

"Please," Danae said. "Please, can I be alone with her now?"

Jane stood up. "I'll go. I'm so sorry."

Gemma followed her out, giving details of what they had learned to the police.

Gemma chattered, fast and furious, about what had happened and how bad her shoulder hurt as they drove away. Jane didn't listen.

Solving mysteries uncovered so much ugliness. Did she really want to do that with her life? Didn't she want to clean sin with the gospel instead? Or just simply clean dirt for her clients? So much hurt and ugliness in the world. Was she strong enough to do this?

And what if no one could ever prove her theory was correct?

"I am going to need to seriously alternate hot and cold on this shoulder," Gemma said. "I can't believe how much it hurts!"

Jane glanced at the injured shoulder; it was deep red and already swollen. "What you need is a frosty cold smoothie."

CHAPTER 25

THE DRIVE TO THE MALL would have been quiet if Jane had had her way. But Gemma recounted every moment of their confrontation at a 100 words per minute. By the time they arrived at the mall Jane was ready to abandon Gemma to the first person she saw.

That person was Jake. "This is my cousin Gemma, and she has suffered a serious injury in the name of justice. What drink do you suggest for heroes?" Jane pushed her cousin forward.

Jake looked Gemma up and down. He whistled. "Jane's cousin, eh? Then let me mix you a special."

"I'm allergic to strawberries," Gemma offered. She looked over at Jane, one eyebrow lifted. "He's cute," she whispered.

"Gemma's a doula with a heart for God," Jane said.

"Work with pregnant ladies and stuff?" he asked as he handed over two smoothies.

"Usually." Gemma sipped her drink. "That's good."

"Make sure to get your free smoothies while you can, Gem. Jake's moving back to Thailand soon to rescue women from sex slavery."

Gemma smiled at Jake. "I'll be sure to come back while I can."

Jake winked at Jane. "I know what you did there."

She shrugged. "Just trying to make the world a better place." She led Gemma from the food court. Now that she had distracted her cousin and calmed her down a bit, what she really wanted was wise counsel. "I'm going to go see my mentor. Would you like to come?"

"Nah. I need to get home. I'll pack up Stephanie's stuff so she can be ready to leave as soon as she shows up." Gemma sipped her drink. "Hey, I'm sorry."

"For what?"

"For letting someone into our house who was planning to hurt you."

In her heartache for Stephanie, that part had slipped her mind. "How could you know? I don't blame you."

Jane took Gemma back to the apartment and then went to Paula's without calling first.

Paula answered her door in her bathrobe. Her face was haggard, with deep shadows under her eyes. "Please, come in." She managed a small smile.

Her house was immaculate. "Thank you for letting me drop by. I'm sorry to bother you."

"It's okay. You're just what I need today." Paula poured two cups of coffee and then joined Jane in the living room. "I'm a little rough today. I'm sorry."

"Don't apologize." The stress of the morning, the fear and sadness, and now a grief that pierced her as she looked at Paula brought tears to her eyes.

"It's hard to change from caregiver to someone who needs care." Paula tucked her feet under her and relaxed back into her chair. "You have something weighing heavily on your heart. It's written all over your face. But can I share something with you?"

Jane sipped her coffee. "Of course."

"All of my life, I knew I was going to be a wife." She choked on her words a little. "While at school, my friends all got married. The ones I was most jealous of got married and then went on the mission field. I'd ask God why I hadn't met my husband yet and He wouldn't answer. I went to India and I worked for what felt like my whole life. At no point in my life did I ever feel like God was telling me I was going to be single forever, but I have to say, turning forty as a single woman made me wonder just a little."

Jane couldn't take her eyes off of Paula.

"And then one year, I came home on furlough and I met Mark. And God said, 'This is why you hadn't met your husband before now.'"

Jane didn't have any words, but she felt like the discoveries of the morning were somehow smaller than whatever Paula had to say.

"And, Jane, I feel like this is you. You will be a missionary someday. I wouldn't dare predict when, or where, or for how long. Maybe you will be like my mom and dad and spend a lifetime together. Or maybe you'll be like Mark and I."

Jane chewed on her bottom lip.

"I waited a long time, but it was perfect. It was short, but it was perfect." Paula wiped her eyes with a white handkerchief. "That's all. You may have to wait. And it may not be what you expected. But if you really do believe God wants this for you, it will happen, and it will be exactly what it was supposed to be."

Jane's mouth felt sealed shut. She had a thousand questions, from how Paula and Mark met to why she had come home from the mission field to how she dealt with the disappointment for all those years while she waited, but she couldn't speak. Paula's face was beatified, almost. She was broken, but her eyes shone with a glow that only comes from trusting and waiting your whole life. It would be twenty more years before Jane could understand the real answers to her questions.

"You wanted to talk about something though, right?" Paula pushed her handkerchief into her pocket. "Even though you aren't looking at full time missionary work right now, I'd be proud to continue to mentor you."

"I'm okay." The words came out before Jane could weigh what she wanted to say. "I had a rough morning, but I think you just answered all of my questions." She set her cup on the coffee table and stood up. "I can't thank you enough."

Paula hugged Jane tight. "Thank you, kiddo. I really needed you guys right now. You don't know how much."

Later that week, the news reported an arrest in the case of the death of Douglas Swanson. His son had been taken in for questioning. He hadn't confessed, but the news report online said that there was possible DNA evidence connecting Matthew Swanson to the scene of the crime, as well as physical evidence in the trunk of his rental car. Jane was pretty sure that would be the missing hamper and towels.

Gemma, Amy, Danae, Stephanie, and Jane herself had all been down to the station to report what had happened at the pool house. Making statements was becoming second nature to Jane.

She had Isaac on speaker phone while she doodled logos at her desk. He was talking about the school in Montreal. "If you stay in Portland to finish your degree, you need to start your French classes right away."

Jane erased a magnifying glass she had put over her name. "Yup. I registered for it today."

"You did?"

"Of course. If I have to learn a new language, I'd better start now."

"So you're dead set on staying in Portland one more year?" Isaac was crunching something. Jane liked to think it was chips and salsa, since that's what she was eating.

"Did you really think I'd move to Canada with you before we were married?"

"Not *with* me, but I did think there was a chance you'd transfer there to stay close."

"If wishes were horses." She drew a stick figure in a Sherlock hat, then scribbled it out. She thought about making a joke about a family discount on credits, but she wasn't going to say a word about marriage until he did.

"I'll come back a lot."

"On a teacher's wages?"

"I'll come back as much as I can."

"We'll buy stock in Skype."

"Good move."

Jane checked her watch. It was time to meet with the advisor for the Portland State University School of Criminal Justice. French wasn't the only thing she was adding to her schedule this year. "I've got to run. I love you."

"I love you, Jane. Call me when you get back, okay? I want to hear all about detective school."

And so did she. She might not start all over again, but if she was going to solve any more murders, she wanted to do it right.

Now Available

TRACI TYNE HILTON

BRIGHT NEW MURDER

A Plain Jane Mystery

CHAPTER 1

JANE ADLER SAT ON THE COLD, wet hood of Isaac's car. She leaned away from him, her arms crossed. Their spot on the top of Mount Scott gave them a good view of the city lights. The day's light rain had turned to softly falling snow as night fell.

She was damp, cold, and beyond irritated with her boyfriend.

"If you keep changing your degree, you'll never finish school." The vein in Isaac's temple throbbed, and he flexed his jaw.

"Again: I have not changed my degree. And I'll still graduate this spring even with the extra classes." Jane exhaled slowly. Isaac had only been home a week, and they had already had this argument four times.

"You've changed your degree twice since I met you." Isaac leaned back on his elbows. "It's like you don't want to finish."

"You're exaggerating, and it's not fair. I finished Bible school and I started a bachelor's degree in business. That is not the same thing as changing my degree."

"And now criminal science."

"Yes. I added a couple of criminal science classes to my schedule. As well as French. It's more work, but I'll get it all done."

Isaac leaned over to bump shoulders with Jane. "See, that's the thing. You don't even speak the language. How are you going to be a detective in Montreal?"

Jane didn't answer. She couldn't say what she was really thinking—that she hoped she *wouldn't* ever be a detective in Montreal.

"Talk to me, Jane."

"Why? You only hear what you want to hear."

"Just help me understand why you're making it harder to finish. Are you trying to come up with reasons to stay here? To not move to Canada with me?"

"You may not stay there forever."

Isaac leaned over and brushed her cheek with his lips. "I hope I do. It's my dream job." His voice was a low, sexy rumble in his throat.

She pushed him away. "Don't kiss me while we're fighting."

"I haven't seen you since August." He tried to set his hand on her knee, but she moved a little. All of his little caresses and kisses were making the inevitable harder for her.

"You saw me yesterday."

"And we had this same fight yesterday." Isaac turned her gently by the chin and kissed her lips.

Jane froze, a hairsbreadth from his closed eyes and slightly parted mouth. "Then quit bringing it up."

Isaac pulled a small square box out of the pocket of his ski jacket. He set it on the hood of the car, right between them. "I keep bringing it up, because I have something to ask you."

Jane stared at the box.

The box.

The box she had been waiting to see since his last visit home. The box she had been dreaming of since she fell for him at first sight, a year and a half ago. The box every Christian girl hopes to get before she turns twenty-three.

Jane stared at the box and felt sick to her stomach.

"Jane…I want you to marry me. Move to Montreal this spring. Be a professor's wife. Don't ever worry about cleaning, or detecting, or anything ever again. Make Montreal your mission field." He opened the box and held it out to her.

One large diamond, with a swirl of smaller diamonds cascading away from it, down both sides of the ring.

"Say yes." He stroked the back of her head with his strong fingers and pulled her close, his forehead bumping hers. He went for the kiss, but hesitated—a pause that gave Jane the chance she needed to act.

She pushed him away and slid off of the car. "I'm not a prize—not another set of letters to add after your name, Isaac."

"What? What is wrong with you this week?" Isaac held the ring out to her and cocked an eyebrow.

"Nothing is wrong with *me*. *I'm* doing fine. *I'm* working hard to follow my dream and make a difference in the world." She took a deep breath. "What's wrong with *us*? That's the real question. Neither of us seem willing to admit the obvious." She stopped. She had to say it, but it felt like something smashed into her heart. "This is not meant to be." She was too mad to cry, but her whole body shook. Right now, at this moment, she should be slipping that diamond ring on her finger and kissing her fiancé. The man she loved. Not yelling at him. Not...breaking up.

"What do you mean this isn't meant to be?" He shoved the ring forward. "It's right here. I'm asking you to marry me. We'll go have adventures in French Canada. You can keep doing the career student thing. What don't you like about this?"

"That!" The word felt like a knife in her throat. "That's what I don't like! I'm not doing a 'career student' thing. I've been a key player in successfully solving two murder investigations, and I want to do more of it. I plan on cleaning houses and solving murders for as long as I can, but it's like you don't believe me."

"You wanted to be a missionary too, and you're not doing that anymore." His cocky voice made Jane want to punch him in the face.

"Who says I'm not going to be a missionary?"

"You just did. You said you're going to be a detective."

"Right now. I'm going to be a detective right now."

"And for as long as you can. You *just* said that, Jane. You don't know yourself very well at all, do you?"

"Well, if I don't know myself, then I have no business getting married and moving across the continent, do I? I say no.

No. No. I'm turning down your proposal." She clamped her jaw shut and stared at him.

His mouth bobbed open. He shoved the ring box into his pocket. "Fine."

"Fine." She eyed the lone bus stop on top of the hill. Right next to the cemetery. "And I'm taking the bus home."

"Now you're just being stupid. Jane."

Jane yanked her wallet out of her purse. "Don't call." The bus was lumbering up the hill, so she didn't run for it. She didn't want to look like a child, but she did stomp away as fast as she could.

She waited with her back to Isaac.

Merry Christmas to me.

The rank odor of dirty people in the overheated bus combined with her heartache made Jane's gut burn.

After two transfers and an hour and a half of travel, Jane made it the four miles from the hilltop to her apartment. She shoved the door open like it was Isaac and she was pushing him away again. She dropped her purse and her coat in the doorway and threw herself on the couch.

"Look what the cat dragged in!" Jake was sprawled in front of the plug-in electric fireplace. "Trouble in paradise?"

"Shut up." Jane buried her face in a feather pillow. She pressed against it until she couldn't breathe, then she pulled away and punched it.

"Whoa," Jake said. "That's real trouble in paradise."

Gemma padded into the room. She was decked out in leggings and an oversized, hipster ugly Christmas sweater.

Jane stared at it. The image of a cat batting at a tangle of Christmas lights made her want to punch something again, so she hit the pillow a few more times.

"Hey Jane, want some cocoa?"

"Shh. Don't talk to Jane. She's mad," Jake whispered.

"Oh, go home, Jake!" Jane threw the pillow at him. She rolled over and laid her arm across her face.

"What's the matter with her?" Gemma asked.

"Boy trouble, I assume."

Jane curled up like a baby.

"What happened, Jane, didn't he propose?" Gemma rattled in the kitchen, but Jane pressed her arms over her ears.

"Was he going to propose?" Jake raked his hand through his hair. "The plot thickens."

Every word Jake said was like a tap on the head with a ball-peen hammer. Jane wanted to throw more things at him, but she didn't have anything else.

"Was the ring cheap?" Gemma asked.

"He does seem like the kind of guy who would buy a cheap ring, doesn't he?"

Jane squeezed her eyes shut. She had to say something, if only to get them to shut up. "It looked like a very expensive ring."

"But then, it would to you," Jake said. "You're not used to real quality."

Gemma squealed, the sound piercing Jane's skull like a drill.

"Don't get too excited, she didn't say yes."

Jane opened her eyes again. Jake was staring at her, his cheeks slightly flushed, and if she had to bet, she'd say his eyes hinted at actual sympathy.

"What? Never!" Gemma perched on the edge of the couch and stroked Jane's hair.

Jane brushed her hand away.

"She turned him down because the ring was cheap." Jake leaned back again. His face turned brilliant red.

Jane narrowed her eyes. What was his game? He was…embarrassed about his jokes?

"Isaac is her soul mate, Jake. She would never turn him down."

"Soul mate or not, she kicked him to the curb on Christmas night." Jake looked away. "And it was about time."

"What happened, Jane? Don't leave us in the dark like this!" Gemma slid onto the seat, and Jane's hair.

"Ouch." Jane pulled on her hair to free herself.

"It hurts now, like taking off a Band-Aid, but the fresh air will make it heal. That's what my mom always said." Jake was still talking nonsense, but he was staring out the window now, not looking at anyone.

"Shush, Jakey. Let her talk."

"Please. Don't call me 'Jakey.'" He groaned and flopped onto his back. "Anything but 'Jakey.'"

"We talked about the future and he, he just doesn't…" She choked on a sob. Her shoulders shook and hot tears rolled down her cheeks. She couldn't say it. Not yet. Because maybe it was just for tonight. Maybe Isaac would see that he was wrong and come apologize. Maybe he did respect and appreciate what she was trying to do.

"He doesn't love you." Jake cleared his throat.

"He thinks he loves me." Jane wiped her cheeks with her sleeve. "But you're right, I don't believe he really does. He loves the idea of me, but not the actual me."

"And that's not good enough. A husband is supposed to love his wife more than himself. Love her enough to lay his life down for her like Christ laying his life down for us." Jake didn't look away from the window. His voice was a bit husky, almost sincere sounding.

A little sigh escaped from Gemma's slightly parted lips. She stared at Jake with big, moony cow eyes.

Jane sniffled, and held her sleeve to her nose. No point in being ladylike around Jake and Gemma. "You two should go out and let me be miserable. I don't need to ruin this night for you."

Gemma's cheeks flushed a pretty pink. "It is an exciting night."

Jane tried to smile. "I am ruining it. This should be your chance to celebrate all of the hard work. Tomorrow is a big day…"

Gemma slid into her black wool coat.

"It's Christmas night. What are you guys doing hanging out here anyway? Go take Gemma out somewhere nice, Jake. Celebrate everything you guys have accomplished. Make a real date of it without me tagging along."

Jake didn't move. "Sorry. I kissed dating goodbye. You know that."

"Celebrate anyway."

"We'll celebrate after the event. We may have done a lot of work getting ready for the fundraiser, but the real work is all tomorrow." Jake remained perfectly still, as though he were frozen to the rug. "If you're not up to it though, Jane, please be honest. We don't need some sad sack coming around and ruining our fun."

The last hint of sympathy had disappeared from his voice, and it hurt a little. If Gemma and Jake had to stay, flaunting their happy flirtation in front of her, at least they could continue to baby her feelings a little. She flopped back onto the couch. "I'd rather supervise takedown and cleanup of the big fundraiser than stick around this joint by myself."

"That's a good girl, Janey." Jake's unpredictability seemed to be in full swing again, as his voice cracked when he said her name.

She appreciated it.

CHAPTER 2

THE EVENING WAS DARK, like all Portland evenings in winter. Thick pewter clouds that had made a perpetual dusk of the day spewed sleet across the town, making this Boxing Day possibly the ugliest day of the year.

Just perfect.

Jane sat on a stool by the window and watched the sleet slide down the glass in slushy sheets. This was no night for smoothies. But it was too late to worry about that now. Yo-Heaven, the frozen-yogurt smoothie empire Jake had inherited when his father died, was sponsoring a fundraiser for Helping Hands Early Education Center, so smoothies it was. Jake was revealing his New Year's Cookie–flavored smoothies at this evening's event, but…Jane sighed. That would hardly be enough to bring people out in this weather.

She turned her back on the window. The doors were opening in just twenty minutes and everyone was still rushing around, though the place looked perfect to Jane. The Shonley Center had moved them to the smaller banquet room at the last minute. The bad news was that it meant they were stuck at the back of a long, empty hallway. The good news was the room was much smaller, so the event would feel like a success even if it failed to meet their projections.

Jane jumped off the stool and wandered into the kitchen. Technically, she didn't have to work until she directed the volunteers during teardown, but helping was better than sitting.

"Hey, Jane. Any word from Isaac?" Gemma licked the spatula she was holding.

"Shut up, Gemma, jeeze." Phoebe Crawford rolled her eyes. "Jane, toss me that towel."

Jane tossed the towel.

Phoebe rolled it up and smacked Gemma.

"Oh, he'll call. It doesn't matter what you think. He cannot live without her."

Jake walked past with a tray full of smoothie samples. He didn't say a word, but winked as he pushed open the door into the banquet room.

"He's not the only one." Phoebe hefted a big steel bowl onto her hip and carried it away.

"I wish you'd stop asking me about him. I don't know if he'll call or not. He's kind of...I don't know how to put it."

"Sullen? Pouty? Brokenhearted?"

"He's the strong, silent type. He might never call again." Jane traced the faux granite design of the laminate counter with her fingertip. "And that's fine, too. It's not like I'm going to take him back or anything. This was the right decision for us."

"You say that now, but wait until New Year's Eve. You'll change your tune by New Year's."

"Phoebe...do you need a hand with anything?" Jane called out.

"Yeah, out front. Go ask Jake. He's got a huge list to do in the next few minutes."

A tuxedo-clad server pushed his way past Jane.

"Never mind that." Gemma tossed her spatula in a bowl. "You stay here and start washing up. Might as well get some of it done beforehand. I can go help Jake."

Jane carried the bowl to the sink. Gemma was right. It wouldn't hurt to get some of the washing done in advance. And she preferred to leave Gemma and Jake to each other. Two birds with one stone.

"You're a dope," Phoebe said. "Why dump Coach Isaac? Is there a hotter man in this town?"

"He's not *in* this town. Well, he is, but not for long."

"Yeah, that. He does have a lame job. I mean, how much money can a *professor* really make?"

Jane curled her lip up in disgust. It wasn't about the money, or lack of money, or even the location. It was about the lack of...respect.

It was about the lack of *mutual* respect. She had as little interest in being a supportive college wife as he had in being the husband of a private detective, or missionary, or...

That was the other problem. He couldn't see that her two dreams were just as important as his one. But the mutual part, yes, she was as much to blame as he was. She liked having a boyfriend…a handsome, important boyfriend. It had made a good change from no boyfriend at all. But, when it came down to brass tacks and diamond rings…

A sob was working its way up from her heart. She squeezed her eyes shut and held her breath for a minute. Lack of mutual respect aside, she couldn't imagine him not calling today. And not coming by this evening, and not cradling her in his arms so she could rest her head on his shoulder while they watched TV, their fingers laced together, him nuzzling her ear. She turned on the hot water and took a deep breath. He was very nice to have around, but that wasn't the same thing as being the one she was supposed to marry.

Once guests began arriving, the banquet hall filled up fast, and it looked like they ought to have had the large ballroom after all. Jane had to hand it to Jake. He knew his events. She had doubted the kind of draw the local preschool-for-children-of-homeless-families could have, but her heart was warmed to see the hundred or more people jostling each other for a taster cup of smoothies and the chance to donate to needy kids. She hadn't signed on as a server, but she carried trays and filled cups and tossed away the empties anyway.

But she kept thinking she saw Isaac out of the corner of her eye. Every time a dark head appeared to the side of the room, she just knew it was him, come to say they could make it work. That he believed she could do something important and exciting with her life. But even though she turned, every time, it was never him.

About an hour into the event, Jane spotted a man with a big camera on his shoulder following a woman in a red dress with stiff hair. TV news? It seemed likely. Jane sidled up behind the cameraman to listen to the reporter's take on the event.

"The folks inside aren't letting the weather, or the protesters, dampen their enthusiasm for this worthy cause." The reporter's face only moved slightly as she spoke, her eyebrows frozen in a look of mild astonishment.

Protesters?

"Excuse me." A man tugged Jane's elbow. "Will there be real food here tonight?"

"What? Yes, of course." Jane squinted towards the kitchen. Some kind of sandwich-and-salad thing was supposed to be coming out before the night was over. "Just give it a few minutes, okay?" She gave him a quick nod and slid away through the crowd. She opened the door a crack and peered into the hallway.

A dozen hippies and punks and hipsters were gathered in the hall with tattered cardboard signs. The sleet had battered them on their way into the event, but their message was clear. And so was the person in charge.

Rose of Sharon Willis.

The "Helpers" had arrived.

Jane scratched her head. The Human Liberation Party was all about eating right, but what was wrong with smoothies? Or educating homeless preschoolers? Jane slipped out of the door so she could hear better.

Rose of Sharon stood on top of an old-fashioned soapbox, her banged-up red megaphone at her lips. The hubbub in the crowd made it hard to hear, but Jane made out a few choice sentiments.

"We're not baby COWS! We're NOT baby cows! WE'RE not baby cows!" The emphasis was on a different word each time, but the point was clear. Rose of Sharon had a problem with milk. Rose of Sharon turned on her box and seemed to catch Jane's eye. "Are YOU a baby cow?"

Jane wanted to duck and cover, but instead, she shook her head no.

"That's a good girl!" Rose of Sharon spun on her box to call out to a janitor that was passing by.

Jane exhaled slowly. HLP wasn't doing any harm. They hadn't prevented anyone from getting to the fundraiser. Kids would get their preschool, and that's what was important.

Rose of Sharon dragged her soapbox right in front of the door and pushed it open. Megaphone to mouth, she began her favorite protest song. "I like to eat apples and bananas."

Jane sidled through the crowd, but couldn't get past the soapbox. Jake hovered near the door, just on the other side, and she managed to catch his eye.

He pulled a chair up to the doorway and stood eye to eye with Rose of Sharon. "What do you have against the children, Rose? What did they ever do to you?"

Jane was pushed aside as the reporter and her cameraman took her spot near the action.

Rose of Sharon's thin, leathery face was beet red. "Why are you poisoning the children? Why are you using the children to poison the city? We thought you'd learned your lesson, Crawford. We thought you'd changed your ways, but you keep trying to kill us!"

"I'd kill for a hamburger right about now, that's true," Jake said with a smirk that was captured on the reporter's camera. In fact, Jake was turned towards the camera on purpose, as far as Jane could tell.

"You'll kill us all if you don't quit forcing your animal products on our fragile bodies."

Jake cupped his hands around his mouth like he was going to begin his own chant, but Jane shook her head.

Jake shrugged and stepped off of the chair, his eyes narrowed.

Jane managed to wheedle her way through the crowd to Jake.

"I'm not trying to kill people, Jane. Just trying to help out your cousin's charity." Jake lowered his voice.

"I know, Jake, I know." Jane turned to Rose of Sharon. "Listen, Rose, can you take this outside? I don't want to have to call security, but I will if I need to."

"But you're not a baby cow!"

"Of course I'm not, Rose. But…it's not like it's high-fructose corn syrup, right?"

Jake cleared his throat.

"Never mind."

Jane dragged Jake back to the table of smoothie samples. The party had begun to deteriorate.

A red-faced man with a bald head yelled at a younger, taller man in a suit.

A woman with bobbed black hair pushed another woman with bobbed black hair out of her way.

A man in a sweater with leather patches on the sleeves punched one of the hippies holding the door open. Punched him right in the face.

Then a woman screamed.

Jane froze. The room went completely silent.

Jake climbed back on his chair so he could see over the top of the crowd. "Who was that? Does anyone know who that was? Is everyone okay?" His voice had turned serious, manly, and in charge. She had never seen him like that before. Not once. "This event was meant to benefit the most vulnerable children in our community. It was not meant to insult our friends who believe in a different way of eating, or to harm anyone. That scream sounded like someone was really hurt. Everyone look around, and holler if someone near you has been injured."

A low murmur spread across the room, then another woman screamed.

The crowd jumped to life, and Jake pushed his way through the people with Jane right behind him.

A woman in a denim skirt and Christmas sweater knelt beside another woman, who lay on the ground, a pool of blood forming on her sweater.

The woman kneeling on the floor rocked back and forth, sobbing.

Jake checked the pulse of the injured woman. "Jane, call 911."

Jane pressed the phone to her ear and ducked through the crowd. She told them what little she knew: injured, bleeding, unconscious, and where they were located, and then she hung up. She needed to breathe.

The volume in the packed room had gone back to a loud roar. A man in a red-and-green Christmas sweater whose head was just above, and almost directly over, Jane's own kept shouting, "No, let's go home NOW." Jane tried to maneuver around him, but the woman he was shouting at reached for him and caught Jane in her arms.

"Excuse me," Jane whispered.

"Well!" The woman kept a tight grip on the sweater man with one hand, but let Jane go free.

The room had seemed pleasantly full when the party was new, but with everyone jostling to get out but being repulsed by the protesters, and the fear and yelling, it was a bedlam that made Jane's head spin.

"Excuse me!" Rose of Sharon had climbed up on the table full of smoothie samples. "EXCUSE ME!"

The room simmered to a low boil.

"It has come to my attention that someone in this room has been seriously injured. I have taken the responsibility to keep everyone present in the situation. No one has left the room through the main door. The paramedics will be here as soon as they can—any minute. I need everyone to take a seat along the walls, leaving a center aisle through the room to the injured party, do you understand?"

The people seemed to want a leader, and though they murmured in frustration, they shuffled to the sides of the room, and some people even sat down.

"Thank you."

Jane jerked her head up. Rose of Sharon had thanked them?

"In times of crisis, people need to come together and work with their enemies for the greater good. Because we are here protesting, it is of utmost importance that the authorities arrive to a calm scene. Any kind of chaos and my friends and I will be arrested."

"Let them be arrested!" a deep voice from the back of the room interrupted her.

"Yeah!" A throaty female voice joined his.

Jake hopped up on the table with Rose of Sharon, though Jane hadn't seen how he got there. "That's enough. For better or worse, the lady is right. We need to be calm so that the medics can treat the injured woman as quickly as possible. Right now, I'd like to know if someone can tell me who she is."

"I've never seen her before at all!" The speaker was a woman applying pressure to the wound. "Does anyone know this woman?"

Before anyone could answer, four paramedics barreled into the room. They paused in the door just long enough to spot the party they needed to help.

A pair of policemen stationed themselves at the door.

Jake climbed down from the table and joined Jane. He leaned close, his warm breath on her ear. "Now's your chance, Janey. Someone stabbed that poor woman. But whodunit, and why?"

ABOUT THE AUTHOR

When not writing, Traci accompanies her mandolin-playing husband on the spoons and knits socks.

She is the author of the Tillgiven Romantic Mysteries, the Plain Jane Mystery Series, the Mitzy Neuhaus Mysteries, and *Hearts to God,* a Christian historical romance novella. She was the Mystery/Suspense Category winner for the 2012 Christian Writers of the West Phoenix Rattler Contest and has a Drammy from the Portland Civic Theatre Guild. Traci served as the vice president of the Portland chapter of the American Christian Fiction Writers Association.

Traci earned a degree in history from Portland State University and still lives in the rainiest part of the Pacific Northwest with her husband, their two daughters, and their dogs, Dr. Watson and Archie.

Traci's photo by Jessie Kirk Photography.

Find all Traci's books and sign up for her newsletter at TraciHilton.com.

Connect with Traci at Facebook.com/TraciTHilton or tracityne@hotmail.com.

Made in the USA
Lexington, KY
15 December 2016